The Wolf vs the Monster

THE HIDDEN CITY SUPERNATURAL SLEUTH

LAURETTA HIGNETT

Copyright © 2025 by Lauretta Hignett

All rights reserved.

No part of this publication may be reproduced, distributed, or transmitted in any form or by any means, including photocopying, recording, or other electronic or mechanical methods, without the prior written permission of the publisher, except as permitted by U.S. copyright law. For permission requests, contact Lauretta Hignett info@laurettahignett.com

The story, all names, characters, and incidents portrayed in this production are fictitious. No identification with actual persons (living or deceased), places, buildings, and products is intended or should be inferred.

No generative AI was used at any time in the story and artworks of this book.

Editing by Cissell Ink

Book Cover by Atra Luna Graphic Design

First Edition 2025

CAST OF CHARACTERS

Daphne Ironclaw: Unhinged defective werewolf with a heart of gold. Poor Daphne is a bundle of confusion right now — battered and bruised after her nemesis Christopher tried to summon a Greek god but ended up blowing the Jupiter mansion to smithereens, she's now (rightly) under investigation for the murder of Wesley Jupiter.

Romeo Zarayan: The Warlock, High Priest, Lord of Shadows, currently very injured from the aforementioned Christopher Jupiter shenanigans, but unlike Daphne who has a proper job, he's a billionaire who has the luxury of staying at home to recover.

Dwayne: Master of Mayhem, Archangel of Anarchy, Commander of Chaos, Supreme Sultan of Shenanigans.

Dr Johan Van Eiken: the new nestmaster of Philadelphia, Azerad's protegee. Literally a Nazi vampire mad scientist.

Marie: Seventeen-year-old nerd girl, now a brand-new vampire. Marie is less Buffy and more Big Bang Theory.

The Soul Stealer/Stephen: Pompous scumbag witch pretending to be a pigeon shifter.

Myf: A seriously depressed dragon shifter and a *very* mean drunk.

Lennox Arran: Alpha Shifter of Philadelphia, world champion boxer, rich playboy and total fuckboy. Is convinced Daphne should be his princess and doesn't really believe in consent.

Sergeant Hart: A bear shifter, beat cop, and a lovely man.

Monica: Daphne's boss, the manager of the Otherworld department of the CPS. Never stops moving, and is ninety-nine percent made up of caffeine.

Judy: Daphne's colleague. Nosy witch, office bitch.

James: A lovely hardworking O-CPS colleague of Daphne.

Cindy: A gothflower pixie and Otherworld Drug and Alcohol counsellor, last seen flying out the window trying to get away from the Warlock.

Countess Ebadorathea Greenwood: A sorceress with a terrible (and deserved) reputation.

Valerie: A confused and somewhat pathetic vampire. She's not doing great, but everyone is rooting for her.

Asherah: the Fae Diplomat of Philadelphia, Dwayne's current main squeeze. Asherah is still away on a trip home to Faerie, and she's still an absolute psychopath.

Christopher Jupiter: the oldest Jupiter brother, an absolute monster. Incorrectly presumed dead.

Mina and Wesley Jupiter: Christopher's parents, former High Priest and High Priestess of Philadelphia. Don't worry, they're both actually dead.

Troy Jupiter: The youngest Jupiter son and Daphne's lying, cheating ex-boyfriend.

Holly LeBeaux: Hot-shot lawyer, smoking-hot witch and Troy's ex-fiancée.

Levi: A witch, covenmate and devoted acolyte of Romeo Zarayan.

Micah: Former assassin and another covenmate. Not a witch, but actually a sexy raven-haired vampire.

Cole: Another loyal covenmate, again, not actually a witch, but a stocky, sandy-haired cheerful lynx shifter.

Brandon: The final covenmate, another former assassin and, surprise surprise, not actually a witch, but a dragon shifter.

Azerad: The Vampire nestmaster of New York. He's not in this one, but is lurking behind the scenes, up to no good.

Alexei Minoff: Former Alpha Shifter, polar bear shifter, still dead!

Zofia: Former vampire Nestmaster of Philadelphia. She's still dead too but rates a mention.

Bella: Romeo Zarayan's foster sister and best friend. Also still dead!

CHAPTER
ONE

"It's okay. There's no need to be nervous." The detective gave me a fake reassuring smile. "You can relax, Daphne. Now, tell me. How many times did you stab Wesley Jupiter?"

I was already confused and unsettled as hell. The gory accusation combined with his pleasant smile threw me off even more. "I-I didn't stab him," I stammered.

Enough, my brain added cheerfully. *We didn't stab him enough. Honestly, we could have stabbed him a whole lot more.*

"It's alright," Detective Boggs nodded encouragingly. "You can tell us."

I swallowed. My head was pounding along with my heart. The remnants of the concussion I got only a day ago made it hard for me to think clearly. I healed quickly, but I needed sleep to do it, and I hadn't gotten much last night at all. "I don't know what you're talking about," I managed.

A sickening, squirming feeling writhed in my gut. I hated lying. And worse, I was really bad at it.

Even worse than that, both these detectives were really good at their jobs, so they knew I was lying. The thinner, lanky one, Detective Hartshorn, leaned up against the wall of the interview room with his arms crossed over his chest, highlighting the wrinkles in his shirt. He watched every little twitch and blink I made. Hartshorn was reading me like a book, I could tell.

Bald, bullish Detective Boggs, sitting at the table across from me, chuckled lightly, as if I'd said something really amusing. "Come on, now, Daphne. There's no need to be coy. We know you killed him. We just want to know how many times you stabbed him, that's all."

I swallowed roughly, trying to force some moisture into my parched throat, while Brain-Daphne answered the detective happily. *We stabbed that fucker Wesley only once, actually. Twice, if you count the fact that we twisted the blade in his kidney. If we had time, we would have stabbed him a whole bunch more. We could have turned him into a sieve.*

Stop it, I silently begged her. We're in deep trouble.

No, we're not. This case will get turned over to the Otherworld authorities any second. It doesn't matter what these cops think.

But it did. The detectives were right; I did kill Wesley Jupiter. There were extenuating circumstances, though. He and his wife had been trying to kill me and Romeo while their son Christopher summoned a dangerous god to share his body.

Luckily for all of us, Christopher had failed in spectacular fashion. Unluckily, though, he blew a hole in the Hellenic pocket dimension, which imploded with us still inside.

We escaped by the skin of our teeth. The mansion collapsed into a sinkhole and was now an unrecognizable pile of smoldering bricks and splintered wood. The only body they'd recovered was Wesley Jupiter, and, for some unfathomable reason, the human authorities were handling the case as a standard homicide.

I couldn't understand why. All supernatural crime was automatically handed over to the Otherworld authorities to deal with. We had our own enforcers, court system, and punishments. We had our own magical means of establishing guilt, and we had ways to cover up evidence that found its way into human hands. I had no business being in here, questioned by two human detectives who had no idea the Otherworld existed.

It never occurred to me that I'd ever have to answer for Wesley's death in the first place. The fact that he'd been trying to kill his own High Priest at the time was enough to have the whole mess metaphorically swept under the rug, never to be spoken of ever again.

Hmm. Brain-Daphne sounded uncharacteristically pensive. *That's a good point, actually. Why did this case land in the human system?*

I had no idea, but the fact that it had made me very nervous. It was obviously an administrative error, but the Otherworld Liaison—a neutral, non-corruptible Orbiter, who was usually a lieutenant on the human police force—should have transferred the case to the Otherworld authorities already. It was his job to monitor all the police reports, pick up any rare supe cases that slipped through to the human system, and send them to the appropriate Otherworld departments, then remove any trace of them from the human records.

In fact, this case should never have accidentally slipped through to any human in the first place. The Jupiters were witches, everyone knew that, so the Otherworld should have picked it up immediately. These two human detectives shouldn't have ever gotten involved. It was a mistake that should have been fixed already.

You might be right. This is a little disturbing, Brain-Daphne said nervously. *Not exactly unprecedented either.*

It was rare, but it did happen. I'd heard stories of supernatural creatures mistakenly getting arrested by human cops and stuck in human jails, and the stories always ended disastrously.

Last year, a drunk young vampire in Baltimore got hauled in for harassment and burned to a crisp in the midday sun after being forced out into the exercise yard. A few months back, a half-pixie in Tulsa almost died of iron poisoning after being shanked by an old pipe in the dining hall.

In prison, having supernatural powers didn't help at all. The sentient magic of the Great Agreement made it almost impossible to use any magic in public, and if there were more than three sets of human eyeballs watching you, you were in public. We stayed in the shadows to maintain the balance between us supernaturals. It was the law. The Agreement would choke you to death if you defied it.

The detectives were still looking at me. Hartshorn, leaning against the wall, had a soft, pleasant smile on his face. Boggs nodded at me encouragingly. "It's fine, Daphne. You can answer the question."

"Wh— what was the question?" I'd been busy dissociating, and I'd forgotten what they'd asked me.

Boggs smiled. "How many times did you stab Wesley Jupiter?"

"I didn't!"

"Come on," he chuckled. "We know you did."

I shifted in my chair, my discomfort suddenly becoming unbearable. My Orion blades—the murder weapons—were burning a hole in the hidden sheathes at my back. If the detectives decided to arrest me, I'd be searched, and they'd have a concrete piece of evidence, something to match to the stab wounds in Wesley's kidney.

I'd be trapped. Trapped in a concrete box with evil humans. *Evils.*

Suddenly, my gut clenched so hard, it hurt, and I let out a little gasp before I swallowed it down. It was such a visceral response, it shocked and confused me even more.

What the hell was wrong with me? I was used to being scared. I'd spent most of my childhood and adolescence absolutely terrified, running from things that wanted to enslave me, use me, eat me... you name it. Tumbling through hundreds of wild-magic realms and running from demons and beasts made me an expert at dealing with fear.

But this was something new. The feeling squirming in the pit of my stomach was a brand-new anxiety I'd never felt before. Icy cold fear set in, making it hard for me to think.

I'd been an Otherworlder my whole life. Apart from the odd bit of liaising with Orbiters I had to do, I had no experience with humans and the human system. I had no idea what was happening, I had no idea why it was happening, and I was—irrational or not—absolutely terrified.

Brain-Daphne flicked me in the sinuses; the sudden pain snapped me out of my downward spiral. *Suck it up, princess. We're stuck in the human system for now. Let's just behave like a human until we can get this mess sorted out.*

My pulse slowed down a little. My brain was right. I'd seen a handful of cop shows and true crime dramas. What did humans do when they got in legal trouble?

Kill all the witnesses?

That might be a bit extreme. Let's start at the beginning. I opened my mouth. "I think I want a lawyer," I croaked.

No, you fool, you demand a lawyer!

I licked my lips. "I demand a lawyer."

"Why would you need a lawyer, Daphne?" Hartshorn

said, his voice pleasant. He didn't move from his spot, leaning casually against the wall of the interview room. "You're not in trouble. I'm sure there was a good reason you killed him. We're just interested, that's all."

"There's... I didn't..."

"We know about your relationship with Troy Jupiter," Boggs murmured, still smiling across the table at me. "We know Troy dumped you because his family didn't approve of you. You moved all the way from California to be with him, right?"

"Y– yeah..." That was true. My mind was racing. How much did they know about me? How much *could* they know?

"And Troy dumped you the second you showed up," Boggs continued. "Word on the street was that he was embarrassed to be caught with you, a poor nobody. And Troy's mom, Mina, was horrified. She told everyone you were a scheming gold digger." His voice became gentle. "But she was wrong, wasn't she? You were just a woman in love." He shrugged his massive, bullish shoulders. "Honestly, honey, I get it. I love my wife; there's nothing I wouldn't do for her. I know how far you'll go to be with the one you love." He leaned back, his movements deliberately casual. "What did you do with Mina's body?"

I jerked in my seat like I'd been electrocuted. "What?"

"Where did you bury her?" Hartshorn chipped in from the corner. "You must have taken her out at the same time. Where did you put her body?"

Holy guacamole! They think we killed Mina and Wesley because of Troy. This is insane.

But very plausible, my brain muttered. *Think about it. If this was a true crime drama, it would go like this: the human cops find Wesley's body full of stab wounds in a pile of rubble that used to be the Jupiter mansion. Mina hasn't been seen since. They check the CCTV of the street outside and see us two hours before the whole thing collapses. They check the list of suspects and decide that Romeo is untouchable, but we're the one that has the biggest motive, so they drag us in for questioning—*

"Where's Mina's body, Daphne?"

I stammered, "I-I didn't..."

Boggs smiled at me conspiratorially. "We know you did. We're not just shooting the breeze here, sweetie. We know you killed Wesley. You don't have to play pretend."

Brain-Daphne noted the confident smile, the sureness in Detective Bogg's eyes. *They've got something on us. Video footage. Forensic evidence. Proof. Fuck.*

They would have already arrested me, though, if they had something. And they'd be far meaner. They're playing good-cop-good-cop, trying to get a confession. Why?

It takes time for forensic evidence to be processed, maybe? They're probably waiting for results to come back. They're trying to get a quick confession just to save some time.

I had no idea what to do. My heart began to thump in my chest as all the implications set in. The case hadn't been referred to Otherworld authorities, so there was a good chance it wouldn't *ever* get transferred.

I couldn't go to human jail. The thought made me want to tear my own skin off. My breath quickened. It was irrational, but I was starting to panic again.

Calm down. What evidence could they possibly have?

There was none that I could think of, so my brain ran the scene back so we could both watch it. In that beautiful little apple orchard at the top of Hyperion's pillar, I left Romeo to dispatch Mina and snuck up on Wesley from behind. I stabbed him in the back, twisted the blade, muttered something melodramatic, and rushed off. No part of me had touched him, I was sure of that. So why were these two detectives so adamant it was me who'd killed Wesley?

Oh, gods. I was going to jail. Human jail. At best, I'd get attacked by a human at some point and be forced to defend myself. If I even used a tiny bit of my wolf powers in front of the humans, the Great Agreement would choke me to death. At worst, I'd be stuck in a concrete box for years, possibly centuries. The thought of being held captive made sweat break out on my forehead.

Bogg's saw it. His eyes lit up.

I swallowed my anxiety. They didn't have anything concrete on me. If they did, they would have arrested me already. "I didn't kill Wesley Jupiter," I said firmly.

Boggs tilted his head. "We know you did, honey. It's okay. You can tell us all about it." His tone slipped around a little, moving from casual concern to downright patronizing.

Hartshorn was getting impatient too—the easy smile had dropped from his face. My eyes flicked over to him, and I watched as he carefully arranged his expression into one of father-like concern. "You know, Daphne, sweetheart, it's only going to be worse for you if you drag this out."

This is unbearably insulting. They actually think we're dumb enough that this will work?

Apparently, they did. Glancing from Hartshorn and back to Boggs, I suddenly realized what their game was. And then I felt stupid for not realizing it sooner.

"Can you help us out here, sweetie?" Hartshorn asked. "We just need to get to the bottom of this."

We can't be too hard on ourselves. We've never been questioned by the human police, so we have no idea how to act. Plus, the whole concussion thing...

Boggs and Hartshorn actually thought if they empathized with poor, dumb little old me, they'd get me to admit I killed Wesley Jupiter out of spite, just because he made Troy dump me.

I suppose I shouldn't have been surprised. People had been underestimating me my entire life. I'd been caught off guard because I'd been expecting violence and threats.

Boggs leaned forward, trying to catch my eye. His tone turned serious. "A pretty girl like you wouldn't cope in jail, Daphne. Now, I know you're a new social worker. Please don't take this the wrong way, but you guys are really idealistic, and you think the system will protect you like it protects your kids."

I almost laughed. The system had so many bad apples rotting the barrel, it was enough to make you cry. Only last week I had to pick up a runaway shifter kid from a precinct in South Philly who had bruises all over his neck from the dirty cop who manhandled him while hauling him in.

"We're on your side, honey," Hartshorn said, his voice gentle. "We just want to know what went on in that house before it collapsed. Can you fill us in?"

I kept my mouth shut, watching them. I caught the moment when Hartshorn decided to throw a little jab from the corner. He clearly needed to get a reaction out of me. "We know you were dating Troy. Were you sleeping with Wesley too? Daphne, you can tell us."

Okay, that's enough. I'm taking over.

I felt my face harden. "Are we done here? Because I'm getting bored, and I have quite a lot of work to do."

Boggs's eyes flashed. "You haven't answered our questions."

"Yes, I have." I sandwiched my mouth shut and stared back at him, unflinching.

A full minute of silence passed while I watched his expression change in tiny, minute ways. Both detectives were obviously sure that this was the right tactic to take with me. Be nice, be empathetic, build rapport, and I'd confess to murdering Wesley because I was obviously just a dumb, unhinged lovestruck girl out for revenge.

And they were certain I'd done it. My brain was right, they had hard evidence, and it wasn't circumstantial.

Hartshorn shifted, uncrossing his arms and crossing them again. "Great, got one of those split personality girls on our hands," he muttered under his breath. I wasn't supposed to hear him, but I did.

They thought I was crazy.

We are crazy. And we did kill Wesley.

Yes, but—

It was justified, yeah. That doesn't matter. Humans don't play like this, you know, it's all black and white to these people. Brain-Daphne huffed out an irritated breath. *We have to figure out a game plan, babe, because as much as I'd love to stab both of these fuckers and moonwalk out of here, that kind of shit doesn't wash in the human world. If we kill them, the humans will come after us. If we give them any reason to think they're right—and we did kill Wesley—they will arrest us, and they'll have their hands on the murder weapon before we can even blink. We need to find out what they've got on us, and we need to get out of here. As soon as we're out of here, we get hold of Romeo and find out why the case hasn't been transferred to Otherworld authorities. He'll be able to get the case transferred.* Brain-Daphne's confidence wavered a little.

Maybe Romeo couldn't get the case transferred. The Otherworld Liaison was impartial—they had to be. The supernatural leaders couldn't influence them at all.

My intuition was screaming at me that this was on purpose. I'd been thrown to the humans, and I might be stuck here for good.

Well, fuck, my brain said miserably. *Let's just deal with what we can right now. So, let's get out of here. Play into it, and pull the uno reverse card. See what you can get out of them, and let's blow this popsicle stand.*

Boggs took a deep breath and sighed, sounding very disappointed. "Come on, Daphne. Let's not do this. We know it was you. Please, just be honest with us."

I echoed his sigh. "Listen, Detective Boggs, I was trying to be nice and helpful, but y'all are obviously new to this whole detective thing. You're being really weird. I don't know why you keep asking me strange questions. I understand you're trying to do a job, because people are dead, and it's noble of you to try and sort that all out." I nodded seriously. "Good for you. But... Perhaps you need to talk to someone a bit more experienced in homicide cases. Get a mentor or something. There's no shame in admitting you need professional development, you know."

A flash of fury sparked in Bogg's eyes. Whoops. Too far?

"Oh, we know what we're doing, honey," Hartshorn called from the corner. "Don't you worry about that. We're just interested in what you're doing. Why were you at Jupiter's mansion yesterday?"

I shrugged. "I wasn't."

Nice. Now, glue those lips together so you're not tempted to unleash verbal diarrhea to fill the awkward silence, and undo my very admirable attempt at lying.

I did as my brain directed. Hartshorn gave a little growl before he stopped himself. "We know you went there. We got you on CCTV crossing the street."

I laughed. "In Rittenhouse Square? It's one of the main tourist areas in Philadelphia."

The detectives lapsed into silence for a second, both staring at me with carefully blank expressions. They had something on me; I could tell. They were too confident they had the right suspect. And it wasn't just that they spotted me in the area. It was something else.

Boggs took a deep breath through his nose. "Come on, sweetheart. You were right across the street from the mansion."

I widened my eyes. "In a public park? Along with how many other hundred people?" A thought occurred to me. If they caught me on camera, they would have gotten Romeo too.

Is this about him?

Everything was about Romeo. The Jupiter mansion was his property. He had a very public beef with Mina and Wesley. The detectives should have hauled him in for questioning by now. But these two assholes were absolutely sure I was the one who'd killed Wesley, and they were ignoring Romeo like he didn't exist.

I smell a conspiracy.

I agreed with Brain-Daphne's assessment. Someone wanted me to go down, and they were very carefully leaving Romeo out of it.

Boggs sighed again heavily. "We know you killed him, Daphne. It's only a matter of time before everything is confirmed by forensics."

Aha, they do have something concrete. Maybe we left a fleck of spit on Wesley when we stabbed him.

Boggs let his eyebrows droop, leaning into the "disappointed dad" persona. "I was hoping we could talk about this like reasonable, mature people."

I stayed quiet. The silence became more uncomfortable with every second that ticked by.

I knew what was coming next. As soon as Boggs and Hartshorn realized they weren't going to get an easy confession out of me, they'd give up the "disappointed dad" schtick and change tactics.

They'd get mean.

I'd been interrogated a bunch of times, and "disappointed dad" was my favorite. My least favorite was "psychotic sadist scientist." I'd seen it all, and knowing what might be coming just made everything worse.

Relax, my brain told me. *They're humans. The only advantage in being trapped in the human system is they're not allowed to do "psychotic sadist scientist" anymore.*

I ground my teeth, answering my brain internally. Do you not remember that little incident with that secret military black-ops department when I was a kid?

Brain-Daphne chuckled awkwardly. *I forgot about that. They were Orbiters, though, and these are normie cops.*

It wasn't much of a consolation. The detectives couldn't beat me up or experiment on me, but psychological torture wasn't off the table. I braced myself for the inevitable—the point in which they started digging up the details of my relationship with Troy. They'd ask me intimate details about our sex life and what it felt like to be humiliated and dumped. They'd find a sore spot and poke at it over and over. Anything to get a reaction. Trying to find a chink in my armor.

My attention drifted. Outside the interview room, I could hear the sound of rapid, heavy footsteps charging down the corridor. The air buzzed with tension. Multiple officers were rushing somewhere. If I strained my ears, I could just make out the crackle of static and abrupt orders being given over the radio.

Hartshorn's phone vibrated. He ignored it and straightened up, inhaling deeply through his nose. "We'd be far more inclined to be understanding if you came clean right now, Daphne. We just want to get some clarity and move on, so we can take down the real bad guys."

They were acting as if they would just scold me for Wesley's murder, spank me a couple of times, and let me go. They really thought they could get me to confess to murder just by acting like disappointed dads.

I don't like this.

You don't like not being able to stab people for the tiniest of reasons.

That's insulting. I've never stabbed anyone without a good reason. And now we can't! Brain-Daphne whined. *I've never felt so helpless in my life. Being stuck in the human system is the worst.*

Patience. We'll get this sorted out.

What if we don't? What if we're stuck here forever? And... is that a whiff of smoke?

Someone knocked at the door. Hartshorn strode over and pulled it open. "Yes?"

A young man spoke. "The building is being evacuated, sir."

Hartshorn glared at whoever was beyond the door. "Why?" he snapped.

"There's some kind of riot going on right outside."

"A riot? Who the hell is rioting?"

"We're not sure, sir," the officer said, the quiver in his tone betraying his panic. "We're assuming gang activity, but we can't get confirmation on the perps just yet. We've got multiple officers down and several cruisers flipped and on fire out back. All available units are on their way, and we're all being asked to evacuate the building. Please leave through the front—the back exit seems to be under attack."

Some of the dread swirling in the pit of my stomach eased. That was a stroke of luck. Now that the door was open, I could hear the activity in the corridor a lot clearer. Radios blared static and orders. Shouts and thumping boots raced back and forth. In the crack of the open door, I caught a glimpse of a squad thundering past wearing riot gear and holding shields.

Hartshorn let out an exasperated grunt. "Fine." He slammed the door on the poor kid, and turned, exchanging a loaded glance with Boggs. "Let's wrap this up."

Boggs glared at me. "I'm disappointed, Daphne. Maybe we gave you too much credit. I was hoping you'd do the right thing."

Relief flooded me. They weren't going to arrest me just yet. Whatever forensic evidence they had, it wasn't enough to hold me yet.

I just had to find out *what* they had. I had to find out who the hell was pulling strings to keep this case in the human system and why they were keeping Romeo out of it.

Hartshorn was already halfway out the door. "Don't leave town."

CHAPTER
TWO

I breathed a sigh of relief as I walked down the steps of the station. Some of the tightness in my chest eased, but the swirling anxiety in my gut hadn't quite vanished. My natural optimism was struggling to reassert itself.

It didn't help that the weather was terrible. Winter still held the city in its icy grasp, refusing to let go and give way to the hope of an early spring. The pretty banks of white snow were long gone, leaving sad piles of chilly, dirty mush in the streets. The sky above me was the same color as the concrete buildings surrounding me—no fluffy clouds or peek of dazzling blue. I could almost hear the sun whining miserably, stuck behind the solid gray curtain. It was trapped—like I could have been if the detectives had arrested me. Stuck in a concrete box, surrounded by human witnesses, unable to use any of my wolf strength or speed to defend myself. Trapped. Unable to escape. Unable to move.

Suddenly, my heart thudded. Despair surged within me. Something about the idea of being trapped in a box was triggering my nervous system and sending a rush of adrenaline through my bloodstream.

Holy shit. What is happening? Why are we so fucking scared?

I had no idea, and I didn't know how to stop it. This wasn't a simple panic attack. I was spiraling, the despair overwhelming me.

The edges of my vision darkened. The steps of the station started to swim in front of my eyes. Blackness threatened to consume me. It was right there. Pain. Suffering.

Evil.

Brain-Daphne kicked me in the temple, sending me reeling back a step. *Breathe! Deep breath and hold it!*

I gulped in a deep breath, forcing the air into my too-tight chest.

Gratitude list, now!

With enormous effort, I wrenched faces out of the blackness before it devoured me completely—faces that had saved me many times before.

Chloe. Uncle Nate. The countess, reluctantly dragging me out of trouble, and Dwayne, cheerfully getting me into it. Aunt Marche, making cookies in the giant kitchen in Castlemaine. Romeo, his lips buried in my neck, his hands tangled in my hair.

The darkness receded. *Good, good. Keep holding that breath. More faces. The ones you haven't seen in ages.*

Prue surged out of the blackness, emerging in my mind's eye from a memory when she'd last come to visit before I got lost—running full-speed down the main street in Castlemaine in her skeleton form, laughing like a hyena, before turning into a giant squid and tackling Norma in the lake.

I'd had so much fun with Prue on her short visits to

Castlemaine. She was the one who taught me how to see the joy in everything. Chloe taught me resilience, Prue taught me joy, Sandy and Aunt Marche gave me the gift of letting myself be mothered.

They all loved me so much.

I let that feeling fill me. Gratitude, love, respect. It was the bright light that chased away the darkness.

That's it, my brain said encouragingly. *Now, exhale. Release the lingering fear. Get it all out.*

Exhaling in a big whoosh, I mentally pushed all of the negative emotions out, releasing the confusion, the doubt, the despair. I had no idea why I'd gotten so overwhelmed at the idea of being locked up. That thought had never bothered me before.

Or had it? Something was niggling at me, but I couldn't quite put my finger on it, and it had nothing to do with the detective's accusations.

Maybe it was the sounds of the riot behind the police station. I could still hear faint shouts and the odd scream of twisted metal and smell the acrid stench of smoke.

After a few more deep, slow breaths, I opened my eyes. I felt better. The day was still gray and cold, but it had to be like this sometimes, because it made the sunny days even brighter. And besides, with that thick cloud cover, Valerie, my addled vampire friend, would be able to head out of the Hidden City to stock up on supplies. As usual, she'd mugged me on the way through the park on the way to work. I kept a roll of twenties just for her.

There was always a silver lining; you just had to look for it. The cold, empty streets just made the indoors cozier. The chill in the air made your cheeks rosy. Spring would be here soon. It was inevitable.

A low baritone voice sang softly from behind me. "Well,

hello pretty baby, how you doing today? You know you drive me crazy, please don't send me away..."

Stephen, the soul-stealer, was back to serenade me. I'd been so lost in my downward spiral, I'd missed the scent of street trash and death.

Goddamnit, my brain hissed. *I went to all that effort to get your good mood back, and this soul-stealing bastard had to ruin it again.*

The scratchy sound of pigeon claws on concrete moved beside me. The soul-stealer was closer to me than he'd been lately, which was unusual for him. He'd learned quickly I wasn't above killing the ride he'd stolen as soon as he was in reach.

I gritted my teeth and plastered a smile on my face. "Nope, I'm not letting you ruin this for me."

The soul-stealer tapped his little claws, getting closer, and sung again, faster this time. "You gotta give me your number baby, so we can do the dirty, let's do the flirty, baby, and I know you won't hurt me."

Curiosity pricked me. Stephen seemed to favor cheesy country songs from the early nineties, but this was an oddly sped-up version.

"Just stay still and listen to it," Stephen hissed in his normal tone, then he sang quickly again. "Put your arms around me, and rub them up and down me, baby, you changed me forever, I know you won't leave me like you found me—"

Despite my irritation, a grin pricked my lips. "Lennox ordered you to sing the whole song, didn't he?"

Lennox Arran, the new Alpha Shifter of Philadelphia, clearly hadn't given up his quest to win me over. He was under the impression that if he got the soul-stealer to follow me around and serenade me, I'd eventually realize what I was missing and fall into his arms.

"Believe me, child," Stephen whispered. "I am enjoying this just as much as you are."

"Well, you can stop at any time, you know."

"Then I would not enjoy the privileges I receive under the Alpha. I enjoy having the ear of one of the supernatural leaders of this city, child. We are magical creatures. We all must bow to someone. What do you expect me to do, bend the knee to that ghastly boyfriend of yours?" He shuddered dramatically.

I shrugged. "You could. You *should*. You're a witch, and he's the High Priest."

"You know as well as I do, he would kill me the second he got his hands on my mortal body."

That was true. Stephen had committed too many unforgivable crimes. Still... "Romeo's not a monster, Stephen."

The pigeon sneered at me. "We're all monsters, child. Perspective is everything. Even Alpha Arran called you a monster this morning, because, as he quite colorfully put it, you have refused to open your legs. You are, apparently, withholding that sweet pussy from him, and that makes you a monster."

I grimaced. At some point, I'd have to do something about Lennox. "What I meant was, Romeo does make allowances for those who seek redemption."

"Redemption?" Stephen snorted.

"You could stop being such a despicable bastard and start helping people instead of sneaking around and spying on them. It's not too late to try to be a better person."

"I am a perfectly respectable person."

"You're a witch using low-level blood magic to power your necromancy. Those pigeons suffer terribly when you kick them out of their bodies, you know."

"Pish. They are dumb beasts who are here to be used as tools for our benefit." He scowled at the ground. "Just like the new Alpha. Eventually, I will figure out how to push his buttons so he will cease sending me on these ridiculous errands."

"You won't," I told him. "You're underestimating him just like you underestimated me. Yes, Lennox is bombastic and vain and narcissistic, but he's not a fool. He knows what he wants, and he's not going to stop until he gets it..." I trailed off, my heart sinking.

What Lennox wanted was me. He wasn't going to stop.

"Can't you try and push him to do something else with his time?" I heard the whine in my voice, but I couldn't stop myself. "I don't know, become a philanthropist or something?"

Stephen let out a bark of laughter. "I don't even think that man understands the concept of charity. The only thing—other than you, of course—that has been consuming his time is his new career path. Now that he has retired from boxing, he is trying to decide between becoming a reality TV star or throwing his hat in the ring to become the new mayor of Philadelphia."

My shoulders slumped. Politics? God help us all. "Stephen, you don't have to do this," I moaned. "You could be doing something worthy with your magic, you know. Something for the good of society."

"I am! I am trying to climb my way back up the ladder to the Alpha's favor so that I can continue to make money to feed myself. Do I have to remind you that it's entirely your fault I have to do this?"

"I meant for charity."

"Charity begins at home. Anyway, child. Stay still and listen to this wretched song, so I can truthfully tell him I completed the task he set for me." He cleared his throat, singing so fast the words blurred together. "Let's get nakey, baby, let's get freaky, baby, let's roll in the hay all day, okaaaay..."

I turned my head so nobody on the street below could see me scolding a pigeon and raised my voice, cutting him off. "Stephen, stop. This is absurd. You're better than this. You're smart. There's so many better things you could be doing with your talents—"

"Child." The pigeon stopped and cocked his head. "You're delusional. Our powers don't grant us freedom. They're a cage. Just because I know how to work a cleaning spell to wipe the sweat stains out of my—" He cut himself off and inhaled deeply through his beak.

I tried one more time. "You can do better. I know you can."

The pigeon watched me carefully for a second. "No, you're not delusional. You're willfully ignorant. At least I can face the truth." A dark fire blazed in his beady little eyes. "We live in the Otherworld. Nothing is fair. We are at the whim of those who are more magically powerful than us by fortune of birth. Our talents are not our own, girl, they're to be used by those stronger than us. I serve the Alpha Shifter because it is the more palatable option for me."

There was no getting through to him. The soul-stealer was so irredeemably selfish, he had resigned himself to do humiliating errands for the Alpha rather than to use his magic to help other people.

"That's not true at all," I said.

"You actually think you have autonomy. Ha! Child, you are only free to walk these streets as a creature of the Otherworld because you have a pretty face and big breasts. You're too stupid to realize our leaders grant you that freedom." A sneer twisted his little face. "I suppose you'd rather lie to yourself and pretend that you sleep with all those powerful men because you *love* them, don't you?'

A hot fury gripped me; my pulse roared in my ears, almost drowning out the soul-stealer's disgusting diatribe.

His voice thickened. "You found a Jupiter boy in Castlemaine, and of course you let him warm your bed, then a better option came along when Lennox Arran decided he'd take you. And now you're opening your legs for the Warlock, just to hedge your bets."

My fists clenched, but I felt frozen to the spot as darkness threatened to overwhelm me again. I was almost paralyzed with rage.

He chuckled. "You might have everyone else fooled, but not me, not anymore. You're just like me, girl. Debasing yourself for your master's favor. At least I'm not as bad as you. I'm surprised you can hold a conversation after having so many men's dicks in your mouth—"

Let me.

My foot kicked out, catching the pigeon in the chest, flinging him against the concrete wall beside me. A split-second later I stomped on his head, crushing it under my boot.

CHAPTER
THREE

The darkness swamped me.

The soul-stealer was gone, but his words echoed in my head, bouncing around, sending eddies of pain and despair whenever they hit the walls of my psyche, and flinging me back into the dark pit within me that swirled with the horrors of my past. Doubt. Suffering. Confusion. Rage.

Evils.

My legs wobbled. The concrete steps of the police precinct stretched out below me, threatening my equilibrium and promising pain and suffering if I fell. Brain-Daphne screamed, urging me to breathe, but I just *couldn't*.

I couldn't see. I couldn't breathe. For a long moment, I was lost.

Hey. The voice echoed through the filter of pain. **Baby girl.**

Dwayne. He was here. Desperately, I hung on, listening to his voice inside my head.

What's the difference between your mom and a bowling ball?

He was beside me. *Thank the gods.* I panted. "Wha—What?"

You can only get three fingers in a bowling ball.

Slowly, the black agony drained from my head, letting in a sliver of light. I took a shallow breath and huffed it out. Then another one.

You can do better than that.

I could. I inhaled deeply. It felt like my cage had opened, and I was finally free. The sensation felt so good, I dived into it headfirst, savoring it. I was alive, I had my best friend beside me, and I had freedom.

I blinked a few times, clearing my vision. The city street still lay before me. I was still standing on the concrete steps of the police station. It was still cold, the day was still gray, but I was alive.

That soul-stealing fucker was wrong, my brain seethed, pissed at her failure to yank me out of my panic attack. It didn't feel like a panic attack, though. It felt... apocalyptic. *Why did we let him get to us?*

I had no idea, but I wasn't going to dwell on it right now. Turning my head, I smiled down at Dwayne, standing right beside me. I held my smile until it felt less forced, less panicked, more natural. "Where did you come from?"

He wrinkled his beak—a stunning feat, since it was diamond-hard and razor-sharp. **No idea. I'm pretty sure I was formed instantly from the explosion within the primordial goop that sparked life in my home universe.** He waved his wing idly. **I was, and always will be, yada yada yada.**

"No, I mean, where were you? Last time I saw you, you were flirting with that old blind woman who works at the DMV across the street from our department."

She's visually impaired, actually, little one. And

she's an Oracle. You can hardly blame me. I'm bored, and Asherah isn't back yet.

Dwayne's girlfriend, the fae Diplomat, was on extended leave and had gone home to Faerie for a few weeks. He'd been horribly depressed about it. At first, I thought he missed her, but it turns out he was just feeling guilty.

Eventually he confessed to me that Asherah had asked him to join her in Faerie. Dwayne, who didn't want to go, lied and told her he had to stay here to look after me. Naturally, Asherah took this to mean he loved me more than her and had flown into a jealous rage. Luckily, she had to leave for Faerie before she could track me down and kill me.

It wasn't the first time one of Dwayne's girlfriends got so jealous they tried to destroy me. Norma used to try to eat me all the time. I raised an eyebrow. "Asherah will murder the Oracle if she hears about you flirting with her."

That's why I'm hitting on the Oracle. At least she'll see Asherah coming.

I stifled my smile. Dwayne always knew how to drag me out of the darkness. "That's very thoughtful of you."

I'm a thoughtful kind of guy. Besides, you'll be happy to know I sorted out things with Asherah, so she's not going to kill you anymore.

That was a piece of good news I sorely needed to hear. "Really?"

Yeah. Sent her some love letters, smoothed it all over. She's cool.

"When did you do that?" It was only yesterday morning that he confessed he'd thrown me under the bus.

Right after I told you. Went straight to a porter-sorter post office in Harlem.

So *that's* what he'd been doing in Harlem. "Right." I eyeballed him suspiciously. There was a good chance he'd made everything worse. "What did you tell her?"

He let out a sad honk-sigh. **I confessed that I lied to her. I told her I didn't really have to stay here and look after you. I admitted that I don't even like you that much, and I only used you as an excuse to stay home because I was scared of meeting her mom.**

Asherah's mom was Queen Maeve, the ruler of all the Unseelie, a woman so powerful and terrible—

Well, Dwayne would definitely try to shag her, too. It was a *really* good thing he didn't go. But he should have thought about what lie he wanted to give Asherah before he refused.

I told her I was worried her mom wouldn't approve of me, Dwayne went on, laying it on thick. **I was scared that she wouldn't think I was good enough for her little girl. I'm so honest and vulnerable,** he honked sadly. **And sweet.**

I frowned. "You just didn't want to go because you hate Faerie. Too much glitter and not enough beer, you said."

Fae wine makes me gassy. Anyway, Asherah is fine now. The crazy jealous bomb has been deactivated. I *may* have floated the idea of an open relationship, but I backtracked on that one before she flipped her lid.

I pressed my lips together. "That was probably wise, sir."

Anyway, she's not going to kill you, and she's cool about being long-distance until she comes back. Let's change the subject. You got arrested, huh?

"No, just questioned." I took a deep breath and let out a heavy sigh. "I think I'm in trouble, Dwayne. The human cops found Wesley Jupiter's body in the rubble of the mansion."

Just his? Dwayne frowned. **Didn't we leave a whole trail of bodies in there?**

"Yeah, but Wesley's was the only one that was still

intact. The rest of the bodies were in tiny pieces. Romeo turned Mina to marble and blew her up. The two Russian mages both got hit with explosives. And Christopher Jupiter probably got vaporized when the Star Door went supernova." A wave of exhaustion hit me; I dropped into a crouch so I could sit on the cold concrete steps of the precinct next to Dwayne.

Gods, I was tired. And hungry. I had sacrificed breakfast this morning in favor of a bit more sleep before limping to work. I'd been hoping to grab something at the office, but the tiny gap between this morning's clients had been taken up by Monica, my boss, who scolded me non-stop for missing the emergency callouts over the weekend. I was on call, and I'd forgotten.

Tired, hungry, broken... and in trouble with the human police. With no time to recover at all.

No wonder I was spiraling. I sighed wearily. "I'm guessing the remains of all the other bodies were mixed up with the rubble. When the pocket dimension imploded, it all got sucked back to the Hellenic realm, along with the rest of the creatures they'd summoned."

Dwayne wrinkled his beak. **Probably a good thing. That cyclops smelled even worse dead than he did alive.**

I gave a little shudder, remembering how Dwayne had flown me out of the imploding pocket dimension wrapped up in the cyclops's dirty loincloth. A dry heave lurched in my gut. Urgh.

In my mind's eye, Brain-Daphne picked up that memory, squeezed it into a little ball, and slam-dunked it into the sludgy darkness within me, dusted off her hands, and gave a little huff of satisfaction.

"But Wesley's body was intact, and it didn't belong to that realm," I continued, feeling less nauseous. "So, it was pushed out and left behind in the rubble of the mansion.

The cops found it—with the stab wounds I gave him—and now I'm the number one suspect for his murder."

Well. Dwayne gave a little goosey shrug. **I suppose you *did* kill him.**

"Yeah, I did. I just can't figure out how they know that, though." I narrowed my eyes, peering off into the distance of the city. I had to get moving soon, but I couldn't bring myself to stand up just yet. I was too sore, too tired. "Apparently, the cops have something on me," I mumbled, rubbing my hands together to keep them warm. "Forensic evidence. I just don't know what it is. If they searched me, they'd have the murder weapon, and I'd be screwed. I was lucky that the building was evacuated so they let me go for now."

Evacuated, you say? Dwayne's voice in my head was too casual. **That was a stroke of luck.**

Suspicion pricked me. I glanced down at him and ran my eyes over his magnificent white feathers.

Soot dusted his tail. A smear of bright-red blood stained the tip of his wings.

"Dwayne..." I glared down at him. "Did you know I was hauled in for questioning? Did you start the riot just to get me out of the building?"

No. Dwayne narrowed his eyes at me and frowned, clearly offended. **Of course not.**

"Oh."

I never need a reason to start a riot with the cops, baby girl. You should know that. He balled his wing into a fist. **ACAB forever.**

I tried not to smile. "Okay."

Actually, though, I did them a favor. Their emergency response training is horrific. I barely did anything. I just flipped a couple of cruisers and set fire to some old trash in the alleyway out back of the station.

"Really?" I peered down at him. "Because I was *sure* I heard screams and reports of several officers down—"

He blew a raspberry. **That's what I'm talking about. Those idiots tripped over their own feet. One of them actually fell into one of the burning cruisers. Another guy had an asthma attack and couldn't remember where he put his inhaler. Who *does* that?**

I stared at him for a moment.

Dwayne shrugged. **I might have swooped a couple of them. Threw a soup can or two. If their whole unit goes to hell and they have to evacuate the building just because one little goose decides to fuck some shit up in the alley, then they need to sharpen up.**

As usual, Dwayne made several good points. "Well... in that case.... Thanks." I smiled down at him. "I appreciate you getting me out of there."

He gave a little honk. **Oh, thank you, little one. It was fun. I hope to do it again sometime soon.**

"You might get your wish." I put my elbows on my knees, resting my head in my hands.

Why?

"There's a good chance I'm going to get hauled in again soon," I said gloomily. "The detectives investigating Wesley's murder aren't done with me. For some reason, the case hasn't been automatically handed over to Otherworld authorities."

That's weird.

"Yeah, it's very weird. Because of all the high-profile players in this game, I'm going to assume that the Otherworld Liaison is blocking the transfer for some reason." I gnawed on my lip for a second. "The Liaison is supposed to be impartial and above reproach. Something fishy is going on."

Well, I like eating fish. So, what's the plan?

"I need to talk to Romeo," I said. "I've already called him. I tried when the detectives were walking me into the station, but he hasn't called me back yet."

I didn't want to seem desperate or needy, so I didn't message him again. Worry squirmed in my gut, mingling with the gnawing hunger.

Romeo had been injured badly when the Star Door exploded and threw us fifty yards into an apple orchard. I was still feeling the effects of a torn labrum, a slight concussion, and countless itchy, healing cuts, scrapes, and burns.

And Romeo didn't have my advanced shifter healing. He'd taken all the potions he had on-hand and fell asleep with me cuddled up beside him while Levi worked some regenerative spells.

A tingle of unease poked me with icy fingers. Romeo would always call me back as soon as he was physically able to. The man had torn a hole in a pocket dimension for me. He'd shadow-jumped out of a plane and across a quarter of the country just to make sure I was okay.

But he hadn't called me back.

Even Brain-Daphne was suddenly nervous. *He was pretty fucked up in that explosion.*

Again, it was because he'd been covering me with his body when the Star Door went supernova. He'd been protecting me. Again.

No, he was fine. He had to be. His strength was phenomenal. This morning when I dragged myself out of his bed, Romeo had woken up to kiss me goodbye. He was still battered and bruised, but the broken bones were almost healed, and his concussion had faded.

Unfortunately, I didn't have the luxury of being able to stay with him. Not only was I physically much better, but I also had to go to work. I had clients to see and vulnerable children to check on. And I felt so guilty about missing the emergency call outs yesterday, I couldn't bring myself to blow off work and stay in bed.

My phone buzzed in my pocket. I yanked it out, excited, but my heart dropped as soon as I saw the message from Levi.

"Romeo is still asleep," I said to Dwayne. "Levi says Romeo's healing fine, but Levi wants to know if he can help me with whatever I need instead." The cold concrete beneath me was freezing my butt, but I was too tired to get up just yet. I rocked from side-to-side and grimaced. "I can read between the lines. The guys want him to rest as much as possible." It would be awful of me to dump another problem into Romeo's lap while he was recovering from life-threatening injuries.

I blew out a long exhale, watching it turn to vapor in the cold air. "In the grand scheme of things, my petty legal drama isn't urgent. It can wait."

Unless the detectives arrested me. I might not be able to contact Romeo. I could disappear forever. I was sure I'd heard of that happening in the human system before. Deported, disappeared...

A tendril of darkness writhed in my gut.

Dwayne swiveled his magnificent neck around until he was facing me. Glaring, actually. **You're injured. You need rest, too, little one. You're gonna get burned out.**

"Yeah, but I need to get back to work. I've got two clients in the office in ten minutes."

I know about burnout. If you work too hard and don't take time to recover, you burn out. He eyed me sternly and pointed at me with his wingtip. **And the only cure for it is setting fire to things.**

"Uh..." I frowned. "I don't think that's right."

Trust me, I'm an expert. I can help. Do you want me to burn down your office building for you?

I thought of Judy, smirking while listening to Monica ream me out for missing my emergency callouts and, for a second, I was tempted. "No, thanks." I shook my head. "It won't help, anyway. I've got home visits in the afternoon, and I'm still on call. If the office is burned down, I'll still have work to do."

Well, the offer is there. Say the word, and I'll—

"It's okay." I forced another smile. "I have to head back. We'll have to figure this all out later. Everything will be fine," I said, trying to hold the smile without grimacing. "Things will be better tomorrow."

CHAPTER
FOUR

It was tomorrow, and I was *not* better. If anything, I was much worse.

I'd barely slept a wink. My eyes were gritty, my hip was still sore, my healing cuts and burns itched like crazy, and my head felt like it was stuffed with cotton.

Even climbing the steps of my office building exhausted me. I rode my motorcycle into the office today, hoping a quick burst of speed would make me feel better, but my riding leathers already felt like a heavy suit of armor. To be fair, armor would be appropriate; I was heading into a battle I was dreading.

I walked back into the Department of Human Services double-fisting two mega-grande cups of espresso. Neither of them were for me. I'd already consumed all the caffeine I could manage, and none of it had made a dent in my exhaustion.

Dwayne followed right behind me, waddling through the human office, fiddling with the police radio he'd stolen during the riot and stashed under his wing. He was oddly attached to it. I didn't want to tell him it made me jump every time it blared static.

Dwayne was right; I was dangerously close to burnout. There was nothing I could do about it right now, though. I had to work.

While I passed through the human office security check, I tried to think about good things to pick my mood up. The only good thing I could think of was Romeo.

I only managed a brief phone call with him last night. He was healing well. The intense yearning I felt for him was bittersweet. It would have been a lot sweeter if Cole hadn't called first, begging me to leave Romeo alone and let him rest for a day or two. "I know what he's like, Daphne," Cole had pleaded. "It's not you, it's him. Rome is obsessed with you. He won't rest if you're here; I know that for a fact. He won't be able to keep his hands off you, and we need him firing on all cylinders as soon as possible. It's either this, or Levi's gonna take one for the team and drop a knock-out spell into Romeo's coffee. And then, of course, Romeo will kill him when he wakes up. Do you want Levi's death on your hands, Daphne? Do you?"

Cole was dramatic but not entirely wrong.

I spent the rest of the night with extreme emotions— intense yearning and overwhelming guilt—warring within me. I wanted to go to him so badly. He'd asked me to come over. If I did, he'd fix all my problems.

But Cole was right; Romeo had to rest. I did too.

But I couldn't.

While I was on my way home from my last client's house, Monica had called me late in the afternoon to ask me about my run-in with the human detectives. I was hoping I could pretend I was assisting them with a case and not have to tell her what was going on, but someone had clearly ratted me out. She'd requested a meeting first thing this morning.

Dwayne and I headed to the O-CPS office in the corner

of the floor. The police radio under his wing blared as I opened the door, and I jumped.

Not wanting to explain it to my colleagues, I gave Dwayne a meaningful stare as I walked to my desk. He turned down the volume on the police radio, tucked it back under his wing, hopped up on my desk, and lay down to preen his feathers.

Judy, my witch colleague, paused her game of Minecraft, looked up from her laptop, saw the cups of coffee in my hands, and smirked. "A bribe, Daphne? Really?"

"It's not a bribe. Just a gift." I certainly hoped an offering of twenty-two shots of espresso would placate Monica, at least a little bit. The woman was made up of mostly caffeine, so it should see her through until the end of the day. "I'm just trying to be nice."

"You're not fooling anyone." Judy chuckled nastily, her eyes glittering with satisfaction. "And I think you're seriously underestimating how much trouble you're in." She turned back to her laptop, mumbling under her breath with a smile on her face. "... can't wait to hear all about how you've fucked up this time. Your new 'boyfriend' won't even be able to save you now." She sniggered.

I heard her put audible quote marks around the word "boyfriend." I didn't want to think about what she meant by it. Whatever it was, it was bound to be really mean.

I glanced towards my boss's office. As usual, Monica was pacing back and forth behind her desk like a tiger with her headset on, talking to one of the other department managers. Despite Monica's unpunctuated, rapid-fire speech, I could hear her quite clearly. She was wrapping up the call.

Time to face the music. I put down the coffee cups, took off my backpack, and placed it on my chair. Judy watched me out of the corner of her eye and abruptly paused her game when I picked the coffee cups back up. She leaned over on her desk and adjusted a little crystal-and-twig pyramid set up on the corner, moving the quartz points to face Monica's office. A whiff of cranberry-flavored magic told me it was an audio enhancing spell.

Judy was planning on listening in on my meeting with Monica, and she didn't care that I knew. She let out another gleeful chuckle and unpaused her game.

I huffed out a breath. Judy hated me, and I had no idea why. As an unapologetic people-pleaser, it drove me insane. I'd tried to figure out why she had it in for me, but after a month in the job I realized that Judy hated everyone. She even despised her friends.

At first, I felt sorry for her. I assumed she was a general, free-floating misery-guts type of person who couldn't find joy in anything. I understood it as a defense mechanism—nobody could ever hurt you if you beat them to it by being as mean and unhappy as possible, all the time.

She had gotten worse with me the longer I worked with her, though. The jabs and insults became more targeted to the point where she was actively trying to get me fired almost every day. Her awful bitchiness wasn't just a defense mechanism. She wasn't as mean to James, our other colleague; she practically ignored him. Soon, I realized that she was jealous of me. It gave an extra punch to her meanness.

Despite all this, I still felt sorry for her. Judy was only really happy when everyone else was miserable. I'd much rather be happy than not, and the power to choose lay entirely within ourselves.

It was the second time in two days I'd had to confront someone who deliberately chose to have a miserable life. Like the soul-stealer, Judy didn't have to be like this. She didn't have to be a jealous, selfish, bitter harpy. She could devote herself to educating the parents who so desperately needed help. She could choose compassion, empathy, service, and love, and her whole life would change for the better.

But she didn't want to. She wanted to play Minecraft and amuse herself by listening to Monica yell at me.

The glass office door banged, and I jumped. One of these days Monica was going to shatter it completely. She glared at me from the doorway. For a split second, her eyes dropped to the cups in my hand, then focused back on me. "You. In here. Now."

I scuttled in, handing her both coffee cups on the way past her. She took one in each hand, and, like a woman dying of thirst, took a huge swig out of one, then the other, then moved back behind her desk and began pacing back and forth in the way that reminded me of a videogame character stuck on an inescapable level.

"Daphne..." Monica's voice quivered and suddenly I realized she was almost vibrating with anxiety. "I'm trying to remain cool here, trying not to blow up or break down or explode completely, dear, and I know you understand how stressful this job can be—"

"I do," I murmured, nodding seriously. Monica's machine-gun staccato speech patterns made it difficult to know when it was a good time to talk, but I wanted her to know I was actively listening to her.

"—and it can be incredibly stressful at the best of times, we're understaffed, overworked, under resourced, overwhelmed, underfunded, over inspected, underestimated, overextended, undervalued, overutilized—"

I nodded along patiently, wondering if something in her head was broken. She was twitching like a short-circuiting robot. Stressed was Monica's default mode, but this was something else.

"And that's normal, love, that's natural for the Department of Human Resources, but now, of course, the government is slashing everything around here, nobody wants to fund any sort of government department anymore, our budgets are worn down to nothing because those silver-tongued devils up in the capitol decided it was a good idea to campaign on the notion that anyone who receives any help from social services is a lazy layabout stealing your hard-earned tax dollars, the general public is eating it up, they got the average person thinking—"

Monica paced faster. Back and forth, back and forth. My gaze drifted down. She'd worn a path in the carpet all the way down to the bare concrete underneath. "—and now there are people out there who call themselves Christians who will turn their heads away from a starving orphaned child and refuse to help because they don't want their tax dollars going towards helping the little kiddos, *nooo*, they'd rather it go towards tax cuts for billionaires or bailing out another failing bank or to prop up an already overfunded bloated military budget—"

I worked hard to keep my expression blank and kept nodding, while Brain-Daphne made a yeesh face. *Look at her go. Our boss is on the verge of rolling out the guillotine. Paint an A for Anarchy symbol on the back of her snazzy blazer and stick a Molotov cocktail in her hand.*

I kept my response internal, while I watched Monica whizz back and forth behind her desk. If Monica wanted to weed out the bloated bureaucrats who took advantage of the system, she could start by firing Judy. That woman did barely any O-CPS work, and what little she does makes everything worse.

Except Judy has contacts in government, remember? That's

why she hasn't been fired already. Kinda hard to drain the swamp when the swamp creatures are actually the ones holding all the power.

Monica's voice reached a fever pitch. "... trying to balance the budget and work with what we've been given but at this stage, our budget has been slashed so much we might as well start considering our jobs as volunteer work because goodness knows I'd make more money working the drive-thru at Burrito Burgerama..."

I glanced at my watch. I had client meetings starting soon—three of them, back-to-back, then I still needed to do a home visit in the Hidden City once I was done for the day. While I appreciated Monica's sudden crusading social justice rant, I needed to get moving. I just needed to wait for her to take a breath so I could cut in and interrupt her.

Monica, unfortunately, seemed to have a never-ending supply of oxygen for talking. "Cindy's addicts are ringing all day and all night, wondering when she'll be back so they can come for their meetings again, she had three big meetings scheduled today and all of them needed to be pushed back because she's not coming in today or tomorrow and now of course all the recovering addicts are losing their minds because she hasn't told me when she'll be back..."

Brain-Daphne twitched. *Cindy's away?*

That wasn't like her. The meeting room planner was always filled in with her little squares, marking out the times she'd booked the room for her drug and alcohol counselling session. Cindy, a no-nonsense, straight-shooting gothflower pixie, took her job very seriously. As a recovered addict herself, she'd devoted herself to helping other supes with dependency and addiction issues.

I hadn't known Cindy for very long, but I liked her a lot. She had a strong work ethic, and she genuinely cared about people. I knew it wasn't like her to cancel her meetings without warning. I hoped she was okay.

A squirm in my gut made me uncomfortable. My intuition was poking me.

Was it my intuition, though, or just bog-standard anxiety borne from years of worrying about people who had mysteriously vanished?

I racked my brains. The last time I'd seen her was Saturday, four days ago, when she screeched like a banshee and zoomed out the window, trying to get away from Romeo Zarayan.

I kept forgetting that most supes were terrified of him. And for good reason, too, since he was insanely powerful, wealthy, ferocious, mysterious, *and* he'd blown the former High Priestess to a fine mist during a formal challenge.

Having Romeo show up in our office out of the blue was enough to make anyone nervous. Cindy had run away as soon as she saw him, zooming straight out the window, in fact, before I had the chance to explain to her he wasn't as bad as his reputation made him out to be. Yes, Romeo Zarayan was ruthless and merciless, but only when he had to be.

When Cindy came back, I'd talk to her. I'd introduce her to Romeo and explain about Aunt Marche.

He's probably okay with sharing the truth about what happened between them now that bitch Bella's influence had gone.

I certainly hoped so. Eventually, I hoped to introduce him to my friends and family as my boyfriend. I was acutely aware it wouldn't go very well if they still thought he'd murdered our beloved Aunt Marche in cold blood.

I tuned back to my boss. "... not only do I have a laundry list of addicts calling me day and night wondering when Cindy will be back, we've also got a new list of a small handful of missing human children that may or may not have mysteriously disappeared due to supernatural involvement, James is busy cross-checking the list to see if there's any connection to anyone on the supe records, and of course you know that's just what we need at a time like this, kids go missing because of magical means, we're getting squeezed by the humans on all sides right now—"

I cleared my throat. "Monica, I'm so sorry to interrupt, but I have clients coming in a minute."

"Of course, of course," Monica's pacing slowed a fraction. "I'll get straight to the point, Daphne dear." She whirled around to face me directly and drained one of the coffee cups, then the other, before slamming both down on her desk. "The human police suspect you of murdering Wesley Jupiter."

I opened my mouth and shut it again. Then, I opened it. "Yes. But—"

"I don't want to know." Monica started pacing again. "If you did do it, well, good for you, that man was the worst High Priest this city ever had, and he and that bitch of a wife deserve to dance in the fiery pits of hell for the part they played pushing their awful class war against the poor. I'm only an Orbiter, but I know as well as anyone that they were the worst that witchcraft ever had to offer."

My mouth dropped open.

Monica whirled around and pointed at me again. "That's not my point. My point is, Daphne, I can't lose you. You and James are already doing the work of what should be a department of eight O-CPS officers."

"Why would you lose me?"

She exhaled heavily, momentarily lost for words. "Because if the human police don't drop the case quickly, I'll have to fire you."

I gasped. "Monica—"

"My hands are tied, Daphne. You've completed your supervision hours early, and you're a fully qualified social worker now, but your probation period isn't up yet. If the police arrest you for the murder of Wesley Jupiter, I'll have to fire you, and you'll be de-registered. I don't mean if you get convicted in a court. I mean if they even try to take you in, you're done here."

My gut lurched. "But..."

"I have no choice." Monica's sharp eyes softened a little. "I'm getting pressure from above to let you go now, since this homicide case has landed in the humans' laps, and we all know how bad murder looks to the normies. And my direct boss at Otherworld Social Services knows that the longer this stays with the humans, the harder it will be to cover up."

"But—"

"Yes, I know it's a mistake, the case should be dealt with by the Otherworld authorities, but it hasn't been transferred, and because it hasn't, it's made my life a living hell. The optics are bad, I just had an email from one of the Department of Human Services directors asking me why you haven't been fired yet. The humans would never dream of having a murder suspect running around their little normie office. If this doesn't go away, and *soon*, they want you gone." Monica took an uncharacteristic heavy pause. "Daphne, there are no new grads to take your place. If I lose you, then the kids lose."

Dread tightened my chest. Monica wasn't exaggerating.

If I got fired, and there was nobody to replace me, more kids would fall through the cracks. More scared, lonely, abused supe children would have nowhere to turn. I took a breath, then another, suddenly realizing that I was panicking a little, and started to pant. "But, Monica, there has to be someone... something..."

"Nobody wants to work here," she barked. "There's nobody else willing to even submit their resumes. The pay is garbage, the hours are abysmal, the danger is life threatening—and I'm just talking about me and my blood pressure, I don't even go out on home visits. It's not like I'm forced to punch abusive troll moms or slap neglectful goblin dads on a daily basis. Nobody else wants to do this job, Daphne. Nobody else can do it!"

"But..." The words died in my mouth. I didn't know what to say.

Monica's tone softened a little. "The only reason you're here doing this work is because you want to be. This is your calling, Daphne. This is your life purpose, and you're good at it." Her lips quivered for a second. "And I hate this more than I can possibly tell you, but if you don't sort out this mess with those human detectives, then you're going to need to find a new reason for living, because you won't be able to work here at O-CPS anymore."

My lip quivered. "Shit."

"I can't lose you, Daphne. The kids can't lose you." Monica's expression hardened. "So, you need to fix this, and you need to fix it now."

CHAPTER
FIVE

Monica kicked me out of her little glass office two seconds later, ostensibly to make some phone calls begging for more budget money. I stumbled out, feeling shell-shocked.

Judy chuckled softly, not looking at me. "I see your days here are numbered, little girl."

I glanced over at her. My fingers twitched. Brain-Daphne showed me a nice vision of myself stabbing her in the liver in the same way I stabbed Wesley, except this time, I twisted the knife a dozen more times.

My gut squirmed at the vision.

It was supposed to cheer you up. Good gravy, forgive me for trying to lighten the mood.

My gaze drifted out the window to the dull gray concrete buildings and the matching dull gray sky above.

I wonder if this was just karma coming for me? I asked my brain. After all, I did kill Wesley Jupiter. I deserve to be investigated.

Brain-Daphne considered it. *Nah. We're good.*

I'd killed dozens and dozens of sentient creatures in my short time on this earth, and I hadn't answered for a single one of them. The closest I came was when the Otherworld Court was investigating the death of Zofia, the vampire nestmaster, and Romeo had stepped in and taken the blame for that just to keep me out of trouble. I hadn't answered for the death of anyone else, though. Maybe I deserved this?

Wesley was trying to kill us, my brain hissed. *And he was trying to help his evil bastard son summon an evil bastard god into his body so he could do more evil bastard things.*

The urge to respond out loud overwhelmed me. I sat down at my desk and put on my headset so I didn't look insane. "But what, though? What evil bastard things? We still don't know what Christopher Jupiter was trying to achieve by summoning a god from the Hellenic realm."

It doesn't matter. He failed. He blew himself to smithereens, which, honestly is the worst way to be blown. And now all the Jupiters are dead.

"Except Troy," I muttered, opening my laptop. Beside me, Dwayne gave a little *honk-shhhhh*. He'd fallen asleep on my desk. "Troy is the only Jupiter left."

Guilt swamped me again. My ex-boyfriend was an entitled, cheerful, selfish idiot—not necessarily evil, just spoiled.

Now he was a penniless orphan. Last time I saw him, Holly LeBeaux was dragging him off to sign the forms to cancel their marriage contract. So, Troy didn't have her anymore, either.

He'd lost everything because of me. Considering what the Jupiters had done, I shouldn't feel bad about it, but Troy was innocent, so I did.

Maybe karma really was coming for me. I'd destroyed a whole family, now I was, at best, about to lose my purpose in life. Monica was right. I had to fix this, and I had to fix it now.

I checked my phone. I'd called Romeo this morning, but

he hadn't answered. More guilt surged. I should have told him all about this yesterday. Now, I really needed him to help me, and soon, or else I was going to get fired, arrested, trapped in a concrete box...

The darkness squeezed me.

Oi. Brain-Daphne punched me in the temple so hard, my head jerked back. *That's right, bitch, I've learned my lesson from yesterday. There will be no downward spirals today.*

My phone pinged—it was the main CPS reception. Three of my clients were already here, waiting to be taken through to our little Otherworld department.

I sent Romeo another quick message, asking him to check in as soon as he could, and did a quick meditation, counting backwards from two hundred while keeping my breathing deep and even. After a while, I managed to clear the whirling confusion and lingering dread in my mind and went to do my job.

While I still had it.

CHAPTER
SIX

Six hours and one missed lunch break later, Dwayne was still asleep on my desk, the police radio buzzing softly underneath his wing. James was still frantically typing up reports, Judy was still playing Minecraft on her laptop, and Monica was still pacing back and forth in her office.

And Romeo still hadn't called me back. I checked my phone for the millionth time, wondering if he was just ignoring me.

It's been two days since his foster sister got squished into a liquid state. My brain's internal voice sounded much more cheerful than it should have. *That's bound to fuck with his mental health a little bit. He's gone over twenty years being emotionally tied to that conniving bitch. He's probably just adjusting.*

I exhaled slowly. Brain-Daphne was right. He might need some space.

Although I imagine it would be liberating, rather than confusing, she added, suddenly changing tack. *He's feeling his own feelings for the first time since he was a child. He's free to love without Bella's hateful influence tugging on his emotions.*

I grimaced. "Make up your mind."

I am your mind, you dumb cow.

For what felt like the billionth time, my eyes brushed over my phone, willing a message to appear. But there was nothing. Taking a deep breath, I turned back to my laptop. I had eight more reports to submit before I was done for the day, but the words kept swimming in front of my eyes, making it impossible to concentrate.

Judy stood up and stretched. "Okay, I think I'm done." She brushed her fuzzy platinum hair back off her face, snapped her laptop shut, thrust it carelessly into her satchel, swung it over her shoulder, and stood up. Her eyes fell on me, and she smirked. "Don't forget, you're still on call tonight, Daphne."

"I know."

"I'm just trying to look out for you," Judy said, her sugary-sweet voice dripping with sarcasm. "You're on call tonight, tomorrow... Oh, and for the rest of the week."

I forced the words out through gritted teeth. "I know."

"Don't forget to take your phone off do-not-disturb. You can't miss any callouts. We don't want any cold, frightened children left in danger again, do we?"

Bitch, I swear to God I'm going to—

I clenched my fists and tried to ignore her. Judy was trying to get a rise out of me. I was better than that.

Brain-Daphne threw up an image of me, laughing maniacally, punching Judy in the mouth until her teeth broke.

Okay, maybe I'm not better than that. But my moral code dictated that I wouldn't bring a bazooka to a knife fight. Technically, Judy hadn't done anything to me yet. She was just mean and hateful. And I couldn't fight fire with fire, because I didn't have it in me. I wasn't a mean or hateful person.

I didn't want to be one.

Judy smirked at me. "The last thing I want is for you to get into any more trouble, Daphne, sweetie. You look *so* tired, though. You've got dark circles under your eyes."

She wasn't wrong—I looked awful. Thanks to the intense combination of Dwayne's police radio, the threat of being stuck forever in a human jail, my intense yearning for Romeo, and the heavy shroud of guilt that had settled over me, I'd barely gotten any sleep last night.

"I'd hate for you to fall asleep and miss another call-out." Judy's eyes twinkled maliciously. "Maybe I should call you a few times tonight, to make sure you're awake." She left that threat hanging in the air and stomped out of the office, not even bothering to say goodbye to anyone.

I exhaled heavily and glanced at James. He was so quiet, sometimes I forgot he was even here. "How come she's not so mean to you?"

His eyes flicked towards me, and he jerked. "Huh?" He took a tiny earbud out of his ear. "I'm sorry?"

"Oh. That's why. You just ignore her."

His lips twitched into a smile. "Of course I do. I would have strangled Judy years ago if I had to listen to her talk all day. As soon as I realized she wasn't the type to make accommodations for people with disabilities, I actually had Monica tell her I was partially deaf." He shrugged his shoulders. "She barely interacts with me at all. Works like a charm."

"Damn." I exhaled. "I wish I'd thought of that."

A quiet burst of static punctuated the silence. Dwayne, still fast asleep on my desk, jerked. The radio slipped out from underneath his wing and landed on my desk. He let out a little honk-snore and settled his head deep under his wing. I stared at the police radio, wondering how the hell I was going to return it to the station without getting into any more trouble.

Keep it.

Maybe I should. I picked it up and fiddled with the dials, turning the volume up a little. I had superpowered hearing, but it was still really hard to understand the short barks of information that came out of that thing. It was one thing to be able to hear, it was another to comprehend.

I listened to the dispatch for a second, trying to make sense of what the gruff woman's voice was saying. After a moment, her words began to make sense.

"... members of the public requesting urgent assistance to apprehend what appears to be a violent exotic animal loose in Fitler Square..."

Violent exotic animal? My eyes drifted down to Dwayne, sleeping peacefully beside me.

Another burst of static came over the radio, and a man's voice spoke, "Copy, dispatch, I'm on the ground on Pine Street, and I just got another report from a woman running with her children. The animal appears to be some kind of giant insect, or an armadillo or something."

Dispatch answered, "Any other details?"

"The witness was highly distressed, but she said it looks like some kind of alien, and it's attacking the church." The officer's voice started to pant—he was running. "I'm a block away, but I can hear some serious commotion. Gunshots, maybe? I think the civilians are frightened, and they're getting trigger happy, Donna."

"Goddamnit," dispatch muttered. "Sending all available units now."

"Get animal control out here, too."

A cold fear gripped me. Some kind of alien? Attacking a church?

Romeo's church. That's why he hasn't called us back. He's under attack.

Oh, shit.

I shot up out of my chair, sending it rolling back across the small office. Dwayne woke up with a jerk. **Wassup?**

"We gotta go," I told him. "Come on." If there was a violent exotic alien animal attacking the church, then I was going to bring my very own violent exotic animal to level the playing field.

CHAPTER
SEVEN

For once, the speed didn't soothe me.

I rode through the afternoon traffic on my Kawasaki, weaving between cars and trucks with split-second timing, my heart pounding in my chest. At least the speed blew out some of the lingering fog of confusion in my head. Zipping through traffic, I felt I could think a little clearer.

What the hell was attacking the church? A giant insect? An alien?

And why now?

The timing was suspicious. Every single one of the guys was either recuperating from horrific injuries or trying to hold down the fort the best they could. The coven was at their most vulnerable right now. My heart pounded as I shot through the city as fast as I could, riding on the edge of recklessness. If Romeo could see me now, he'd kill me.

So, who was attacking the church right now? And why?

A giant insect. Maybe one of the mythical beasts escaped from the pocket dimension before it collapsed.

I held my breath as I whizzed between two freight

trucks holding up both lanes of traffic. My brain was right, a Greek monster was the most likely possibility. The Jupiters had summoned a bunch of them—the stymphalian birds, the vile hyena-like crocotta, and the cyclops—and sent them to attack us, so it was possible there were other beasts we missed in the labyrinth that might have escaped.

And there were lots of giant insects in Greek mythology. Myrmekes, the giant ants who guarded a gold-filled hill, or Arachne, the former mortal transformed into a spider after foolishly challenging Athena to a spinning contest. There was even one guy who'd been transformed into a grasshopper, but I couldn't remember why. And the Indus worm... although, if it were the Indus worm attacking the church, the mortals would be doing a whole lot more screaming.

A shadow passed low over my head as I turned down Pine Street towards the church—Dwayne was flying above me. He dropped words into my head as he swooped low. **Seeing some smoke from up here, little one. Looks like the church has been firebombed.**

I hit the brakes, spun out, and shot off down the small side-street as my heart thudded in my chest. Firebombed? What kind of giant insect...?

Dwayne shot off into the sky again, flapping his magnificent white wings. I put on a burst of speed, and five seconds later, I skidded out on the gravel path that led to the church. I hit the kill switch, yanked off my helmet, and froze.

Smoke filled my nostrils. Something was on fire. The acrid smell of burned plastic stung my sinuses. Under that, I could smell a musky human man close by. A second later, I heard him crashing through the undergrowth a few yards to my right.

I strained my ears and heard him whispering into his

radio. "... seems to have broken through the gates and entered the church grounds. The gate is a smoking, twisted mess. No animal did that, Donna, it's a weapon of some kind. No idea who is wielding it. No, I don't have eyes on it, but I heard a crash in the church thirty seconds ago. Whoever it is, it's gone inside. I'm going to try and get closer to see if I can spot anything coming out."

It was the cop I'd heard on the radio. Brave guy. I reached out with my senses and tried to catalog every smell I could.

A billion different scents screamed for my attention. Most of them were familiar—Romeo's chocolate, whiskey, and fireworks scent hit me like a punch, making my heart clench in my chest. Then, Levi's candle wax and herby smell, the vampire sand-and-copper of Micah, woodsy, earthy Cole, and Brandon's leather and flame.

Another familiar scent floated by, a gorgeous fiery spiceberry, one I couldn't quite assign a face to in my panic, but knew was a friendly scent. A pizza delivery guy, maybe. Other smells drifted through the smoke, older than the others—a lingering hint of the countess's amethyst and gin martini and Bella's pungent cocktail of mixed-magic punch. When I caught Bella's odor, my gut clenched.

She's dead. Brain-Daphne bared her teeth. *We don't have to worry about her anymore. Anyone in the immediate vicinity? Any giant bugs roaming through the bushes around the church?*

"No," I muttered, sending my senses out wider. "Apart from the cop stumbling through the undergrowth over there, I can't smell anything foreign. Nothing alien, anyway."

Nothing is alien to us, though, she reminded me. *We've been everywhere.*

"There *is* something weird here, though." I tilted my

head, inhaling deeper. "Something really damn strange. It smells... high tech."

Brain-Daphne frowned. *What?*

"Like..." I chewed on my lip. "It smells like explosives but not quite. Like something that has been burned at a super-high temperature." I screwed up my nose, frustrated. "I don't remember what the Star Door smelled like when it exploded. I was too focused on running away. But when that beam of light shot into the air..." I huffed out a breath, trying to remember. "The thing I can smell right now reminds me of it. A highly explosive, concentrated light beam."

So, we are looking for a beast that escaped from the Hellenic realm?

"Possibly. Most probably, actually." I got off my bike, hit the kickstand, and dumped my helmet. "Whatever it is, I think it's gone. Because I'm sure I'd be able to smell a giant bug rampaging through the church right now. There's nothing, though." Panic clawed at my chest. What the hell was attacking Romeo? Was he okay? I couldn't hear a thing.

Let's check it out.

Wildly aware that there was a nervous, trigger-happy cop stumbling through the bushes off the path to my right, I slunk to the left and disappeared into the undergrowth. I moved into a familiar low-lying gait, adjusting my posture to the one I used when I was trying to survive in the wild-magic realms of my childhood, stepping on the balls of my feet, creeping forward silently, tasting the air on my tongue, my eyes noting every flicker of movement around me.

I reached the wrought-iron fence and crouched down, still hidden. The cop was right—whatever had attacked had smashed the church gates open with devastating force.

Looks like some psychopath drove a bulldozer through here again, my brain snickered.

It did. The iron gate was mangled and twisted, but it also smoked slightly. The smell of burning metal hurt my nose.

It's not like it was when we did it, though. Whatever smashed through here was on fire, my brain noted. *A giant burning insect?*

"That doesn't feel right," I whispered nervously. Whatever it was, it had gotten through Romeo's wards.

His fortress had been breached. Adrenaline flooded me. I had to get in there and find Romeo.

Sirens sounded in the distance, maybe a few blocks away. Backup was coming. The cop lingered near the fence line; he was staying still for now. I reached out with my senses one more time, straining to check for danger, then darted onto the path and through the tangled metal of the gate.

I shivered as I passed through the wards. That surprised me—they were still intact. The first, a no-human ward, tied to the gate might have bent when the gates were destroyed. But the second one, the ill-intent ward, still held fast. The creature had gotten through anyway.

Maybe it didn't intend to do any harm, my brain whispered. *Maybe it really was just a dumb bug under a compulsion, so it'd eluded the magic of the ward that way.*

There was no time to dwell on it. I had to find him, and now.

I dashed up the path and into the church grounds. My stomach sank when I saw the heavy oak door at the top of the church steps, now a smoking, destroyed wreck.

Please be okay. Please.

I bolted up the steps, light on my feet, and took a peek inside.

The place had been trashed. The entrance to the church, now Romeo's living room, looked like it had been ransacked by a whole team of burglars—sofas flipped, bookshelves tipped over, potted plants smashed on the ground. That acrid burned scent was everywhere. The whole place was deathly silent, though.

I sniffed carefully. Nothing odd, nothing foreign. Certainly no weird alien bug smell.

This is so damn weird, Brain-Daphne said, puzzled.

She was right; it was weird. No sounds, no bizarre scents, apart from that strange scent I seemed to associate with high-tech weaponry. The church was so quiet, I could almost hear the sound of Father Benedict's ghost harrumphing.

Come to think of it, I could smell him, too. The ghost's very faint smoky-ozone scent had become familiar to me. But I couldn't smell a giant insect.

I crept inside, heading further into the church, moving silently through the trashed living room. To my left, a cross-section of the church had been sealed off to create a climate-controlled library. The glass doors were broken, but thankfully not shattered. They hung uselessly off their hinges. I peeked inside and saw whole sections of books had been swept off the shelves. The thing had been in there, too.

A noise broke the deathly silence. *Tshhh.*

I ducked down, taking cover, and froze. The noise was coming from the kitchen, directly opposite me in the other cross-section of the church.

Thump. Glug glug glug glug....

I knew that sound. I frowned, stood up, and looked.

Dwayne was in the kitchen, perched on the counter. As I suspected, he'd opened a can of beer, kicked it over, and was now lapping it up off the countertop with his barbed tongue.

I sighed.

He glanced up. **Don't look at me like that. The fridge was already tipped over when I got here.** He bent his head down and sipped at the puddle. **It's only going to get warm.**

"Can you not take anything seriously?" Panic made my voice shoot through several octaves. Quickly, I bolted down the hallway and checked the rest of the church, sticking my head into the bedrooms and scouting the gym area at the rear. Only the living room had been destroyed, but Romeo's room showed signs of disarray—his bed had been shoved one foot to the right, several books had fallen off the shelf, and the photo of Aunt Marche on the windowsill by the loveseat was gone.

"He's not here," I mumbled. My lips felt numb.

Nobody is here, baby girl. Whatever busted in here is gone. I think we might have only just missed it, though.

"Did you see anything?"

Nah. But the little gate at the back was busted and still glowing orange a little when I flew over, so I guess whatever burned through it had only just gone.

I ran back to the kitchen, pulling out my phone on the way. No calls, no texts. I dialed Romeo's number and waited, my pulse pounding in my ears.

A faint buzz thrummed through the room. It was coming from an alcove just off the living room. I raced over and opened a door in a built-in cupboard and found an electronic safe. "His phone is in there. Why is his phone in a safe?"

Dwayne shrugged and sipped at his beer. **Kids these days.**

At least that explained why Romeo hadn't called me back yet. Dread still swamped me. "Did it take him? Did the freaky giant alien bug take him somewhere?"

I doubt it. Dwayne cracked open another beer with his

beak and kicked it over. **We would have heard screaming, at least.**

I let out a little moan.

Oi. My brain kicked me. *Take some deep breaths; you're panicking. You're not thinking properly.*

I did as she told me. Breathe in, breathe out. After a second, I felt a little calmer.

That's better. So, let's think this through. A giant bug attacked the church, busted through the gates, breeched the wards, and trashed the church. Romeo isn't here. Now, the man was a little banged up, but he wasn't incapacitated. Who else was here?

It took me a second to rummage through my thoughts. "Brandon and Micah were staying with him today. He told me that last night. Levi was going out first thing this morning on coven business, and Cole had to go downtown to sit in on one of the Jupiter companies board meetings in Romeo's place."

So, the big guy wasn't alone. He had a shifter and a vampire with him to protect him.

"A sunburned vampire who was in his death-sleep and a dragon shifter who can't shift!"

Welp, nobody is here now. Dwayne guzzled up the last of the puddle of beer and hopped down off the counter, heading back to the fridge. **They left in a hurry when the monster breached the wards, I guess.**

"Romeo wouldn't run away." My voice shook. "This is his fortress. He would have stayed and defended it even if something breached the wards."

Dwayne paused on his way to the refrigerator and gave me a look. **He's no fool, little one. You're not thinking clearly. If he was injured, and if he didn't know what he was fighting, and he had his coven brothers to protect...**

I exhaled. "You're right. He would have left to save them at the very least." My intuition was still screaming at me. Romeo was hurt, I knew it in my bones, and the knowledge made me panic. "I have no idea where he is, and it's freaking me out."

Dwayne chuckled. **Baby girl, you worry too much. He's a big boy. His crib got smashed, and he made a strategic withdrawal.**

I waved my hands in the air frantically, trying to expel some of my panic. "Well, forgive me, sir, but my senses are still on high alert from the last time someone tried to kill us! Which, I have to remind you, was only a couple days ago!"

A siren outside gave a little *whoop whoop*, and I flinched. "I need to figure this out quickly, because we need to move. This place will be crawling with cops in a second."

Nah. You're forgetting who your boyfriend is. He's not a limp-dick coward wet-blanket like your ex. No cop will set foot on his property without his permission. They'll dance around the gate, but they won't be coming in. But you'll have to sneak out the back.

I crossed my arms over my chest and rubbed, hugging myself and trying to give myself comfort. "I can't shake the feeling that he's hurt, Dwayne," I said, hating the whimper in my voice.

Do you smell any blood?

"A little." That's why my intuition was screaming. I could smell Romeo's blood—just a drop, but enough to make me freak out. "Judging by the mess in here, he definitely tried to fight." I took a deep breath. Realization dawned. "He shadow-jumped them out of here."

Of course he did.

"Where did he go?"

Dwayne rolled his eyes. **You're an idiot.**

"Oh." A warm glow chased away some of the ice in my veins. "He'd go somewhere he felt safe."

He felt safe with me.

"The Hidden City," I said. "That's where he's gone. He went to find me."

CHAPTER
EIGHT

I lost Dwayne somewhere on the way to the Hidden City. Or he might not have even followed me. He might still be in Romeo's kitchen, drinking all his beer.

I pulled off my helmet the second I moved into the pocket dimension. I didn't want any of my senses stifled right now. The weather in the Hidden City mirrored the outside world, so the sky above me was a sad, uniform iron gray. The cold weather kept most of the residents indoors. Only a handful of creatures scuttled along the path—mostly shifters in both human and animal form and vampires with their arms loaded with supplies, their skin glistening with SPF.

The chill in the air brushed my cheeks and made my nose tingle and run. Nevertheless, I caught a hint of Romeo's scent on the path, and my heart leapt in my chest. He was here. Brandon and Micah, too, were with him. I felt a pulse of gratitude for the cold, gray day and the thick cloud cover above me. Micah's skin wouldn't burn.

I sped down the path towards the West Tower, parked my bike right outside, and dashed into the elevator, tapping my foot impatiently as the doors took their sweet time closing.

We should have taken the stairs.

My gut clenched. Brain-Daphne was just as worried as I was.

Of course I'm worried. This whole thing is fucked up. A monster attacked our lover, and I haven't had a chance to bite him and see what his flesh tastes like yet.

The elevator crept upwards slowly. I tapped my foot compulsively.

Finally, we reached the forty-fourth floor, and I smacked my shoulder against the doors as I rushed out, heading down the hallway towards my apartment.

What the hell...?

My footsteps faltered. There was a dagger stuck into my door, right below the peephole. I came to a halt, sending out my senses to check for danger.

There was none, apart from the knife in my door. Double-bladed, perfectly balanced, and curved, like the haladie Bella used. This one, though, wasn't a mortal realm dagger like hers had been, which were originally used by the Rajput warriors in India. I could smell the components of the dagger from here quite clearly. The hilt was bozan bone, an indestructible substance made from the thigh of a rhino-like fae creature. A bozan blade.

I'd seen a weapon like that before. Each side of the blade had different thicknesses, so you could stab and slice a variety of creatures. They were popular in Faerie, usually used to do terrible things like puncture the thick skin of a troll with one side and delicately slice a finger off a pixie with the other side.

Why was this dagger sticking out of my door?

I crept forward, senses on high alert, and inhaled carefully. There was a slight fruity-wine odor lingering in the hallway, but it wasn't unfamiliar. Whoever stuck the knife in my door was either masking their scent, or it was someone who lived in my building.

But another scent overpowered everything—Romeo. He was here.

I rushed to the door, cracked it open, sniffing carefully. Suddenly, it was ripped out of my grip. Strong, warm arms pulled me inside, wrapping me up and cocooning me in heat and safety. I surrendered. Every muscle in my body melted.

Romeo lifted me off my feet like I weighed nothing. I clung to him as he slammed the door behind me and pushed me against the wall. I wrapped my legs around his waist and ground myself into him.

I couldn't get close enough.

Stubble brushed my cheeks, sending eddies of pure sensual pleasure colliding with the intense relief I felt at seeing him and feeling him—it was so overwhelming and delicious, my eyes rolled into the back of my head. His cool breath washed over the nape of my neck, tickling my earlobe, as he breathed out in relief and inhaled me.

I buried my face in him. "Romeo," I gasped.

He let out a low, masculine noise. "Daphne." His voice rumbled through me. "Thank the goddess you're okay."

I cupped his hard jaw and buried my lips in his, desperate to have his mouth on mine. The kiss was frantic, possessive, desperate. The space between us was still too big.

"Get a room, ya skanky hoe-bag," a voice slurred from the pantry.

I barely registered her words. As far as danger went, my drunk pantry-dwelling roommate was low on the scale of things I had to worry about right now.

I fell back into Romeo's kiss, finding that little moment

of sweet pleasure, and lost myself in it for another few seconds. All the confusion and anxiety of the day melted away in the comfort of his body, the hard muscles under his soft hoodie and sweatpants, the heat of his mouth, his tongue, his hands...

Romeo flinched.

A tingle of unease ran through me. Something was wrong. It took a few seconds for my brain to catch up with my nose. "You're hurt."

He pulled back, his gray eyes glittering silver. He didn't want to stop kissing me, either.

"Sluts," Myf's voice echoed from the pantry. "Big whorey slutbags, the both of you."

The moment was gone. "Put me down."

His jaw hardened, and his huge biceps tightened around me. "I don't want to."

Wiggling, I escaped his arms and climbed down him like he was a tree. "You're hurt," I said again. "Where?"

He didn't answer me. I glanced around.

Micah stood in the corner of the living room, leaning against the wall with his arms crossed, looming like a specter in black sweats and a heavy black hoodie. Brandon sat on the couch in casual jeans and a tan sweater, leaning forward, wringing his hands compulsively. The contents of my first-aid kit were scattered over my little coffee table.

My focus zoomed in on Brandon's expression. He seemed upset about something, almost frantic. After a second, he leapt to his feet and gestured to the sofa. "Boss," he pleaded. "Please sit down. We gotta close that cut."

A tingle ran up my spine. I could smell it quite clearly. Romeo had been stabbed by something with a very high iron content.

He'd been poisoned.

A regular knife wouldn't have bothered him. Nobody

used pure iron for blades anymore, not since the late eighteen-hundreds, it was too soft and prone to rust. But someone had slashed Romeo with a pure iron blade, sending tiny fragments of the poisonous metal into his bloodstream, and it was slowly killing him.

Well, fuck. Brain-Daphne whistled through her teeth. *Not this again. He still doesn't know he's part-fae.*

I almost groaned out loud. Too many things were happening all at once, and I couldn't deal with it all. Too many secrets, too many lies. I'd only just managed to expose Bella as a bound witch who'd been using her magical tie to Romeo to manipulate him into loving her for the last twenty years. There was no way I could drop the truth of his heritage on him like this.

Romeo was like a storm—a wild, powerful force of nature. The events of the last few days had pushed him to the very brink. Emotionally, mentally, physically... he'd taken a beating on every level, and he'd still managed to shadow-jump himself and two of his covenmates out of the church to get here to me. Instead of being beaten down when things overwhelmed him, he got more explosive.

More violent. I did, too, so I knew what it was like. The difference between us was that he was a witch, and he could fall to blood magic when there were no other options.

He'd used a little before, when he was a kid, egged on by his vile foster sister. He knew how heady the power was and how corrupting it could be. Blood magic ate at your soul until there was nothing left.

Romeo Zarayan was the strongest person I'd ever met in my entire life, but the lingering temptation of blood magic was always there. Always within reach.

He'd just been through hell with me in the Jupiter mansion. He'd barely recovered, and now he'd been attacked by a mysterious creature and stabbed with an iron blade.

I pulled on his arm, dragged him back to the sofa, and pushed him. It was like trying to manhandle a giant oak tree. He submitted and sank into the seat.

"What happened?" I asked.

"A monster attacked the church." He sounded exhausted.

"Yeah, I figured that." My nose quickly found the source of the iron poisoning. I lifted his shirt. Sluggish red blood oozed out of a deep red slash over his ribs. "Ouch."

"It should have stopped bleeding by now," Brandon said, scowling. "It's a fairly shallow cut. And it was the least of his injuries." He passed me a wad of gauze. I pressed it against the cut.

Romeo flinched. "Please don't tell me you went to the church."

"Of course I did," I said. "I heard about the attack on a police radio, and I freaked out. I've been trying to get hold of you all morning."

Romeo made a gruff noise. "Levi locked my phone in the safe and changed the code before he left. He insisted I needed to rest."

"Yeah, I figured that out when I heard it buzzing in the safe," I said dryly. I lifted the gauze. The blood seeped out again immediately. It wouldn't stop. His body was trying to expel the iron, but it was already inside him. Already poisoning him, very slowly.

Romeo sighed roughly. "The fact that Levi was so worried about me that he was prepared to risk a beating for taking my phone makes it harder to be so mad at him." His eyes suddenly narrowed. "Wait. Why have you been trying to get hold of me?"

He knew me too well. I wouldn't have disturbed him

today unless it was urgent. I gave him a weak smile. "It's not important."

He stared at me for a moment. "You really are a terrible liar."

"Yeah, I am, but what I meant was, it's not important right now. I'll tell you in a minute." First, I had to get some polelizard tongues so I could cure his iron poisoning. Lodestone, goblin urine...

I cleared my throat. "Our first priority is figuring out what monster just attacked the church, because if it got in there, it could get in here."

"It can't get inside the apartment. The wards are too strong," Romeo said. "But it's been here in the City."

My hands clutched the gauze. "What?"

"I didn't just shadow-jump out of the church to run away, Daphne. I needed to see where it went once it left, so I could figure out what we were dealing with. We were chasing it. It came here."

You idiot. You big, hunky, sexy idiot.

I blinked. "Where did it go?"

He hitched his massive shoulders in a shrug. "No idea. It disappeared as soon as it moved through the entrance of the Hidden City. We've only been here for ten minutes, but there's no trace of it anywhere. I've got some witch residents searching for it right now, but so far, nothing."

So. Freaking. Weird. "What was it?"

"I don't know what it is. It's a monster of some kind, a weird cross between a crab and a spider. It's bigger than my bike, it's got a hard carapace, so it's naturally armored, and it's got bioweapons."

"Weapons?"

"Yeah. High-tech photon blasters," Brandon chipped in. "It's intelligent. It can handle tools. It picked up an antique ceremonial athame from our display case and slashed Rome with it."

Ah, so that was the source of his poisoning. I'd been worried it was a deliberate attack from someone who knew what Romeo was. If the athame belonged to the coven, then the poisoning probably wasn't pre-planned.

I blew out an exasperated breath. "It must be a monster left over from when the Hellenic realm imploded. It's gotta be a mythical Greek beast. The Jupiters sent them to target us, so maybe it was still following the magical compulsion to find and destroy you."

But Romeo shook his head. "I don't think it's a Hellenic monster."

"How do you know?"

"I'm sure I've seen it before." He leaned his head on the back of the sofa and closed his eyes.

"When?"

"Years ago," he mumbled.

I squinted. "Years?"

"Yeah. It's attacked me once before. Maybe not the same one, but a monster that looked just like it. I think I told you... just after I became High Priest..." He exhaled heavily.

I smoothed a dark smudge on his cheek, feeling frustrated and helpless. So many people had tried to kill him over the years. In fact, two of his assassins were standing in the room with me right now.

Three, if you counted me.

Everyone was trying to kill him. Everyone, everywhere, all of the time. The injustice churned hot like acid in the pit of my stomach. "It's not fair."

He hitched his huge shoulders in another shrug, wincing. "It is what it is."

"You've seen this monster before?" I prompted. "What do you remember?"

"I don't know if it was the same one. It didn't have laser guns before. But something almost exactly like it came at me once, just after I became High Priest. Attacked me in an alleyway. I managed to shadow-jump away then, too, and it didn't follow me. So, I figured when it showed up at the church and busted through, it was safe to travel through the shadows again."

"It's not a Hellenic monster," I muttered. "It's definitely not a fae creature." I'd never heard of a giant spider-crab with photon blasters in all my time in Faerie. "It has nothing to do with Christopher Jupiter or the Star Door. Or Bella," I added, glancing up at his face.

He met my eyes and read the depth of emotion in my expression.

A million words were exchanged in a fraction of a second. I was so, so sorry for everything that had happened.

He saw it. He understood.

It had always been like this with us; we understood each other. Romeo's face softened. He was okay. "I'm sure it's not anything to do with the Jupiters or Bella. This is something else."

"It still could be something to do with the Jupiters." Micah jerked his chin up. "Someone has obviously sent an alien assassin to kill you. The Jupiters were always fond of sending assassins to kill you."

"The Jupiters are all dead." I lifted the gauze off the wound on his ribs again. Bright-red blood still oozed. "But I suppose they could have contracted this monster assassin before they died." The flesh around the edges of the wound was a little gray. I should fix this now, or he'd just get sicker. "This cut isn't sealing. It might have dripped some kind of venom on the blade before it cut you. I need to grab some supplies from next door," I said, keeping my voice casual. "I'll need the countess's help for this."

"She's out." Myf's voice slurred from the pantry. "That bitch is *outtt*."

"Myf." My tone came out far growly than I meant it to. "What did you do?"

"Nothing! Well, I raided her liquor cabinet a little. She's not happy with me. Had to head out to get some supplies." A gulping noise and the spicy smell of whiskey told me that Myf was still drinking in the pantry.

I sighed. The Countess Ebadorathea Greenwood had been looking after Myf while I was busy dealing with the whole "Christopher Jupiter summoning a god into his body thing," but I knew it was a very temporary Band-Aid solution. I knew it was a terrible idea to have a high-functioning alcoholic look after a girl determined to drown her considerable sorrows.

Myf needed help in the worst way, and I felt so guilty I couldn't give it to her. The most I could do was arrange some counselling.

A thought occurred to me. "Did Cindy get in touch with you, Myf?" I called out.

"Yeah-huh." She knocked something over in the pantry. "Called earlier and canceled on me, the little emo birdbitch."

I raised my eyebrows. "You were supposed to have a therapy session?"

"Tonight," Myf confirmed, knocking something else over. "But she's had to go out of town." A sob cut her off. "I couldn't handle sitting in here feeling sorry for myself, so I raided the countess's liquor cabinet. Now, she's mad with me, and I'm drunk sitting in the fucking pantry again like a coward." She gave a little mournful howl. "Like the coward that I *aaaaam*."

I glanced over at Brandon and raised my eyebrows.

He made a face. "I tried," he hissed at me. "I know we're both dragons, Daph, but apart from that, we've got nothing in common. Our stories and our trauma are very different." For a second, an expression of outrage crossed his face. "And she doesn't appear to like me at all."

"It's not you," Myf shouted. "It's men in general. *All* men. All ye revolting bastards make me sick."

I took a deep breath and exhaled, suddenly feeling exhausted. Brandon was right; I could see how Myf wouldn't be able to relate to him. Her main problem was a childhood filled with the threat of sexual violence due to her gender, and, mostly, an excess of survivor guilt. Both of these were something Brandon never had. And besides, he took a potion to inhibit the shift, so he couldn't even turn into a dragon anymore. Myf was much more traumatized and far more powerful than Brandon ever was.

There's a metaphor for womanhood in there somewhere.

"All you cunts got it easy," Myf slurred. "With ye big floppy penises and no uterus to speak of, and no nurturing emotions to deal with. Yers can piss where you want to, but you can't even grow a small baby out of food. Useless."

I suppose that will do.

Sighing heavily again, I got up and filled a glass of water, dropped a hydration tablet in, and watched it fizz. "Don't worry about the countess," I said to her, putting the glass on the floor next to the pantry door. "She's got bottles of liquor to spare. If she's mad, it's because she's worried about you."

"You're a terrible liar, Daph," Myf gulped. "You know that, right? Totally shithouse."

Micah pushed himself off the wall. "If it's okay, boss, I'm going to head out and see if we can find any trace of the creature."

Romeo didn't open his eyes. "Go ahead. Bran, you go too. Stick together."

"We will. You already know it's not us it's after."

I frowned. "What does that mean?"

"When it busted into the church, we tried everything we could to divert its attention to keep it from attacking Romeo," Micah explained. "It barely even noticed us. It went straight for him. I managed to get a couple of good punches in—not that it did any good, with that rock-hard armor on its body. It just shook me off and kept coming for him. Stalking him, and making a weird clacking-gurgling noise, like it was trying to shout at him."

"It felt..." Brandon paused and shuddered. "Furious. Like it was so angry, it could barely hold itself together. I know what that feeling is like, so I recognized it." He glanced at me. "Keep him safe."

"Of course," I replied. Brandon trusted me. That was nice. "No enemy is getting in here, don't worry."

But an odd feeling had settled in my gut. There was something I was missing.

That's right. "Wait. I almost forgot. Did you stick that bozan blade into my door?"

"That double-bladed knife?" Romeo gave a gruff rumble. "I was really hoping you did that yourself."

"I didn't." Fabulous. Another mystery on my plate. "Well," I exhaled roughly. "I suppose this is the safest place for us right now."

"That's what we thought about the church." Brandon glanced at his phone. "Although Levi and Cole are there now. Levi is putting the wards back up and reinforcing them. We'll do a sweep of the City and come back and get you, boss, then head home."

Brandon opened my front door. Micah stuck his head out and checked the hallway.

The elevator dinged, and the countess's voice called out. "Well, hello, fresh meat!"

Both men cringed. "Good afternoon, your grace," they muttered.

"Well, don't just stand there." A tinkling clink of bottles sounded down the corridor. "Come and help me with my groceries. I swear, you'd think chivalry was dead and buried six feet under."

I squeezed Romeo's hand and got up off the sofa, heading to the door. The countess sashayed down the hallway towards me, impeccably dressed as always, wearing an emerald-green suede pantsuit with a fluffy fur collar and matching gloves and hat. She held a giant cardboard box balanced in one hand. She handed it off to Brandon, who gave a little *oof* as he took its weight.

"Countess," I said urgently.

"Hello, dear." She didn't pause. "Busy day?"

"Um, yeah." I waited by the door and took the box off Brandon. He and Micah melted away down the corridor. "I don't suppose you were the one that put that there?" I asked the countess, jerking my head towards the bozan blade, still sticking out of my door.

The countess frowned. "No, I didn't. I thought you must have left it there."

"Nope. Was it there when you left to go and get your supplies?"

"My dear, it was there when I came to check on your curmudgeonly hobgoblin at lunchtime."

My brain whistled. *So it happened before the monster attacked Romeo. It's another little mystery to add to the piles of mysteries.*

She surveyed the blade with interest. "Fascinating placement."

It wasn't fascinating, it was maddening. It wasn't from

the Hellenic realm. It was definitely a weapon that originated from Faerie. The monster didn't sound like anything from Faerie; it was still most likely from the Hellenic realm. Both the monster and the blade had shown up roughly at the same time, though, so they were probably linked.

I pinched my eyes closed and mentally swept everything out of my brain. One thing at a time. *Let's do triage. What's most urgent?*

"Countess." I took a deep breath. "I need your help."

She eyeballed me stonily, pursing her lips. "I'm afraid I'm going to have to respectfully decline, dear. There's a reason I didn't have children of my own, you know; I have no patience for that kind of conflict."

"No, I—"

"The answer is still no. I don't mind checking on her, but I can't babysit that thieving mopey teenager for a second longer. Normally, I like teenagers, but I cannot eat a whole one. I have my figure to consider, you know."

"Countess—"

"That wasn't a joke, dear. There's a handful of things I'm fond of in this world. One of them is cocktail hour, which she ruined, and the other is my wardrobe, and that will be in jeopardy if I am forced to fight her. I'm telling you right now, if she singes any of my clothes with her dragon breath, I will rip her tongue out of her throat, season it with salt, pepper, bay leaves, onion and garlic, and *I will eat it.*"

Her icy-blue eyes flashed. She meant every word. Sometimes, I forgot who my friends were.

"It's not Myf," I said. I'd have to look after her myself.

"Good." The countess stared at me. "Don't get me wrong, dear, I quite enjoy her company when she's not being a raging bitch. So..." She tilted her head. "What is it?"

I licked my lips. "I need some polelizard tongues."

There was really only one thing the tongues were used

for. "Oh." She blinked. "Did you have a tiff with the Warlock?"

I sighed. "It wasn't me."

"Of course it wasn't," she murmured, opening her apartment door with a flourish.

I followed her inside, set the box on her dining room table, and quickly filled her in on the monster that had attacked Romeo's church. "Any ideas what it might be?"

"Well," she huffed, moving a giant jar filled with little eyeballs out of the way so she could reach a bottle filled with golden liquid. "That doesn't sound like any creature I've heard of before." She thrust the bottle into my arms; I tried not to shudder. Goblin urine. Luckily for us, goblins weren't fussy about who they gave their pee to. All I needed was the urine, some lodestone, and a handful of polelizard tongues, and I'd be able to purge the iron from Romeo's bloodstream before it did any permanent damage.

The countess peered into a cupboard. "And the monster managed to break through the Warlock's wards?"

"Yeah. That's not an easy thing to do."

"My dear, you can do it. That means anyone can do it."

"I put a lot of effort into learning how, though. Chloe and Prue taught me the basics before I got lost off-world, but it took me years to figure out how to hold an intention hard enough to trick the ward into letting me through. A giant alien beast should not be able to crash through several wards that easily." I blew out an exasperated breath. "A giant insect with embedded bioweapons that can hold iron blades in its claws? It's straight out of a sci-fi movie."

The countess rummaged through the rest of her jars, looking for the polelizard tongues. "Do you think it came here to find you first? It could have left the bozan blade in your door."

I wrinkled my nose. "It doesn't feel right."

"Well, you must always follow your gut, dear."

"Except my gut is telling me that *none* of this is related. It's all a bunch of separate terrible things that are happening all at once, which makes no sense at all. And..." I squirmed a little. "I feel terrible that I haven't told Romeo the truth about his fae heritage yet. He's just got so damned much on his plate right now, and he's injured."

The countess yanked a leather satchel off the shelf. It rattled ominously. "Not for long, if I can help it."

"He's still reeling from having the emotional tie with Bella severed," I said. "I can't imagine what he's going through right now."

"Your capacity for empathy is your greatest strength—as well as your biggest weakness." The countess turned and faced me, her expression serious. "You want to shield him from pain and suffering, but you cannot do that forever, dear. You can only postpone it and run the risk of making everything worse. The hard truth is that there will *never* be a good time to tell him difficult things. He will always have too much on his plate." She paused. "You will, too. That is never going to stop."

I stared at her.

A moment passed. Her face softened. "And I consider that a good thing. There's nobody else in the world who can do what you two can do, and unfortunately, it means you will *always* be targeted. Universes will rise and fall beneath your feet, and you will endure, because you are brave and kind, and you always know what's best." She gave me a gentle smile. "I don't *think* you are capable of greatness, Daphne. I know you are. I see the evidence right before me, every single day."

A loaded silence fell between us. I stared at her, then narrowed my eyes. "Are you drunk?"

"No. That awful hobgoblin drank all my spirits, remember?" The countess paused. "But I did share a joint with a banshee in the park before I came home, though." Her thin lips stretched up in a slightly manic, snake-like smile. "Unprompted motivational speeches are rather uncharacteristic of me, aren't they? I feel a little..." She shuddered. "Goody-two-shoes. I'm not sure I like it."

"Yes," I nodded. "*I* like it, though. It means a lot, your grace."

"Here." She shoved a little jar filled with tiny tongues into my hand and dropped the leather pouch on top. "Go and heal your boyfriend. I'm not using my tools to whizz up the potion. The last time I did it, it took forever to get the stench of goblin urine out of my blender."

CHAPTER NINE

I blended the mixture of goblin urine, soft lodestone, and polelizard tongues in my own blender for a whole minute and waited for it to turn clear before handing it to Romeo to drink. He stared at the vial. "What is it?"

"The countess's special blend," I lied uncomfortably. "Broad-spectrum antivenom, healing potion, a coagulant, some electrolytes." I didn't add them in. Goblin urine naturally had lots of electrolytes.

Tell him!

I'm going to. I'll just wait for a minute until he feels better. "You can trust the countess," I told him. "The potion will help."

"I don't trust her." Romeo tossed the contents of the vial into his mouth. "But I trust you." He swallowed, let out a sigh, and rested his head back against the sofa again, closing his eyes. Some of the tension melted out of his shoulders.

I moved a little closer. "Do you feel better?"

"Just being with you makes me feel better." A corner of his perfect lips curved up into a crooked smile. "A screaming mob could be outside with pitchforks, demanding our heads, and I'd feel perfectly at ease sitting in here with you." The half-smile disappeared abruptly, and he frowned. "Is that bozan blade still stuck in your door?"

"Yeah." I didn't want to move it just yet. I didn't even want to touch it.

A low growl left his lips. "Someone is threatening you."

I didn't want to say it out loud, but it looked like it. "Maybe. It could be a practical joke. It could be a challenge. It could be a gift."

"It's a fae blade."

"Yeah." That was undisputed.

"A high fae warrior weapon." Romeo's voice turned dark and cold. "I don't think I've ever had a good interaction with any of those asshole high fae." His eyes opened, and he turned his head slightly to look at me. "Daphne, if one of those bastards is coming for you..."

"Romeo, no."

"I know that you lived in Faerie for a while—"

"Not *lived*. Held captive might be a better descriptor," I admitted.

"I knew it. I felt it as soon as I saw that damned thing in your door. Someone misses you. They want you back." His jaw hardened. "I know it. I can feel it in my gut."

"Whoa." My eyes widened. "This whole jealousy thing is nice and all, but I doubt any of the nobles who kept me and used me as a stable hand or a handmaiden—or even the one who made me sew piles of straw into gold, which, by the way, took a lot of smooth-talking to get out of—none of them would ever go to the trouble of coming here and demanding me back."

"I bet they would," he rumbled, closing his eyes again. "You've barely told me anything about the time you were lost, but somehow, every single story ends up with you, a highly prized, valuable servant, running away from your master."

"Not *every* story."

"How about when you were making mnemosynes with that dark elf sorcerer? Or when you were a champion erlyn racer? And how many fae warlords locked you in towers, hoping to marry you the next morning?"

I kept my lips shut, but the answer was twenty-three. Fae warlords loved locking pretty girls in towers so they could wed them against their will.

Romeo growled again. "If one of them is coming for you, if anyone tries to take you away... I'll burn their entire realm down. The fae are not to be trusted. Trickery and arrogance are in their blood. They're born monsters."

I squirmed. *Yeah, maybe we shouldn't tell him about his fae heritage right now.* "They're not all bad," I said out loud.

"No... but the high fae are. They're dangerous, arrogant and unpredictable. And you know it."

This conversation was getting more uncomfortable by the second. "You get on okay with Asherah—" My eyes flew wide as the thought hit me. "Oh my gosh! Asherah! It could be her!"

Romeo frowned. "Why would it be her?"

"In all the madness of Christopher Jupiter blowing everything to smithereens, I forgot to tell you she might try to kill me!"

He closed his eyes, grimacing. "You're going to have to fill me in a little more."

"I should have told you already, and I'm sorry. Asherah invited Dwayne home with her to visit the Winter Court. He respectfully declined and told her that I'm the reason why. He explained he had to stay here to take care of me."

"Hmm." Romeo understood. "And Asherah was consumed with bitter jealousy and now wants to kill you?"

I waved my hand. "Naturally."

Romeo huffed out a breath. "I'll take care of it."

"No. You won't."

"Yes, I will. I can and I will. Asherah is my colleague. We have a professional relationship."

"That's like saying you have a professional relationship with a tornado."

He opened his eyes again and turned his head to look down at me. His eyes were calmer now—back to light gray. "I'll make sure she understands that you're off-limits."

"And will this involve you locked in a magical battle with her?"

He tilted his head, considering it. "Possibly."

"No," I said firmly. "If you fought Asherah, it could cause a diplomatic nightmare, and you know it."

I didn't have to say anything else. I'd promised Asherah I wouldn't tell anyone she was the exiled princess of the Winter Court, but Romeo wasn't a fool. He would have guessed she was a royal of some sort. "I don't want you involved. This is my problem." I glared at him. "And besides, I think it's fixed, anyway. Dwayne told me he took care of it already. He apologized to Asherah, told her a fun new version of the truth, and smoothed things over. It's not Asherah. That thing in my door is a fae blade, but it's not from her. The monster who attacked you probably came here first."

"But the monster isn't a fae creature." Romeo's face hardened. "And Asherah is insane. I don't trust her."

"You shouldn't. But then again, you don't trust any of the leaders you deal with." It was time to change the subject. "Is Azerad still giving you hell?"

Romeo sighed. "Yeah. He's insisting we accept the new nestmaster he's installed here in Philly, but from all accounts, this new guy is even worse than Zofia was."

"How so?"

"He's young."

I grimaced. New vampires were almost as bad as the ancient ones. After a thousand years, vampires tended to go a little crazy. They forgot all their ties to humanity and decided they were gods. Several genocides in history were actually due to an ancient vampire losing their marbles.

New vampires—especially the men—were often overwhelmed with their new magical powers, the speed, strength, and the hypnotic compulsion abilities. Sometimes, the more foolish ones acted almost exactly like ancient vampires.

Romeo went on. "The new guy's name is Johan Van Eiken. He's in his early forties in human years, but only a year old as a vampire. He's Azerad's own child, chosen and turned specifically because Johan's just like him—arrogant, ambitious, entitled, racist, and sexist. Azerad found him in a boxing gym in South Africa. Johan is a medical doctor, an anesthetist, but he lost his license to practice a few years back."

"How come?"

"Multiple complaints and investigations spanning over a decade. Apparently, it was common practice for him to refuse to sedate his female patients before invasive procedures. He insisted that they didn't require pain relief anyway, and it was a waste of resources. Only the women, though."

"Of course," I managed. I already had a very good picture of what this new nestmaster was like, and I didn't like the image in my head.

"He got caught administering paralytic drugs without the anesthesia, so his patients were aware and could feel every little thing during surgery, but they couldn't move or scream. In court, he argued that his victims were being dramatic babies who were exaggerating their pain because they were bitter, man-hating, drug-addicted harpies."

I ground my teeth. This stunning display of mental gymnastics was not uncommon for the worst misogynists in this world. They enjoyed watching women suffer and held the belief that women were supposed to suffer, while at the same time believed women were blowing their pain out of proportion and weren't suffering much anyway.

Romeo went on. "He was using the boxing gym as a cover to recruit young men to join his grandfather's secret fascist white-nationalist movement. The Pureblood Brotherhood."

"Wow." It just got worse and worse. "A Nazi, huh?" I whistled through my teeth. "He's ticking all the boxes. Well, this is fun. We've got a vampire Nazi sadist disgraced doctor as the new nestmaster of Philadelphia."

"Azerad brought him here to America to help expand his territory. I did a little digging when he tried to present Johan to me as the new nestmaster. I refused to recognize him based on..." Romeo trailed off and waved his hand.

"The fact that he's a Nazi sadist disgraced doctor?"

"Right. Not that it did any good. He's here in Philly, already acting as nestmaster. I've been trying to find out what he's up to, and so far, I've got nothing. But a vampire like him is only interested in domination. He won't look after anyone other than the white male vamps. The rest will be his slaves."

I huffed out a weary breath. "He sounds like a peach."

"He's an absolute monster." Romeo sounded just as tired as I did. "But I've got nothing concrete on him yet, just rumors and whispers. He's put together a new Pureblood Brotherhood with the remaining male vamps here in Philly, and he's hyped them up to start a 'new era' of supremacy."

Romeo's fists clenched involuntarily. "The only reason I'm not prioritizing this is because—"

"Because of Christopher Jupiter, the alien bug-monster attacking you, and the fact that you've barely healed from the battle that took place only a couple of days ago?"

"Yes, exactly. But apart from all that, there's hardly any vampires left in Philadelphia anyway, a couple of dozen at the most."

My brain gave me a tickle. *What's the bet that this new nestmaster will be looking to create as many vampires as possible to bolster the vamp population, just like Zofia had? More slaves and cannon fodder for his new Nazi Pureblood Brotherhood?*

I frowned. Zofia had been an ancient vampire, and only the oldest ones were able to turn new vampires. She'd concocted a plan to store as much of her blood as possible so she could turn a bunch of kids all at once, deliberately choosing young adults who had only just gone through puberty so she could skirt supe laws and avoid detection.

Monica did mention a new handful of human kids missing.

Human, not Orbiter. Zofia had abducted Orbiter children so she could manipulate them and prep them for the change without being bound to the restrictions of the Great Agreement. This Johan guy wasn't an Ancient, so he didn't have enough pathogen-rich blood to change anyone in a hurry.

He'll find a way. Nazis are bullies. He'll need more followers to boss around.

But if he forced the change on more than one human at a time, he'd be choked to death by the Great Agreement before they turned into vampires. The vamp-metamorphosis took days—three bites to receive enough pathogen, then a massive blood transfusion, and finally, a day of deathsleep for the new vamp before the metamorphosis could be completed.

Romeo was watching me, a patient expression on his face. He was waiting for me to finish my conversation with Brain-Daphne before he went on. "Sorry," I said. "Go ahead."

"I wished I didn't have to deal with this whole Johan Van Eiken mess in the first place. I was hoping that the Vampire King would be back to reign him in."

"Rafael's not out of Delaware yet." I'd gotten a short message from Imogen, the Vampire Queen Consort, saying they were dealing with a last minute hellmouth problem. Some West Coast demon worshippers had decided to make a pilgrimage to Delaware to try and crack open the freshly closed hellmouth. The seal was still new and vulnerable, and Chloe's special thought-reading abilities were needed to find the worshippers and stamp them out before the worst could happen.

Imogen said Prue and Max were heading home to deal with some new crisis, but the vamp royals were staying to finish the job, so my Uncle Nate, with his girlfriend Amelia, Chloe, and Malik were still on-site at Hellmouth Central. In her message, Imogen told me Chloe demanded I call her as soon as possible, but when I tried, the call didn't connect.

I missed them all so much. Heaving a rough sigh, I slunk down further into the sofa, burrowing into Romeo's huge body for comfort. "I got a nice pep talk from the countess just before. She made it sound like we could handle all these terrible things easily. And now, another one just got dumped on our plate. The new nestmaster," I grumbled. "As soon as we get rid of one megalomaniac dictator, another one slips into their place. Zofia and Johan. Alexei and Lennox. At least Asherah's still away."

"Say the word, and I'll burn down the whole of Faerie for you, and she'll never come back," Romeo said, his voice low.

"So romantic." I nuzzled into him. "We can't set fire to all our problems, though. There's too many of them. Mysterious alien assassins, Nazi nestmasters, insane fae diplomats..." I lapsed into silence.

"And?" Romeo prompted.

"What?"

"I felt you tense up just then. What else?" Romeo opened his eyes for a second and peered down at me. "Okay, out with it."

"Out with what?"

"Why were you trying to get hold of me earlier?"

I opened my mouth, hesitated, then sighed. If he would burn down the whole of Faerie for me, what would he do to two human detectives? "If I tell you, you have to promise you won't kill anyone. You'll let me deal with it myself."

"No." He shook his head once. "No deal."

"You know what, this is probably the least of our worries." I took a deep breath and spoke quickly, getting it all out. "The human police are investigating me for the murder of Wesley Jupiter. They've got something on me, some sort of forensic evidence, and they've already hauled me in for questioning."

"What?" Romeo narrowed his eyes. "But—"

"The case hasn't been transferred to Otherworld authorities—and no, I don't know why, and I don't know if it ever will be. And Monica will fire me if I don't get them to drop it quickly."

Romeo was silent for a second. "Nobody has asked me anything about the Jupiter mansion." He frowned. "That's... weird."

"Yes, it is. I'm guessing they're deliberately leaving you out of it, but they've got something on me, so they're trying to get me to confess. It felt very urgent this morning, but now, with a strange alien monster running around trying to kill you, with the fae bozan blade dug into my door frame, and this new Nazi sadist vampire nestmaster looming in the background, it's been relegated to the bottom of my worries list."

I didn't mention the very mentally unwell drunk dragon shifter in the pantry in case she heard me.

Romeo let out a low grunt deep in his chest. "I don't like this. I'll make a few inquiries to see why the case hasn't been transferred yet. Once it gets to the Otherworld authorities, they'll leave you alone."

"That's what I figured. I wasn't too worried about being put in human jail for human murder, but Monica says she'll have to fire me if I get arrested. In fact," I heaved a sigh. "It would be nice to be locked away for a few days so I could rest."

I'd been joking, trying to lighten the mood, but suddenly, panic scored its icy claws into my chest. *No, I don't think it would be nice to be locked up in human jail. Squished in like sardines in a concrete box. We've never been claustrophobic before. Have we?*

"Actually, no," I said, wildly aware my pulse had started to race, and Romeo could feel it. "Scrap that. I'd still worry about what was going on outside if I was stuck in jail, and it would drive me crazy."

That's not it, but that's a good point. Something else is driving us crazy, but I can't put my finger on it.

Romeo pulled me closer. His warmth melted the sudden stiffness in my limbs. He pulled something out of his pocket —a beautiful raw quartz point secured by filigree wire on a gold chain—and handed it to me. "Here."

I ran the chain between my fingers, examining the rough crystal with a clear shining point. It wasn't just a pretty piece of jewelry. It felt alive. "What is it?"

"It's a tool. I don't want you to worry about me. When

I'm not with you, I worry about you all the time, and I know what it's like. I hate it. Smartphones can only do so much."

"And yours isn't doing anything while it's locked in a safe."

"I'm going to crack Levi's skull for that," Romeo growled. "But you could have called one of the guys."

"I did," I said. "None of them answered."

Romeo glared for a second. "Well, you see what I mean. Electronics don't work during heavy magical interference, and even with the new tower boosters, sometimes you can't get a signal from outside the Hidden City. It hurts me to worry about you, but somehow the thought of you worrying about me all the time is worse. I made these for us." He pulled an identical chain out of his pocket, pulled it over his head, and touched the point of his crystal. "This is your necklace's twin. They're synced to the wearer, and they're keyed to each other. Your crystal will glow purple if I have an elevated heart rate, indicating danger, and turn red if I'm badly injured. You'll always be able to find me if you place the quartz on your palm and follow the direction the point moves in, just like a compass. Now, I'm not asking you to wear it—"

I put mine over my head immediately, touching the sharp point of the crystal. "It's beautiful. I love it." I leaned over and kissed him.

He mumbled a curse against my lips, and suddenly, I was wrapped in his arms.

The shock of his mouth on mine was so intoxicating, I didn't pull back. He cupped my face, moving one hand to the back of my neck and gently fisting my hair in a delicious grip. I moaned.

I could kiss Romeo forever. This was pure bliss.

"Oi! Stop that shit," Myf screeched. "I can see you. I can *hear* you, and it's disgusting."

It was almost easy to ignore her, even when she started making slurpy-sucky noises, mocking us. I lost myself to the ecstasy of Romeo's kiss, his strong hands, his huge hard body corded with muscle. The power coiled within him was like a sleeping tiger in the jungle—it was starting to wake up. And it wanted to play.

But I couldn't ignore my phone. The ringtone suddenly blared loud enough to wake the dead. I'd set it that way on purpose. It pierced the fog of passion, dragging me back down to earth.

It was the on-call number. "I have to take that," I disengaged myself from Romeo's arms reluctantly and pulled my phone out of my pocket. "It's work. I'm on call, and I'm already in trouble." I hit the answer button. "O-CPS, Daphne Ironclaw speaking."

"Daphne? It's Hart." Sergeant Hart's low, growly bear-shifter voice rolled out of the phone.

I relaxed a fraction. "Hey, Sergeant. What's up?"

"Honey, I'm going to need you downtown as soon as possible." His tone was grim. "Got an emergency here, and your services are required."

I stifled my groan. "I'm on my way."

CHAPTER
TEN

I gazed down at the severed head of the Nazi sadist vampire nestmaster and nudged it with my toe. Shaved blonde hair, square jaw, dead blue eyes like marbles. The head rolled a few inches, then rolled back, his bulging eyeballs facing me again. An odd feeling, one I had no name for, gripped me.

It's dissatisfaction, I think. Brain-Daphne rubbed her chin thoughtfully. *Anticlimax, maybe?*

Johan Van Eiken's cold, dead blue eyes stared back up at me. His mouth was twisted in a snarl. He was such a new vampire he hadn't even started turning ashy yet, although a little of the skin on his ruddy face was starting to flake away.

We only just heard about his existence, and now, here's his severed head. I got all excited. Mr. Nazi Vampire Nestmaster was shaping up to be a baddie of epic proportions. I feel ripped off.

"We should be happy about this," I said to myself, feeling a little unsettled. "We've crossed someone off our list before the ink was even dry."

He sounded so bad, she moaned. *So, so bad. I wanted to stab all his internal organs myself—one by one.*

For once, I kind of agreed with Brain-Daphne's bloodthirsty assessment. "On the bright side, now I totally understand what 'giving someone the satisfaction' means."

Exactly. Finding him like this is terribly unsatisfying. Romeo was hyping him up so much. He sounded so evil. I was looking forward to kicking some Nazi sadist doctor vampire ass.

"Hmm. Yeah. I guess it was because there was no room for doubt with this one. He was a rubber-stamped baddie in every single sense of the word—beyond redemption. We don't get a lot of those."

Hogwash. We never feel bad about the people we kill.

"That's because we're always sure they deserve it, and we don't give second chances. But this one I was extra sure of. It feels like a lost opportunity."

This also feels... wrong. Like we've stepped into a movie where someone else is the main character.

"Well, if this was a movie set, then it's definitely a horror movie."

It wasn't just the severed head on the floor. We were standing in the basement level of an old, abandoned orthodontist school. The place couldn't possibly be creepier if it tried.

I shivered, looking around. The walls were a sickly yellow, peeling in places. There were still creepy dentist chairs and trays of torture-like silver implements scattered around.

Sergeant Hart had met me on the street level outside and explained that the three-level standalone building with two underground basement levels had been abandoned for decades. The owners died in the eighties, and the property had been tied up in legal succession battles ever since.

The new nestmaster had been drawn to the creepiness like a moth to a flame and had made the basement levels into his new lair, keeping all the mad-doctor laboratory vibes intact.

Are we sure he's actually dead?

I nudged his severed head with my toe again. Considering the way his entire head had been severed from his body, perfectly cleanly, in fact, it was safe to say Johan Van Eiken was definitely dead. And the rest of his body was burning merrily inside the medical waste incinerator in the corner of the room. It had been chopped into pieces with a hacksaw first.

Definitely dead, Brain-Daphne said gloomily.

Sergeant Hart lumbered over to join me. "That's what tipped the local cops off," he said, pointing at the incinerator. "They saw the smoke coming out the chimney. This place has been abandoned for decades, but security is tight, and the locals know nobody should be here." He pointed at a hole in the wall covered by a plastic sheet. "The new nest-master built a tunnel that leads out to the alleyway behind the building next door. He's been coming and going, using this place as his base for the last few weeks, I'd say."

"What happened to him?"

"He lost his head," the sergeant deadpanned.

I looked at him.

"Sorry, I couldn't help it. But honestly, honey, I don't know. Local cops found him like this, called it in, and we've transferred it to Otherworld. Come on. I'll show you where I found the new vamp kids. It's down on the next level."

Told you, my brain said smugly.

Johan was doing the exact same thing Zofia had planned to do—turn a bunch of kids all at once. The worst part was that he'd succeeded.

"How many are there?" I asked Hart as we walked.

"Five." He made a face as we walked outside, heading down the short corridor. "All girls. I don't want to think about the reasons why he chose to turn five young girls into vampires as soon as possible."

I didn't want to think about it, either.

"Four of them rushed out the second I unlocked the door, and I couldn't catch them. Those damned kids are too fast for me in my human form. I'd need to shift to be fast enough to chase them, and my captain will kill me if I destroy another uniform," Hart added bitterly. "Only one new vamp stayed back. We've got APBs on the rest. Otherworld authorities have been advised, that's why they're not here yet. They're trying to catch the new vamps before they do anything stupid. There are too many hours before sunrise, and these girls are probably terrified." Hart heaved a huge sigh. "And I have no clue how he managed to change five at once."

"I can guess," I muttered.

I figured it all out the second I smelled Zofia's blood in the room. I remembered the dizzying stench of her ancient blood intimately—bags and bags of it had hung in the cool room of her lair, and I'd run through, puncturing them with my blades. But I either missed one, and Johan had managed to retrieve it, or she had more stashed in secondary locations, and Johan had found it when he took over as nestmaster. Or it was possible that Azerad had some, and he gifted it to his new prodigy to bolster his ranks.

Johan had followed Zofia's playbook but with a few minor changes. He'd abducted smaller young adults, so it wouldn't take as much ancient blood to change them, but he'd chosen humans rather than orbiters, so the Otherworld authorities wouldn't get suspicious. And, judging by Johan's previous occupation and the medical paraphernalia left on the counter, he'd kept them drugged unconscious throughout the whole process, so the Great Agreement wouldn't be triggered to stop him. After all, the human kids weren't aware they were being turned into vampires.

And now it was too late. Five brand-new young vampires were running through the streets or huddled in a storage closet, too scared to come out.

"Who took out the nestmaster?" I asked Hart as we walked down the stairs.

"No idea." He gave a shrug. "A rival for the nestmaster job, probably."

"Great," I muttered. "Judging by the severed head and chopped-up body, another complete psychopath is going to pop out of the woodwork at some point."

Brain-Daphne perked up. *Good.*

"Whoever it was left the new vamp kids behind, though," Hart said, shining his flashlight down the corridor for me so I could see.

"Definitely a psychopath, then." My heart gave a squeeze. The poor girl must be terrified. The worst part was that I had no idea what I was going to do with her.

The situation was unprecedented. I never had to deal with vampire kids, so I didn't even know where to start.

Technically, there were *never* any vampire kids. Vampires were sticklers for their laws, and by royal decree, no child was ever permitted to be turned. Unfortunately, that law was made back in the dark ages, when you were considered an adult as soon as you'd gone through puberty. So, there were a handful of vampires who would forever look fourteen years old.

They weren't my problem, though, because they only *looked* fourteen. Some of them were hundreds of years old. Once a supe spent eighteen years living on this green earth, they were considered an adult and no longer required the assistance of Otherworld Child Protective Services.

But these kids were under eighteen, and they'd only just

been turned vampire. Even if the Enforcers managed to catch the ones who ran away... what the hell was I supposed to do with them?

I couldn't send them back to their parents. The normal procedure would be to refer them to their supe leader, who would take care of everything—issue death certificates, concoct a cover story to explain away the lack of body, and arrange for the new vamp to be moved to another city so they wouldn't bump into their mom and dad in the street one night.

But the Philadelphia vampire supe leader was blazing cheerfully in the incinerator, missing his head.

The next closest nestmaster was in New York, and no way was I calling in Azerad for help. This whole mess was entirely his fault.

Mentally, I ran through the short list of vampires I might be able to talk into fostering the runaways once they were found, until I could get in touch with the Vampire King. This last one—the one that was too scared to run— I'd have to take her with me until I could figure out what to do.

Poor thing.

"You might have to keep her down here until the Otherworld cleanup crew gets rid of the body," Hart said, checking his phone. "They're just pulling up now."

"Good idea. We don't want her traumatized any more than she already is."

Hart led me to a door, opened it, and nodded. "Hey, honey. Me again."

"I told you: I don't answer questions." The voice was female, high pitched, and, surprisingly, her tone was calm and even. "I don't talk to cops. I'd like a lawyer, please."

I raised my eyebrows at Hart and mouthed at him. "A lawyer?"

He rolled his eyes and turned back to the door. "I got someone here that you might want to talk to. She ain't a cop, and I told you before, you don't need a lawyer."

"Oh," the girl said. "I suppose there are some benefits to being underage. You have a social worker with you?"

Hart opened the door further, ushering me inside.

A young woman stood in the middle of the room, staring at me expectantly, head held high, back ramrod straight. She was much shorter than me, five one, or five foot even, maybe, with the most translucent-looking peaches and cream skin I'd ever seen in my life. She had thick, dazzlingly bright copper hair flowing over her shoulders and tumbling down to her waist like a waterfall.

The new vamp girl was a true redhead with the delicate skin to match, and the new vampirism had really done a number on her complexion. She was practically glowing. Round, owlish wire-framed glasses sat on her snub nose, and she squinted at me through them.

Why was she still wearing her glasses?

The cute Disney-princess vibe ended at her neck, though. She wore a plaid shirt overtop of a baggy green t-shirt, and huge basketball shorts that came down past her knees, disguising her figure completely. Nike high-tops sheathed her feet. She looked very... comfortable.

She looks like Adam Sandler from the neck down.

"Hi," I said gently. "My name is Daphne."

Her expression remained blank. "I don't answer questions."

"I'm not a cop." I tried to radiate safety and security. "Can you tell me your name?"

"Marie." She glared at me. "Where's the social worker?"

"I'm a social worker."

Marie, the new vampire, stared at me for a moment. Her beautiful emerald eyes scanned me from the top of my head to the bottom of my feet, then, she heaved an enormous sigh. "I suppose there have been a lot of budget cuts," she said, sounding resigned. "Let's get the paperwork started, then. I need to hurry this up. I've got to get back to campus as soon as possible."

This was not what I was expecting. "Paperwork?" I frowned. "Campus?"

"Yeah. Professor Qualley needs me to assist with an experiment she's running. We're trying to disprove the double-slit theory as woo-woo hogwash. I'm going to make those particles do what they're supposed to do while we're *not* watching, damn it."

"Um..." I stared at her. "How old are you?"

"Seventeen years, four days and eight hours." She looked at me right in the eyes. "How old are you? Eighteen? Nineteen?"

I met her gaze evenly. It was important not to show fear in front of teenagers. "I'm twenty-two, Marie."

Her eyebrow arched. "Hmm. What college did you go to?"

Hart gave me a nudge. "Makes you wish the others hadn't run away, huh?"

"I told them not to run." Marie sighed like a disappointed mom. "I explained it all in a way I hoped they'd understand, but the girls let their emotions get the better of them. I probably could have done more to stop them, but ultimately, they need to make their own choices in life." She sighed again. "They'll learn better one day."

I stared at her. The girl was so strange. She didn't talk like a normal teenager, and all this direct eye contact was almost unnerving. Most people didn't look you in the eye when they talked to you. They looked away, or at your mouth, or just past you, because staring into someone's eyes was a very intimate thing to do. But Marie's emerald eyes bored into mine unflinchingly.

I reached into my bag and pulled out a notebook. We'd have to find the other new vamps as soon as possible. "Do you know who the other girls were?"

"Molly Tapper, fifteen years old, from Collingswood, New Jersey; Phoebe Bond, fifteen years old, Lansdown, Pennsylvania," Marie deadpanned, rattling off the names like a robot.

I scrambled to write it down.

"Tara Shepherd, sixteen, and Sonda Pike, sixteen, both from Westville, New Jersey." Marie paused and cocked her head. "I can give you their descriptions as well as several hypotheticals of where they might be headed. I did warn them that it would be silly to run away, considering we were about to be in the hands of the relevant authorities. Just between you and me, they weren't exactly making the smartest decisions before all this." She jerked an arm out and waved it around, gesturing to the room in general.

I didn't know what to say. "Um... how so?"

"Tara and Sonda were both suffering from abuse at home, so rather than report it to the authorities, they ran away. The last thing either of them remember, they were at a nightclub in Queen Village, which is where our captor must have found them. Molly was manipulated by her much older boyfriend to lie to her parents and come to the city for the weekend with him, and he left her alone in a car so he could go do drugs in an alleyway somewhere. Our captor scooped her up and brought her here."

"I assumed he drugged all of you. He was keeping you unconscious, right?"

"Yeah, mostly. But I'm a redhead." Marie jerked her shoulders in a shrug. "He clearly didn't adjust for that. I was in and out."

She was not what I expected, but she was still a victim. My heart throbbed. "I'm so sorry, Marie."

"Oh, I know. I *know*," she said, waving her arm dramatically. "You don't have to tell me. I feel like an absolute fool, Daphne, an absolute fool. But when an attractive older man—with a foreign accent, no less, and when they've got a foreign accent, you know they were not schooled here in America, so you tend to take them more seriously, which yes, it's a bias I'm going to work on—when he approaches you and attempts to mansplain the finer points of arch curvature and how it affects load carrying strength, and he gets his math *wrong*... I'm sorry, but I'm going to get into a heated discussion with him. I had no idea he was a psychotic madman, conducting experiments in an abandoned building." Her expression grew furious. "And he refused to let me assist him!"

I looked at Hart. He looked back at me and shrugged. "I'm out. She's all yours, honey. Good luck." He backed out of the room.

I turned back to Marie. Maybe she was being so weird because she was severely scared. "Marie..." I didn't even know where to start. "How are you feeling?"

She made a face. "Traumatized, of course. I was abducted, drugged, held hostage, and experimented on by a mad scientist for three days. I'm going to need some serious therapy after this. My health insurance probably won't cover more than the ten sessions they allow for under my plan, not even under their extenuating circumstances trauma clause." She squinted at me. "Do you think you could get me a grant or something?"

Health insurance? A government grant? The girl was obviously very smart, but she was clearly short-circuiting and holding on to the remnants of her human life.

I opened my mouth. "Well, you can rest assured that the man who did this to you is gone. You're safe now."

"I'll suspend judgement on that for now, Daphne. I'll be honest with you; I have little faith in social services. Especially these days with all the budget cuts."

This was bizarre. "Are you sure you're seventeen?"

"What kind of question is that?"

I blew out a breath. "Well, I'm here to help you, Marie, and I'll try to do that in any way I can. We'll get you somewhere safe. This isn't the end. You can have a great life, I promise."

For a moment, an expression of true horror crossed her face. "You're not taking me home."

"No," I said sadly. "I'm sorry, Marie, I'm not. You can't go home. Never again."

"Thank *God!*" Her perfect posture dissolved, her shoulders slumped, and she exhaled noisily in relief. "I was really worried there for a second. I know I jumped the gun a little when I decided to indulge in my sense of newfound freedom to leave the dorm and go sightseeing for the weekend. I mean, look how that turned out." She waved her hand jerkily again, gesturing to the abandoned dentistry school. "Abducted, drugged, experimented on. You know, I'll admit I never really understood the concept of victim blaming until right now, Daphne," she mused, nodding seriously. "Logically, I know that bad things can happen to anyone, regardless of the safety measures you put in place, but it's so easy to hold a world view that bad things only happen when people do stupid things. And the only stupid thing I did was trust that Dr. Van Eiken really *did* have a whiteboard in his windowless delivery van, and he would indeed listen patiently while I explained why his math was *wrong!*"

"Yeah." I stammered for a second. "Um, Marie..."

"So, you can take me back to Cambridge now, right?" Marie asked cheerfully. "I need to return soon. I don't want Dr. Qualley doing the double-slit experiment without me." Her eyes narrowed furiously. "That bastard Raj will take any opportunity to muscle me out. If I'm not there, he'll be sticking himself like a limpet onto the professor, and it will take me weeks to prise him off again."

"Cambridge?" I asked faintly.

"Harvard," she replied, giving me a *duh* look. "I don't know of any other universities in Cambridge. I can't miss any classes, Daphne. I got a full ride, the physics department was so excited to have me, I finally managed to smooth things over with Dr. Qualley after I misgendered her wife and blew up her voltmeter. It's only my first year; I'm not risking my scholarship for anything."

My eyebrows hit my hairline. Aha. Now it made sense—her attitude, her attention to details, the intense eye contact, her precociousness. Her outfit.

Marie was a child prodigy. A pretty seventeen-year-old nerd girl. But...

"Uh, no, I can't take you there, either," I told her. "You can't go back to Harvard, Marie."

She looked outraged. "Why not? I like it there. MIT didn't offer me a full ride, and no way in hell I'm going to Stanford, Daphne. Their Physics department is a sausage fest, and it's hard enough to be a woman in STEM as it is. No," she said firmly, "I'm staying at Harvard."

Suddenly, it hit me. She didn't know.

Marie didn't know she'd been turned into a vampire.

"Marie," I said tentatively. "What is it you think Dr. Van Eiken did to you?"

She shrugged. "I'm assuming he was trialing a new cocktail of stimulant drugs. Medical bioengineering of some sort. For a while there, I wondered if this was a black-ops military campaign, because damn, I feel good." She extended her arm and clenched her fist. "I haven't experimented yet, but I'd say my muscle strength has increased at least tenfold, and my reflexes have sharpened considerably. My eyesight is fucked, though."

"Take off your glasses," I said quietly.

"Huh? Oh." She removed them from her little snub nose and blinked. "*Wow.* Twenty-twenty." Her eyes zipped around the dark room, flashing deep scarlet where the flashlight bounced off her iris. "No, it's better than that. I'll have to run some tests."

"Marie—"

"I must be burning through nutrients at an accelerated rate, because I'm starving. Got a hankering for steak. I guess it's a protein-based enhancement." She pursed her lips. "I'm assuming there will be a crash when I go through withdrawals, but all this extra strength and speed is incredible. Dr. Van Eiken might have been a cruel, psychotic mad scientist genius, but wow. I'm going to be putting a little more emphasis on the genius part." She made a yeesh face. "Now I'm kinda regretting—" She saw my face and sandwiched her lips together.

"Marie."

"Hmm?"

"Dr. Van Eiken didn't give you stimulant drugs."

"What was it, then? Ooh, have my cells changed permanently on a molecular level?" She narrowed her eyes on me. "Don't tell me it was gamma radiation exposure, Daphne, because I tried that on my hamster when I was ten, and it *really* didn't work. I didn't get a hairy little mini-Hulk, I got a burned hamster who vomited on my Hello Kitty rug and instantly died of radiation sickness." She shifted on her feet guiltily. "I still feel awful about that. I wrote an outraged letter to Stan Lee, threatening a lawsuit and everything."

"Marie—"

"They shouldn't promote stuff like that. It gives little girls ideas. Gamma radiation can lead to mutation, yes, but not the super-strong green-skin Hulk-smash kind of mutation. Spider bites cause necrosis. Don't get me started on Dr. Strange," she said, rolling her eyes. "Half of the freshmen in Theoretical Physics class have been suckered into thinking they'll be able to break the laws of physics with the power of their minds. That's why me and Qualley are so hellbent on disproving the double-slit experiment."

"Marie!"

"The only one with any basis in reality is Iron Man, and that's my one goal in this lifetime, Daphne. It's why I'm doing Experimental Physics at Harvard, you know." Her pretty face screwed up into a determined scowl. "I'm going to be Iron Man. Without the misogyny or the American exceptionalism, of course," she added. "For now, I suppose it'll be fun to be biologically enhanced, like Captain America," she said, clenching her fist again. "I never identified with him much, if I'm being honest with you. He's supposed to be the most moral character, but he comes across as just stupid. He could have just kicked that grenade into a ditch. He didn't have to jump on it."

"Marie!" I shouted.

"What?"

"You're not a superhero," I said firmly. "You're a vampire. Dr. Van Eiken turned you into a vampire."

She only paused for a second. "Right." She stared at me. "Good one."

I blew out a breath. "Dr. Van Eiken wasn't human. He was a vampire. He was trying to create some new vampires to serve him and to boost the ranks of his nest here. He abducted you, flooded your body with a vampire pathogen, then drained all your blood and gave you a massive transfusion of ancient vampire blood. It triggered a metamorphosis."

"Ha, ha," Marie deadpanned.

"Like a butterfly," I said firmly. "The caterpillar turns to goo inside a cocoon. They get rebuilt from scratch and come out with wings. If a caterpillar can do it, why can't a human?"

"Because humans don't have the biological capabilities for complete genetic restructuring." Marie stared at me. "Duh."

"They do if you introduce a foreign pathogen to trigger dormant DNA."

She hesitated. "Hmm. I suppose, theoretically, that *could* be possible..." Her expression turned thoughtful. She tapped her chin. "I'm going to need a sample of this pathogen and a whiteboard."

"Trust me, Marie—"

"I don't trust anyone."

I hissed through my teeth. "Vampires are real," I told her. "Werewolves are real, too, because I'm a werewolf."

"Oh, yeah? Okay. Show me."

Fuck.

"Well..." I shrugged awkwardly, feeling stupid. "I'm a little defective."

"Right." Marie eyed me warily. There was an awkward silence. "Do you think I could possibly get another social worker in here...?"

Brain-Daphne let out a chuckle. *It's hard to feel insulted. She's hilarious.*

I threw my hands in the air, exasperated. "Vampires are real, werewolves are real, witches are real, magic is real. There's a whole Otherworld that sits alongside the human world, and you're part of it now, Marie. You're a vampire."

She eyeballed me and nodded slowly. "Okay. Whatever you say."

I'd have to rip the Band-Aid off, Jacob style. "Sergeant Hart?"

He poked his head back in. "Yeah?"

"The new vamp is a cynic."

"I'm not a cynic," Marie cut in. "I'm a skeptic. A cynic would imply that I'm predisposed to reject outrageous claims. I'm not." She stared at me. "Get me a whiteboard."

"Okay, honey." Sergeant Hart sighed and took off his shirt. "I have to make this quick. Otherworld has already bagged the head and tagged everything; the scene is almost clear, so you can head out now." He shucked his pants. "My wife has made meatloaf, and it's getting cold."

"Whoa," Marie waved her hands in front of her eyes. "What kind of—"

A punch of magic rolled through the room and suddenly, there was a grizzly bear standing in the doorway.

Marie froze.

Hart gave a little growl, then shuffled back out the door.

CHAPTER
ELEVEN

Marie didn't speak again for fifty-nine minutes. I timed her.

I didn't move her. Instead, I waited patiently and used the time to think about what the hell I was going to do.

I wasn't expecting to have to take a brand-new vampire home with me, and since I was still wearing my leathers, I'd stupidly ridden my motorcycle over here. It would be irresponsible of me to take a client on my motorcycle without a helmet, and I'd only draw attention to myself by leading a catatonic girl onto the bus this late at night.

I sat on the floor, passing the time by checking my phone. Romeo had sent me a message to say that Myf was sleeping in the pantry, snoring loudly enough to wake the dead, there was no trace of the giant alien insect in the Hidden City, and he and his covenmates were heading home.

He asked me to join him if I could. I wanted to in the worst way, but...

Myf. I felt so bad I'd neglected her. She needed support, and there was nobody else to give it to her.

Well, there was. Technically, as a shifter, she was the responsibility of the Alpha. There was no way in hell I was going to hand her over to Lennox Arran. I'd seen the gleam in his eye when he spoke to her when he first came to see me. For a bombastic asshole, he sure had an instinct for people he could use. When he met Myf, he had no idea she was a dragon, but he could sense she was something special. Someone he could exploit.

Like me.

He'd marked her as a person of interest, and Lennox didn't give up on the things that interested him.

I had to keep Myf away at all costs. If Lennox had a dragon under his command, then the world was doomed.

I slumped on the floor, feeling defeated. I never thought this job would end up like this. My Otherworld Social Worker course was very clear on protocol—on how things should go. A vulnerable supe child gets referred to me, I make sure they're safe and refer them to the appropriate leader.

Except most of the time, the supe leader was an even worse option. Case in point, the new vamp girl having a mental breakdown right in front of me.

Dealing with one sassy seventeen-year-old redhead was bad enough. Now, in a lovely twist of fate, I had two. I mulled over the problem while I waited for Marie to snap out of her vamp-shock.

Maybe I could send Myf to another state, so another Alpha Shifter could look after her.

That was a good idea. Prue and Max were heading back to D.C. right now. In fact, Max, the Alpha Shifter of the whole East Coast, was the best option I was going to get. I made a mental note to ask Prue if she'd take on a new ward when she got home. Maybe Prue could look after Marie, too.

They're too similar, Brain Daphne muttered.

"They're not similar. Not personality-wise, anyway."

Not Marie and Myf. Marie and Prue. This new vamp girl is a straight shooter with impulse control problems, a morally questionable mindset, disdain for societal expectations, and, judging by what she said about Van Eiken, she appears to find old men attractive—just like Prue. They might get on like a house on fire, but it's more likely they'd clash like cymbals and destroy the whole world.

"Yeah," I muttered to myself. "You're right, but I can't think of any other options. Max will know what to do with Myf, at least. He'll find somewhere safe for her." I just had to wait until he and Prue got back.

Suddenly, Marie twitched and blinked. Her eyes focused on me, then narrowed. "Are you talking to yourself?"

"Yeah." I made a snap decision to be honest with her. "I got lost in a wild-magic realm when I was a kid. I was all alone, and I made the conscious decision to separate my brain from my heart, so I had someone to talk to and debate things with. I separated aspects of myself, so I'd have company. I still do it. It's a stress response and a self-soothing technique."

She whistled. "Voluntary dissociative identity disorder. That's wild. Your psychiatrist must have had a blast with you."

"Are you feeling better?"

"No. I'm still not sure if I believe you, but it all seems very plausible. That cop did turn into a bear right in front of my eyes. I'm super-strong and super-fast, my canines are suddenly very pointy, and I want to eat a bloody steak so much that I'm getting a lady boner just thinking about it." She suddenly pursed her lips. "And Van Eiken's head didn't bleed out as much as I thought it would. I did wonder about that."

"What?"

"I'm willing to keep an open mind." Marie heaved a sigh. "Okay." She held out her arm and made a grasping motion. "Give me the handbook."

"What handbook?"

"The..." Marie frowned. "You know, the handbook that explains everything. The manual."

"What?"

She tilted her head. "The course notes. Otherworld CliffsNotes? Supernatural Creatures for Dummies?"

"Oh." Almost all of us were born into this Otherworld. There wasn't a book that explained everything to newcomers. "We don't have one."

"Well, something specific to me, then. The handbook for the recently vampirized?

"We don't have one of those either." Vampires loved being mysterious too much for that sort of thing.

Marie looked a little panicked. "Look, Daphne, I love a good exploratory experiment as much as the next girl, but I need some parameters to work in. You can't just say 'oh, look, you're a vampire now, go on with your bad self, girl,' and let me loose on the world."

"I'm not going to do that," I reassured her. "You'll stay with me until I find a safe space for you. Like I said, I'm a werewolf, but I'll find you a vampire to show you the ropes." A nice one, I added inside my own head.

"Okay." She squinted up at me. "How come they didn't send a vampire social worker in here?"

"There aren't any."

"Budget cuts, huh?"

"Something like that. Come on." I jerked my head towards the door. "We're going to have to head out through the upper level." That was where Johan Van Eiken had drugged and changed Marie against her will. It was bound to upset her. "Will you be okay with walking through there?"

"Oh, sure," she said, walking next to me. Marie had the most unusual gait; she kind of bounced along, trotting like a cheerful pony—a very un-vampire like walk. She really was a pretty young woman with her almost shockingly beautiful red hair and her glowing peaches-and-cream complexion. "Can we go get something to eat? I'm starving." We walked down the hallway, heading towards the stairs.

I grimaced. Usually, vampires either fed from their Orbiter servants, or they glamored a human, fed on them in a dark alleyway, and vanished into the night. I didn't want to have to teach Marie how to feed on humans.

I can do it, Brain Daphne said cheerfully. *We can turn this into a positive, babes. Let's prime this pretty nerd to prey on evil humans.*

That's a can of worms I don't want to open. "Try and ignore it for now," I said out loud. "I'll find someone who can help soon."

Marie squinted up at me. "No offence, Daphne, but you seem a little out of your depth."

"I am," I said honestly, walking up the stairs, while she bounced along beside me. "There's never been a situation like this, Marie. As an Otherworld CPS officer, I've never had a vampire client before."

"Why?"

"It's against vamp law to turn anyone before puberty, and most new vampires are well looked after by their makers."

A strange expression crossed her face as we climbed the stairs. I glanced at her. We were so close to Van Eiken's monster lab—the place where he'd kept her drugged and restrained while the metamorphosis took place.

"Are you okay?" I asked.

"Yeah. So, uh." Her tone turned ultra-casual. "Is it, uh, can you expand a little on the vamp law thing?"

"What part?"

"Just in general."

"Vampire law is extensive, convoluted, and exhausting," I told her quite truthfully. Maybe this would keep her distracted while we moved through the room where her torturer was decapitated. "You're asking me to condense thousands and thousands of years of complicated history and put it in a nutshell."

"I did ask for a handbook," she said a little moodily. "I read fast."

I bet she did. "There's no handbook," I said patiently. "Ask me a specific question, and I'll try and answer."

We reached the first basement level and made our way through the lines of dentist chairs. The Otherworld authorities had blown through here quickly. A handful of tags and marks, spots where the Otherworld investigations had taken samples, were dotted over the chairs and on the stainless-steel counters. Some of the equipment had been moved around. The vampire who cut off the nestmaster Johan Van Eiken's head would be found eventually. I wondered what kind of overpowered monster managed to decapitate him.

Azerad was going to have a shit fit.

"Okay, fine." Marie huffed out a breath. "If I commit a crime, I'm not going to be put in the human system, right?"

"No." But... maybe. After all, I was stuck in the human justice system for Wesley's murder. There was no point going into that with Marie right now. "It depends on the crime." I hesitated and pointed at her. "I should get this out of the way. You're not allowed to kill humans, Marie. Even if you have to feed from one."

She rolled her eyes. "I'm not that hungry. And that's not what I meant. I'm just trying to get a general understanding of your culture, that's all," she said casually. "Since you can't get me a handbook."

"Honestly, Marie, the Otherworld is a bit more like the Wild West. The strongest are on top, but all the different supe species try to hold each other accountable to keep the balance. If you kill a werewolf, the Alpha Shifter will demand justice. If you squash a pixie, the Fae Diplomat might rip out your lungs and wear them as a waistcoat."

"Right. So, er." She trotted next to me. "What happens if I, uh, kill another vampire?"

"Probably nothing," I told her quite honestly.

"Really?" Marie brightened. "That's *definitely* something that should go in the handbook."

"Well, there is an Otherworld justice system," I said. "The basics are the same as the human justice system. Interspecies crimes get a whole lot messier. The most important thing is that we keep ourselves secret from the human world. For balance." I was about to launch into the whole explanation of the need to keep humans in the dark, but Marie cut me off with a wave.

"Got it." She nodded. "So, with vamp-on-vamp crime, it's not necessarily a felony?"

"We don't have felonies. The penalty for most crimes is death." I frowned. "But most supes deal with their own. If you broke vampire law, you'd be referred to your immediate superior for discipline. Your nestmaster." I cringed as I walked past the place where his head had rolled on the floor. "That was him, right there."

Marie side-eyed the furnace in the corner, which was still glowing. "That's definitely something you should put in the handbook," she said, sounding nervous. "So... what if there's no nestmaster?"

"Well..." I huffed out a breath. "Every case is different. But if nobody is demanding satisfaction or restitution—"

"So, if it's justified, I get away with it." An evil laugh escaped her lips. "Hee hee heee."

Brain Daphne chuckled along with her. *It was her. She did it.*

I hadn't caught up yet. Did what?

Sweetheart, stop and take a look at the evil genius in front of you. Johan Van Eiken met his match.

It took me a second. Oh.

"Marie." I stopped in my tracks, turned and faced her, and frowned. "Did you do this?"

She blinked up at me innocently. "Did I do what?"

"Did you kill Johan Van Eiken?"

She hesitated. "I plead the fifth."

"There is no fifth, Marie," I said wearily. "You're in the Otherworld now. And I'm going to take that as a yes. But..." I shook my head. "*How?* How did you decapitate a full-grown man?"

She shrugged. "It's always easy to defeat your enemies when you know what their Achilles heel is, so I went with the most obvious option."

"Decapitation?"

"To be fair, I didn't know he was a vampire. If I had, I might have gone for something a little more subtle." She squinted at me. "Holy water? Garlic?"

I shook my head. "Nope."

"Huh. Well, *that* should go in the handbook."

I shook my head, bewildered. "So how...?"

"Found some razor wire in a cupboard," she said cheerfully. "Did a few calculations. Van Eiken is six-two, with his head-to-mid-neck being approximately eight inches of that. When he was out last night, I cut it to the exact measurements and used a pulley system to rig a very heavy weight. Had to apply some force to the razor wire to cut through his neck, y'know?" She grinned up at me.

"Right," I said faintly.

"That dentist chair is four hundred and fifty pounds. I just waited until I had the opportunity, and finally, when all the other girls were awake, he gathered us here to explain his grand plan." Her grin faltered. "I probably should have waited to hear what he had to say before I pulled the lever," she admitted. "This whole vampire thing is a bit of a shock."

"Go on," I said tightly.

"Anyway, I pulled the lever, the weight dropped, and the razor wire bisected the room at exactly five feet four inches from the ground. Even if me or any of the other girls were standing up at the time, the razor wire would whizz right over our heads."

Forget Johan Van Eiken, my brain chuckled merrily. *We got another evil genius right here.*

"That's..." I exhaled. "Wow."

"Anyway, I figured I should leave the head for identification purposes, so I rolled it under the table over there. But the body was freaking the other girls out. So, I, uh..." She trailed off and shrugged.

"You cut it into pieces and put it in the furnace."

"I've sat in on a few autopsies, Daphne. It's not like I'm squeamish or anything. I was trying to protect the other girls from having to stare at a headless body." She tilted her head. "You know what? You're sounding a little judgmental right now."

Hell yeah, you are. My brain showed me a memory of me as a seven-year-old girl, throwing the dead bodies of my enemies to Norma so she could strip the flesh off for me, then building a bone sculpture with Dwayne in our front yard.

"I'm not judging you, Marie." I said softly. "I feel bad for you. I get that you were trying to protect the younger girls. It's just..."

"You didn't expect a young human to be so pragmatic when it comes to body disposal." She rolled her eyes. "Before you ask, I've been tested, and I aced all the tests. I'm not on the spectrum, I don't have any personality disorders, I'm not a psychopath, and I do feel empathy. I just have a high propensity for applying logic to emotional situations, that's all. We had a dead body on the floor and the other four girls were freaking out, so I got rid of him. Most of him, anyway."

Something told me that Marie aced all the tests because she was very good at tests. "You cut up the body of the man who abducted you. I don't blame you for that, in fact, I can relate to you. I grew up as a werewolf in a horrible place. Violence was ordinary for me."

"I didn't cut him up *violently*, Daphne. It was methodical. Precise incisions so I could sever the joints easier. It's like deboning a chicken," she added, a little too cheerfully for my liking.

I blinked down at her. "Where did you come from?"

She shrugged. "San Diego."

Brain-Daphne gave an evil chuckle. *She's just like me. Marie could be my own child. It's like I've just given birth to a hyper-intelligent ginger version of myself.* She sighed happily. *My baby.*

And now she's a vampire. Johan Van Eiken had no idea he'd created a monster. Marie was still a kid, though. I shouldn't forget that. I took a deep breath. "Let's get out of here. I'll take you back to my place."

"And then you'll put me on a bus back to school, right?"

"No, honey, I'm sorry," I said. "You can't go back."

Marie let out a chuckle. "Oh, I'm going back to Harvard,

Daphne. I'm not giving up on my life's work. Pointy teeth be damned."

We walked up the second flight of steps and left the building. Sergeant Hart waited on the steps. His expression made my pulse quicken.

"Daphne, honey," he called. "We got a problem." His eyes flicked down to the street.

I smelled the two human detectives before they appeared. Detective Hartshorn jogged up the steps first. Detective Boggs appeared a second later. He stopped, waiting at street level. "Hello, Daphne." Hartshorn fixed me with a hard stare. "We'd like to ask you a few more questions."

CHAPTER
TWELVE

"We went by your place earlier," Hartshorn said, staring at me from across the cold steel table.

The detectives had asked me to answer some questions at a police precinct only a block away and not wanting to cause a scene in front of Marie, who, as a volatile new vampire, could have an emotional breakdown at any point, I complied. I was now stuck in another windowless interview room with my new vamp client waiting just outside.

"Tell me, Daphne." Hartshorn tilted his head. "How come you live in a hotel?"

I licked my lips, trying to gather my thoughts. The detectives hadn't been by my place; they'd just gone to the address they had on file for me. All supes who lived in the Hidden City kept an address outside the City for human-related purposes.

There was a witch-run boutique hotel in Gray's Ferry that provided this service. It was a little like having a Post Office Box. If a human needed to find you, they'd head to the address provided, and the receptionist would nod and confirm that you lived there, but that's as far as it went.

"I'm between places right now," I said.

"We waited a long time, but didn't see any sign of you." This time, Boggs stood by the wall directly behind me. I couldn't see him unless I turned completely around in my seat, so his disembodied voice came out of nowhere. It was designed to unsettle me, and it was working. "Looks like a swanky hotel. Must cost a fortune."

They'd had me under surveillance. It must have taken them a bit of effort to track me down at a crime scene while I was on a callout. Neither detective was perturbed by the fact that it was late, I was working, and I had a minor under my care. Hartshorn, his salt-and-pepper hair messier than usual, just quietly informed me they weren't arresting me; they just wanted to have a quick chat.

Another tactic. They'd tried surveilling me, found nothing, and decided to apply a bit more pressure to see if I would crack.

I want to crack. I'm so tired, Brain-Daphne yawned. *I almost hope they try to search us, so we can stab them and get out of here.*

I couldn't do that. These detectives were just doing their jobs. It wasn't their fault they'd gotten mixed up in Otherworld business.

Marie was waiting right outside the interview room. I was more worried about her than anything else. There was so much I needed to explain to her. If she did something that broke the Great Agreement right now, she could choke to death.

Luckily, she didn't seem bothered at all by being dragged with me to a police station. She was sitting on a bench in the corridor, whistling and kicking her feet. When Hartshorn asked her if she wanted anything to drink, she glared at him stonily and said, "I don't answer questions."

Marie didn't like cops.

I, on the other hand, took the opportunity to chug a whole gallon of water. I hadn't eaten dinner yet, and I'd missed lunch, so I was starving. Lack of food wasn't helping my mental state.

"Daphne," Hartshorn said, his voice sharp.

I flinched. "What?"

"You didn't answer the question."

Do what Marie did, Brain-Daphne hissed. *Tell him you don't answer questions!*

If I did that, then they might arrest me. My chest tightened at the thought. It wasn't just that Monica would fire me. For some reason, the idea of being trapped in a concrete jail cell was still triggering panic.

But... wait.

I blinked at Hartshorn. "You didn't ask me anything."

"I did," Boggs barked from behind me.

"What was it?"

"I said that the hotel sure looked swanky."

I didn't say anything. He walked right into that one.

"Smartass," Boggs rumbled from behind me.

"Gentlemen," I said, leaning forward, trying to calm my pulse. "I'm more than prepared to help you with your case, but can we please hurry this up? As you know, I've got a client with me, and I have to get her to a safe place. It's getting very late. Is there something you want to know?"

"Okay, I'm going to ask you straight out," Boggs's disembodied voice barked from behind me. "Why did Wesley Jupiter have a clump of your hair in his hands when his body was found?"

I reared back in my chair. "What?" I didn't have to fake my surprise.

"We know it was yours. Even without forensics confirming it. Long, purple strands, exactly like what you've got on your head." I felt a sharp tug on my ponytail.

Boggs had pulled my hair.

He touched you, Brain Daphne snarled. *Rip out his entrails and strangle him with them!*

I couldn't. I couldn't move—I couldn't even breathe. Panic clawed at my chest.

"Answer the question, Daphne," Hartshorn said, sensing blood. "Why did Wesley have a clump of your hair in his hands when he died?"

"I— I don't know."

My mind whirled.

So that was the forensic evidence they were waiting for. My hair had been found on the body—in Wesley's hands, no less—so the detectives had sent it to a lab to be tested. The hair would have come up as not human, so the lab's Otherworld agent would have destroyed the sample, shrugged helplessly, and told the detectives that they lost it.

And now the detectives were all riled up. They would have arrested me as soon as they had confirmation it was mine. But it was long and lavender, so it was good enough for them.

Why was my hair in Wesley's hands? He hadn't grabbed me. He didn't touch me. I was being set up. Framed for a crime I didn't commit.

Well, we did commit it.

Hartshorn leaned forward. "That's it? You don't know?"

There was nothing else I could say, and anyway, it was the truth. "No. I don't know."

"Okay." Boggs exhaled heavily through his nose, a bullish snort. "Here's what I think. I think you went into the mansion to fuck him one last time before you killed him."

Urgh, here we go. I braced myself.

"I think you waited until you saw your ex-boyfriend leaving the house with his fiancé," Boggs continued. "And you went inside, and you fucked Wesley. We know you started sleeping with him when Troy broke up with you. You wanted to get into that family no matter what. I get it, Daphne, they're rich; they've got money to spare. You spent so long chipping away at Troy, and you come to Philadelphia to find he'd replaced you. So, you turn to Wesley, and you seduce him. You started fucking him. He was an easier target, anyway, since it's simple to bag an old guy. But Mina came home and caught you." It wasn't a question. Detective Boggs was presenting it like a confirmed statement.

I kept my mouth shut. It was another common interrogation tactic. Make up the worst scenario and present it as fact, so the one being questioned rushes to correct them.

Boggs went on, "Mina caught you and Wesley at it, and she tried to throw you out. But you killed her, then you killed Wesley. Then you triggered an explosion that destroyed the house, and you got lucky enough to have the whole thing fall into a sinkhole." He paused for a second. "We'll find Mina's body eventually, Daphne."

They wouldn't. She'd been turned into marble and blown to smithereens.

"Must have been a shock for her." Hartshorn watched my face carefully. "For Mina, I mean. To walk in and see you fucking her husband. A dignified woman like that. She thought she got rid of you, and she comes home and finds you with her husband's dick in your mouth." He gave a mirthless chuckle. "First the son, then his dad. You've been a busy girl."

Breathe in, breathe out. Brain-Daphne threw up an image of me punching Hartshorn in the face until his nose exploded. *Breathe in, breathe out.*

"You take it in the ass, right?" Boggs chuckled. "I bet you do. It's the best way to hook a man—offer all your holes. Your plan almost worked, until Mina walked in on you."

"Don't worry," Hartshorn added. "I get it. A girl like you is power hungry and insatiable. I hope you swing both ways. You'll go to jail for murder, and you'll get fisted by felons on a daily basis."

My head swam. Evils burrowed into me, and my breath came in short pants.

Breathe!

It was too late—I was spiraling. Darkness pressed in on all sides.

We need a plan, my brain screamed. *We need to get out of here, or I'm going to snap, rip out Hartshorn's throat, punch through Bogg's chest and rip out his still beating heart!*

We can't do anything. If we use our supe strength, we break the Great Agreement. If we don't suffocate to death, we go to human jail for the rest of our life.

"You'll get all your holes filled, just the way you like it." Hartshorn smirked.

What do we do? We need a plan. Think! What would Marie do? Oh, I know—

I opened my mouth.

And vomited all over the table.

CHAPTER
THIRTEEN

Well, that worked a treat.

It did. After I projectile-vomited a gallon of water right into Detective Hartshorn's face, I burst into tears. Loud, noisy tears. I wailed about how disgusting they were to say such awful things.

The vomit broke the detectives' steely resolve much better than just tears would have. They expected me to start crying at some point. They didn't expect me to puke my guts out at their line of questioning.

I'd managed to create a tiny sliver of doubt in their minds. It would have to do for now.

They weren't going to leave me alone, though. The hair sample had been destroyed, but the fact that a long purple hair that looked exactly like mine was found in the dead guys' hand was still concrete evidence. They had a motive, they had me in the area around the time of death. If they kept dragging me in for questioning, they'd eventually search me and get the murder weapon.

But for now, I was free.

I picked up Marie from outside the door. "Come on," I

said wearily. "I'll take you back to my place." It was well after midnight now.

She wrinkled her nose. "You smell awful."

"Yeah," I sighed.

"Can we get something to eat?" For the first time since I met her, Marie sounded unsettled. "I'm really starving."

I sighed. I had neither the knowledge nor the stomach to teach Marie how to compel, hypnotize, and bite a human victim. Especially not now, while I was bone-tired, starving, and splashed with my own vomit.

But Marie needed to eat. I thought for a moment. Vampires could survive off the blood of animals if they had to, and there were wild deer in the Hidden City. Valerie, the addled vamp who lived in the park, exclusively fed from them, because she thought she was a twilight vamp. Deer blood would tide Marie over until I could find a vampire guardian for her.

We walked out the corridor of the station, heading for the exit. "I was experimenting a little while I was waiting for you," Marie continued, sounding a little freaked out. "I thought I might be able to move fast enough to steal a candy bar from one of the officer's desks. But my throat seemed to close over at the thought. For a second, I couldn't breathe."

She wouldn't have been in danger. It was just a warning. "That's the magic of the Great Agreement," I told her. "It's sentient, and it can read intention. You can't use your powers in public." I explained a little about the Great Agreement as we walked out the door, taking the steps down to the street outside.

"It can kill you?" Marie looked outraged. "You need to put that in the manual!"

"There's no manual." Gods, it was cold. I wrapped one arm around myself and hailed a cab with the other one.

"Daph!" A very loud male voice bellowed from across the street. "Hey! Little sis!"

I cringed. Oh, Gods. As if my night couldn't get any worse.

Lennox Arran was coming this way.

He crossed the street with his trademark swagger, stopping traffic, larger than life, head held high, swinging his shoulders, taking up as much space as he could. As usual, his dark blonde hair was shaved at the sides, longer on top, and pulled up in messy braids and tied in a topknot, giving a neo-Viking look. He wore ripped black jeans, an artfully distressed designer t-shirt and a giant leather coat with a black fur collar. His entourage buzzed around him, silent and obedient, taking their places in the background of his life where they belonged.

Lennox looked like a savage. He smiled at me like a lion sighting a plump gazelle by the waterhole.

Next to me, Marie squinted. "Your brother's here. That's good timing, he can give me a ride to the bus stop."

I shuddered. "Ugh. He's not my brother. That's a horrible assumption."

"It wasn't an assumption." Marie sounded outraged. "I don't make assumptions. He looks like you!" Marie waved her hand widely towards Lennox, who was striding directly in front of the cars in the street to get to me. "You have the same eye shape and jaw structure. And finally, Daphne, the key component to what I would say was a very *reasonable* deduction... he called you 'lil sis.'"

I sighed. "It's a pet name."

"You're his pet?" Marie made a face. "Ew, I'm not sure if I like that aspect of this Otherworld business." Suddenly, she brightened. "Hang on, am I allowed to have a pet?"

"Marie," I growled. "Shut up."

"There you are, lil sis!" Lennox swaggered towards me with his arms wide open, a huge grin on his face.

I held up my hand. "That's close enough, Lennox."

He ignored me and wrapped his arms around me, hugging me tight while I ground my teeth and refused to hug him back. We were in public, in the middle of the city, and even though it was past midnight, there were suddenly a lot of humans around.

Just then, I realized. They were following Lennox.

Lennox Arran was more of a celebrity in the human world than he was in the supe world. He was a champion boxer, a showboater, and a bombastic, handsome, overbearing, arrogant bastard.

The human media loved him. He was good for a soundbite and always delivered his lines with the conviction of a man who had never been told no.

I told him no all the time. He just never listened.

"It's so good to see you." He pulled back, leaving his hands clamped on my shoulders so I couldn't wiggle free and grinned down at me. "I know I've been busy with the new Alpha Shifter stuff, babe, but I promise I'll make some time for you." He ran his hands up and down my arms, squeezing my shoulders, invading my personal space. "And you know what? Now is a good time."

"Take your hands off me, Lennox," I said, my voice tight. "Now."

"You don't have to be coy, sis. It's all good." His gaze drifted down to Marie beside me. That telltale twinkle of interest shone in his eyes. "Hey, girl." He smiled at her and winked.

"Ew." Marie wrinkled her nose. "Daphne, your brother is gross."

Lennox laughed out loud. "Oh, I like your sassy vamp friend, babe. You can bring her to the compound. If you want to do the whole 'stepbrother-stepsister' roleplay thing, I'm down."

I took a deep breath, counted backwards from fifty, and spat the words out through clenched teeth. "Lennox, I'm working. She's not my friend—"

"Wow," Marie muttered. "Mean."

"—she's a client. And she's only just turned seventeen."

Lennox threw his head back and laughed. "Daph, babe, you don't have to do this anymore."

"Do what?"

"Pretend you're not interested. You forget, I've got ears everywhere. I know this was your plan all along." He smirked. "You pretend you're not into me, you keep me at arm's length, you pretend to friend-zone me. I told you; you got me. You don't have to play this game. You won." He smoldered. "You won me."

"Lennox. What the hell are you talking about?"

"I know." He gazed into my eyes soulfully. "I know about your plan, Daphne. I heard it all straight from the horse's mouth."

"What horse?" If there was a horse shifter out there talking shit about me... I shook my head, totally bewildered and lost for words. Lennox was completely delusional.

"There's no point denying it. I've never denied our connection." He took my hands, clasping them in his huge grip. "Right from the start, the second I saw you, I knew we had something. You felt it. You can't lie."

He might have a point there, babes, my brain chipped in out of nowhere. *You've always been way too lenient with him, more than any other idiot that hit on you. If it were up to me, I would have stabbed him by now.*

"We're meant to be together, lil sis. You know it. I know that *you* know it." He stroked his thumb down my cheek tenderly. "I appreciate all the effort you went to, you know. The whole plan. Well, like I said, you won."

The soul-stealer. It must have been him. He'd been in Lennox's ear, trying to manipulate him. Rage made my vision blurry. I wanted to stab them all so badly.

Attagirl.

But I couldn't do anything surrounded by normies. I'd just walked out of a police station after being questioned for murder, for Pete's sake. "Get. Your. Hands. Off. Me." I bit the words out. "I don't know who the hell you've been talking to, but you are delusional if you think I've ever been interested in dating you, Lennox."

"Daphne. Sweetheart. You can drop the act now. This is it. You and me. Mated. Married."

I lost my temper, and shoved him away, hard, using some of my shifter strength to make him stagger back a few feet. The sudden constriction in my throat was worth it. "It's not an act! Lennox, I don't want anything to do with you. I've never wanted anything to do with you, and I will *never* want anything to do with you!"

"But—"

"Leave me alone," I snapped. "Or I promise you I'll make you regret it." I grabbed Marie's arm, turned around, and pulled her away down the street.

CHAPTER
FOURTEEN

The cab dropped us off in the far corner of the parking lot in the Devil's Pocket. "This is where a lot of us supes live," I said.

Marie surveyed the crumbling brick building across the parking lot. "You live like homeless people?" She groaned. "This Otherworld thing sucks."

"No." I gave her a very short, very weary explanation of the Great Suffocation and what caused it as we crossed the parking lot.

Marie was horrified. "There are no failsafes? No backups? No trials, no alarms, no protocols? Nobody periodically inspected this Agreement thing to make sure it was all good? And it caused a *genocide?*" She was still ranting when we reached the brick wall. "Is there not some kind of government body overseeing all this stuff?"

I exhaled. Gods, I was tired. I gestured to the ragged brick wall, the entrance of the Hidden City. There was just so much to explain to Marie, and I was doing a terrible job. "Get in."

"Get in what?"

Oh, good grief. I had to explain about the Hidden City,

pocket dimensions, and magical entrances. I opened my mouth, but no words came out. I was too tired.

Let me. Brain-Daphne took over for a split second. My arms shot out, and I pushed Marie through the wall. *Voila.*

"That was mean," I muttered to myself.

Satisfying, though.

I walked through and saw Marie staring in wonder at the park in front of her. "Whoa. So, that was a wormhole of some sort? Higgs-Boson bridge, maybe?" She examined the brick wall behind her, poking her finger back into the entrance.

"This is the Hidden City. You're safe here." The lie felt dusty on my tongue. I better correct it before Marie got the wrong idea. "I mean, you're safe from human eyes. You won't get suffocated by the Great Agreement if you use your powers inside the City. There are no humans allowed in here. But watch out for everyone else. Every supe of every kind lives here."

Marie blinked around the dark City. "Lots to experiment with," she muttered under her breath. "I've got all night before I get on the bus."

"You're not going back to Harvard, Marie," I said patiently.

"Yes, I am," she sang back. "I'm not giving up my life's work for anything."

"You don't have to give up your life's work," I tried. "You just can't go back to Harvard."

"You can't stop me."

"Your nestmaster will—" I cut myself off and grimaced again. No nestmaster. Azerad was the closest one. He'd claimed most of the territory on the upper East Coast. There were smaller nestmasters in most cities, but Azerad had them all under his thumb, right down to Baltimore. "I'll think of something."

Marie trotted along beside me and gave her little evil laugh again.

I smelled Valerie before I saw her and perked up a little. "Aha, good timing. Here's someone who can help you."

Valerie lurched out of the bushes from my left, scuttling sideways in her trademark low, crab-like crouch. Her greasy blonde hair hung ragged over her face. She was thin as a rake, but the countess and I had managed to get her used to wearing warmer clothes. Valerie was under the impression she was made of stone and didn't feel the cold. No amount of frostbite or vamp-hypothermia would change her mind, and the countess and I had found her frozen solid in the undergrowth more times than I could count.

She bared her fangs at us. "Got any casssh?"

"Hi, Valerie!" I said brightly, beaming at her. "This is Marie." I gestured down to the new vamp girl beside me.

Marie wrinkled her nose. "What. Is. That?"

"This is my friend, Valerie. She's a vampire, too." I was wildly aware that I sounded like a kindergarten teacher trying to introduce two new toddlers to each other. "Valerie has been a vampire for a while now. She'll be able to help you. Valerie, this is Marie."

Valerie's eyes swung down to Marie. She gasped dramatically. "A forbidden child," she hissed, her eyes wide.

"Absolutely not." Marie crossed her arms over her chest. "No way in hell."

I ignored her. "She's not a child, Valerie," I said patiently. "Marie's seventeen. She's just short."

"I'm five foot," Marie said indignantly. "It's a perfectly acceptable height for a young woman, goddamnit."

"How long has she been..." Valerie paused dramatically. "Seventeen?"

I managed not to roll my eyes. "Marie is hungry," I said. "She's a brand-new vampire, so I might need some help—"

"Daphne." Marie cut me off. "Save your breath. There is no chance in hell you're leaving me with that woman."

"But—"

"Seriously?" She stared at me. "You want *her* to help *me?*"

It was a good point. I slumped. "Okay, I'll admit, I'm kind of out of options here, Marie. I've called all the vampire contacts I have here in Philly, and nobody has responded yet."

You haven't called Micah yet. And there's a whole-ass library in the church.

Taking a client to my boyfriend's house for the night was seriously unprofessional. I was on the verge of being fired as it was. Besides, the church had been attacked by a giant insect only a few hours ago.

Valerie scuttled closer, waving her hands around Marie as if to try and pat her down. "Got any casssh?"

Marie slapped her hands away, hissing. Valerie hissed back.

The two vampires hissed at each other like angry kittens for a full thirty seconds, while I dithered, wondering what the hell I should do. Hartshorn and Boggs were stalking us, mysterious fae blades were appearing in our doorframe, and the church might not even be safe, because it was being attacked by an assassin.

Should we go into lockdown in our apartment again? We did that when Alexei was after us. It worked fine then. We could hole up for a little while, until the heat dies down.

The thought made me break out in goosebumps. Back then, I didn't mind being stuck in my apartment, but now, my newfound claustrophobia made me want to claw at my neck. I didn't want to be trapped.

Hmm. Brain-Daphne tapped her chin. *Are we on the verge of a nervous breakdown?*

The memory of me puking in Hartshorn's face flooded me. I think that ship sailed a while ago.

"Get away from me, you weirdo!" Marie shrieked.

Valerie clawed her hands. "Forbidden child," she hissed. "I shall inform the Volt—"

"Stop that." I clapped my hands loudly. "Valerie, you can go. Thank you, but we don't need your assistance after all."

"*She* needs assistance," Marie snapped. "She needs food stamps and emergency mental health assistance. I've never met anyone who needs a five-one-five-oh hold more than this psycho!"

Valerie moved into a low crouch, hissed one more time, and crab-walked sideways into the bushes.

I glared down at Marie and huffed out a breath. "What am I going to do with you?"

"Get me a manual. A handbook. Anything!"

I threw up my hands, exasperated. "There's no manual!"

"You must have something that I can read! A... a spellbook. A Book of Shadows. I'd even take an evil grimoire!"

"No!" There was no way in hell I was letting Marie get her hands on a dark magic grimoire.

"Please?" Marie put her hands together. "Just a little grimoire? I've watched reruns of Charmed. Their Book of Shadows had the information on every single witch and shapeshifter and demon in existence. They're real, right? Some of the goths on campus talk about them."

"There's—" The words died in my throat. Of course they were real, but I didn't have any grimoires lying around.

But the countess did. She'd be able to give me something to occupy Marie until I could figure out what to do with her.

"Come on," I said. "Let's head to my apartment. I think I can find something."

We walked down the frozen path towards the West Building. Marie's pony-like trot grew jauntier at the idea of getting her hands on a Book of Shadows.

A weird beeping noise came from her. "Is that you?"

She sighed and pulled a tiny phone out of her pocket. "Yeah."

"You've had your cellphone on you this whole time?"

"Yep."

"And you didn't call the police when Johan Van Eiken abducted you?"

"I did, actually. I called eight times during the brief moments of consciousness. I had no idea where we were, though, and I was too woozy to recalibrate the settings on my VPN, so the dispatcher couldn't track my location."

She cleared her throat, hit the answer button, and put the phone to her ear before I could stop her. "Hey, Deborah," she said, sounding very perky.

Goddamnit. Marie was meant to be dead now. She shouldn't be answering her phone. A female voice shrieked over the line. Marie flinched and turned the volume down. Her ears would be very sensitive. Normally, I could hear someone quite clearly, but I struggled to make out what the woman was saying.

"I'm sorry, Deborah," Marie said in an odd, sing-song voice. "Remember, I did tell you that you might not be able to get ahold of me right away anymore. There's no internet reception at this ashram."

Ashram? What the hell?

Marie continued, "So, what happened?"

Incoherent shrieking squeaked out of the phone. I couldn't make it out.

"Oh, I see. It's okay. Don't cry," Marie said in a soothing tone. "It's going to be okay. Is it still on fire?"

I squinted down at her. What the hell?

Marie kept walking, trotting down the path next to me. "No, no, you're not stupid. Of course not. These things happen. Sometimes, the cardboard is almost exactly the same color as the pizza base, so it's no surprise that you missed it. Just don't open the oven door, Deborah. It will stop soon."

Who is she talking to?

I had no idea.

"I'm sure it will," she soothed. "Fire needs fuel and oxygen to survive." Marie was using the same patronizing kindergarten teacher voice I tried to use on her only moments ago. "If you keep the oven door shut, the fire will use all the oxygen and all the fuel, and it will stop. Has it stopped? Good. Okay, I'm here if you need me. I know, it was scary. You'll be okay, Deborah."

The female's voice squeaked for a few seconds.

"Oh, yes. Of course, you should call in your"—Marie paused and grimaced—"tribe. Why don't you call Julien and Evangeline and have them come down and keep you company? Yes, great idea!" Marie's tone was perky; her face was stone-cold. "Get the whole tribe together. Maybe have Briar and Echo come down and sage the place, just in case. Good. Okay. Love you. Bye."

She hung up and gave a visible shudder.

We walked for a moment in silence. My curiosity killed me. "Who was that?"

"My mom," Marie said casually.

"Your... mom?"

"Yeah."

I hesitated for a second. "Your mom set a pizza on fire in your oven and called... you?"

Marie glared at me. "My family issues are none of your business, Daphne."

I looked down at her. I recognized the well of pain deep in her steely gaze. I'd seen that look so many times. I'd seen it in the eyes of the warthog shifter kid who tried to defend his mom's drinking. I'd seen it in the eyes of a goblin boy who insisted his dad really loved him and would give him food the second he had enough money.

Ooh, yeah. Marie's family life was fucked up. "You can tell me about it," I said gently. "I'm here to help."

"Oh, of course," she said. "I can tell by the way you just tried to offload me to the very first mentally unwell vampire you saw."

"There's no need to be sarcastic. I wasn't trying—" I blew out an exasperated breath. "Look, I already admitted that Valerie was a bad idea. I apologize. I'm doing my best here. Do I have to remind you that this is an unprecedented situation? Now, you know for a fact talking about your problems helps lighten the load. The more I know about you, the more I can help you."

She trotted along next to me in silence for a moment. "Is it privileged? This isn't going anywhere?"

"Marie," I said, "we seem to be stuck on this point. You're a vampire now. Your human life is over. The old Marie is dead." I touched her shoulder. "You're free."

She chuckled bitterly. "As if it would be that easy. No, Daphne. I've got eight years to go. *Then* I'll be free."

"Eight years?" That made no sense. "You're a year off eighteen."

"I am, sure." She hesitated. "My brother is only ten years old, though."

"Tell me about him," I said, my tone gentle.

"No." She clammed up.

I tried another tack. "Tell me about your mom, then."

She huffed. "Urgh, fine. My mom has always been free-spirited. Absent-minded, free-spirited, helpless, haphazard... all those things. She doesn't do 'adulting' very well, as she put it. She loves to dance and sing and laugh and wear clothes with jangly bells. Mom tells anyone she meets that she is an indigo child, a starseed."

"Okay." I had no idea what that meant. "That sounds nice."

"It's not," Marie said bluntly. "It just means she has borderline personality disorder and delusional narcissism."

"Oh." I knew what *that* meant.

"If Deborah doesn't get attention—good or bad—she'll have a breakdown. She never fed me; she never watched me. I've cooked for myself since I was three years old. I only survived infancy because a handful of her friends felt sorry for me, but they'd always disappear once Deborah realized they were giving me more attention than her. She'd always do awful things to push them away."

Marie let out a sigh. "Occasionally, when I was little, she'd use me to bring attention to herself, and it was always nice when she did that. She'd act like she loved me, as if I was the most beautiful thing in the universe, and she would bask in the admiration everyone gave her for her mothering skills. But, of course, if the spotlight swung my way, she'd lash out."

"Oh, that's rough, Marie. And..." I waved my hand towards her. "That explains a lot."

"Yeah, I know," she said. "The good thing was it was never just us two. We bounced around a couple of ashrams when I was a baby and lived in communes all around California. Mom was fond of saying it took a village to raise a baby, and she kept looking for a village so she could palm me off and have a big audience to admire her. But inevitably she would manage to manipulate or isolate everyone in the collective, and we'd be kicked out."

I made a sympathetic noise. "Sounds like hell."

"To be fair, I never knew any different," Marie said, stomping wearily along beside me. "For the longest time, I didn't realize there was anything wrong. I looked after myself and Deborah the best I could, but the narcissistic personality disorder made her act out so badly, and it was hard to keep her out of trouble. She was always looking for attention. She'd put on whole musical shows dedicated to her life story as a starseed, she'd sleep with married men, she'd accuse her commune of crimes they didn't commit, literally anything for validation. I learned very quickly that I had to keep that spotlight on her, or else I'd be in a whole world of pain."

"Oh, Marie..." We reached my building, and I opened the door for her to go in. We stamped the slushy snow off our boots and strode inside, heading for the elevator. "Nobody intervened? No one reported her?"

"Deborah has been reported to CPS for neglect and abuse a bunch of times since I was a baby," Marie explained. "She got investigated five times. I was removed three times, but I always got returned really quickly. My mother was good at convincing people that the neglect was all just a silly misunderstanding. Once I got old enough, I started to understand that these investigations only made her worse. The threat of having me—her scapegoat, spotlight holder, and guardian rolled into one—taken away made her freak out." Marie hesitated. "It's hard, Daphne. She has an illness. I hate her, but she's my mom."

"I know," I said softly.

After a moment, Marie went on. "When I was six, she ripped out a chunk of my hair and dislocated my elbow in a jealous rage. I reported her myself, and the authorities removed me again temporarily. When I came home, she told me that if CPS took me away again, she would kill herself and film it so I could watch it over and over and see exactly what I'd done to her, how much I'd hurt her."

I had no words. I pressed the button for the elevator. The light told me it was at the top of the building, so we'd have to wait a while for it to come down.

Marie continued, "At seven years old, I stopped caring. The thought of her killing herself didn't seem like such a bad thing anymore. She probably sensed it, because that was when she had Ackie."

"Ackie?"

"My brother." A wistful expression came over her face. "I loved him the second I saw him. He's so innocent. Such a sweetheart. That was it for me. I had to stay and look after him and shield him from my mom the best I could. I couldn't report her. I'd run the risk of me and Ackie being separated, and I wasn't going to let that happen."

Her story was breaking my heart. "But things got better, right? Your mom sent you to school?"

Marie scoffed. "Hell, no, Deborah never sent me to school. In her words, she didn't believe in forcing kids to learn things that just aren't true. She tells anyone who will listen that state schools are filled with indoctrinating dark energy."

"Oh, no."

"But to answer your question, yes, things got better. Once Ackie came along, I realized I had to get good at manipulating Deborah so I could save him. There were no books, so I quickly figured out if I gently nudged my mother to date someone that had a house with internet access and that was close to public transport, I was good. I spent every moment I could at the library with Ackie in his stroller." She gave a little huff of laughter. "I remember when I was eight,

I read the comprehensive guide to modern psychiatry, and it talked about gray rocking. I tried gray rocking with Deborah when I was six without knowing what it was. And because I didn't give her any attention, mom ended up knocking me unconscious once and attempting suicide twice."

I whistled through my teeth. "Marie. That's... that's horrific." We got into the elevator, and I pressed the button for the forty-fourth floor.

"Yeah," she said. "Never tried that again. But I worked it all out. Through a very fun combination of blackmailing her various boyfriends for cash, hiring out-of-work actors to give my mom attention, and enlisting the help of the nice homeless woman who lives under the bridge, I got up to date on my vaccine schedule, and finished the entire high school curriculum in a year. I started crashing lectures at Berkeley when I was twelve." She sighed. "Good Will Hunting was an inspiration to me."

"And your mom thinks you're at an ashram right now?"

Marie opened the panel in the elevator underneath the buttons and started fiddling with the wires. "I think I can make this thing go much faster."

"No." I shut the panel door. "Answer the question."

"Deborah thinks I'm only fifteen minutes from our apartment in San Diego. If she knew I'd removed myself from her immediate orbit, she might lash out, and I can't risk anything happening to Ackie. He's safe, but we went to a lot of trouble putting things in place to make sure he's okay while I'm gone. I'm paying a neighbor to look after him and make sure he's fed and he does his homeschooling, and I found a doctor with a gambling addiction who is very happy to write whatever prescriptions I need. We've settled on a subtle combination of antidepressants, mood stabilizers, and antipsychotics, and Ackie makes sure it all gets blended up in Deborah's green smoothie every morning. That shit tastes so bad anyway, she can't tell."

Marie was drugging her mother. I wasn't sure how I felt about that.

Great. We feel great about it. This girl is a genius.

"We've been upping the doses slowly over the past year, so she's the most bearable she's ever been. Ackie is smart, too, not as smart as me, but he knows Mom's deal. He knows how to play her. We just have to hold CPS off for another year."

"Why...?"

"He's my baby." Marie's lips thinned. "Ackie is my kid. I'm doing this for him, and that's it. The second I'm eighteen, I've got a lawyer ready to file for custody of him."

I stared at her. Old soul didn't seem to cover it. Marie was seventeen years old, and she'd lived a hundred lifetimes. "Marie..."

"What?"

"I'm sorry."

"Why?" She looked alarmed. "You didn't do anything."

"You've had a terrible childhood." I had a terrible childhood too, but at least I didn't have a baby to protect while I was still a baby myself.

"I've got Ackie. He's all that matters to me."

"Let me guess. Ackie's favorite superhero is Iron Man."

Marie stared at me for a moment. "You know what? You're smarter than you look, Daphne."

The elevator dinged. The laughter died in my throat as I walked out of the elevator and saw the block of ice on my doorstep.

CHAPTER
FIFTEEN

A rose hung suspended in the block of ice, as if it were floating in pure crystal.

It was a deep purple bloom, with thick, almost fleshy velvet petals and a long, dark-green stem studded with vicious-looking thorns.

If that's not a message, I don't know what is.

Marie frowned down at it. "What's that about?"

"I don't know."

"A rose encased in ice. It's seventy degrees Fahrenheit here, give or take a few degrees." She pursed her lips. "There should be signs of ablation. A tiny puddle, at least. Whoever left it here will still be close by."

"Thank you, Miss Marple." I skirted it carefully. The fresh scent of the creature who left it there had faded until it was just a background smell like the rest of the odors in the hallway, so it had been there for at least a few hours. It was quite possible that whoever left it there came the moment Romeo left my apartment. The bozan blade was gone, at least; Romeo must have taken it with him.

I didn't pick up a new scent. Every single odor in here was familiar to me. I didn't have a super-memory to go with my super-scent, but I could always register when I came across an unfamiliar odor.

Someone was threatening me. The frozen rose was a clear message, just like the dagger had been—*I can get so close to you, you won't even know I'm behind you.*

"Don't worry about it," I said to Marie. "And, uh, don't touch it." I was too tired; I wasn't thinking clearly, so I didn't even want to try. I knocked on the countess's door.

She opened the door with a flourish, wearing royal-blue silk pajamas and her hair in a turban. The countess looked at me, then looked at Marie, then back to me. "Did you bring me a midnight snack, dear?"

"No, your grace—"

"Good, because vampires do not make good snacks. Not even the new ones." She pursed her lips. "They're too crumbly."

Marie, uncharacteristically quiet, stood next to me, eyeballing the countess warily. She was such a smart girl.

Or maybe the psychopath recognizes another psychopath.

"Your grace." I put my hands together in a pleading gesture. "I was just hoping you could help me with—"

"Absolutely not." The countess cut me off with a curt shake of her head. "Not a chance. It's almost two in the morning, and I need my beauty sleep. I will not be babysitting another one of your ginger waifs."

I didn't need another reminder of how late it was—I was so tired, my eyes kept rolling in the back of my head. All I wanted to do was sleep uninterrupted for at least a few hours. Just a few. Marie was nocturnal now, so she wouldn't be getting tired until dawn. If I could settle Marie down with some reading material, I'd be able to get some sorely needed rest. "No, I was just wondering if I could borrow a book from you."

"A book?" She tilted her head. "Which one?"

"Anything. Non-fiction," I amended, remembering the countess's penchant for erotic horror. "Do you have a grimoire I could borrow?"

"No." The countess stared at me like I was nuts. "What need do I have for a grimoire? I already know everything that there is to know."

"Something educational. Anything." My tone ended in almost a whimper.

The countess paused. "Give me a moment." She shut the door in my face.

"Who is that?" Marie whispered to me.

"The Countess Ebadorathea Greenwood," I whispered back. "She's a sorceress, which is like... a turbo-powered witch. Don't do anything to offend her, or she'll eat you."

"No, she won't." Marie sounded so confident.

Everyone was scared of the countess. She had such a ferocious reputation. Normally, I had to work hard to convince my friends that she was a big softie underneath all those hyper-powerful gang tattoos that represented all the soul ties she'd devoured. And now, I was warning a new vamp against her. "I'm not joking, Marie—"

"She just said it herself. Vampires don't make good snacks."

I opened my mouth, then closed it again. "Smartass."

The countess pulled the door open again and tossed a giant leatherbound book into my hands. "Most of my library is in storage back in Castlemaine," she said. "But I have this. It's a history of the vampire wars."

It would have to do. I took it. "Thank you, your grace. I don't suppose you caught sight of whoever left the frozen rose on my doorstep?"

She stuck her head out the door and looked. "Hmm. Well, that's a nasty message if ever I saw one. No, I didn't see or hear anyone, dear. Goodnight." She slammed the door in my face.

Now that I was so close to my apartment, tiredness overwhelmed me. I'd been doing a good job keeping the fatigue under control, but it had been such a long day, and the punches had just kept coming.

I ran back through everything while I listened at my own apartment door for a second. Being questioned for Wesley's murder. Monica threatening to fire me. The giant insect attacking the church and stabbing Romeo with an iron dagger. The bozan blade. Marie. Then, being questioned again by the detectives who I knew were only going to get worse, and now, finding a frozen rose on my doorstep—an obvious threat.

I opened my door and paused. Maybe I'd lie down in my bed and find a horse's severed head in there.

Soft snores came from inside my apartment. Myf was asleep. I glanced at Marie next to me, already flicking through the book. "You have to be quiet."

"Why?"

"I have an agoraphobic teenager asleep in my pantry."

"Okay," Marie said absently, her eyes flicking back and forth over the pages.

We crept inside. I didn't turn the light on. Marie didn't need light to read, but she did need food. I rummaged around in the fridge, looking for something that might tide her over.

Sleep. I needed sleep.

"Wassat? Daphne?" Myf inhaled deeply, sniffing the vampire. "Who's with you?"

"Yeah, it's me. I've got a client with me, Myf. A new vampire named Marie."

Marie didn't glance up from the book. To my horror, I

saw that she was already a quarter of the way through it. "Hey."

"I'm not going back to sleep," Myf mumbled grumpily. "Got a raging headache."

That would be the hangover. Myf thumped around in the pantry for a moment, the telltale sounds of a surly teenager trying to get comfortable. "I can't sleep while there's strangers in here, Daph. This is meant to be my safe space. Get rid of her."

"She's got nowhere else to go," I said, getting a packet of blood sausage out of the fridge. "Please be kind, Myf."

"She can fuck off back to whoever made her."

That got Marie's attention. She lifted her eyes from the pages and arched her eyebrow. "Wow." She caught my eye. "Is she another client of yours?"

"Yes. Myf's a shapeshifter, and she's going through a very hard time right now, so she's staying with me for the time being."

"Don't give her my life story, you eejit," Myf slurred, her Welsh accent heavier than usual. "Can't you do anything right? Just get rid of her. I need to sleep."

"This isn't helpful. It's just political propaganda." Marie snapped the book closed, and cocked her head, gesturing to the pantry. "You let her talk to you like that?"

"She doesn't mean it," I said, wildly aware that I sounded a little pathetic, but I was so tired. "She's hurting, and hurt people hurt people." I put four blood sausages on a plate and put it in the microwave. It would be easier for Marie to stomach if it was heated a little.

"I do mean it, actually," Myf said. "Some people get all the luck in this world, and good ol' Daphne out there was blessed with doe-eyes and big boobs, and the boys are falling over themselves to help her out." Her voice broke. "I've got nothing. No family, no home, no friends. Nothing."

This might have been a bad idea, my brain said wearily.

Of course it was a bad idea. I have no good options.

"You don't have nothing." Marie darted around the room, moving vamp fast, checking the small collection of books on my shelf and dismissing them instantly. "You've got a bad attitude. That's something."

"Tell her to fuck off!"

I took a deep breath. "Myf..."

Marie whizzed off out of the room.

Dwayne was asleep in the middle of my bed; I could hear him snoring very loudly. I was glad he was home, but the chainsaw impersonation was going to make it hard for me to get any sleep.

My phone buzzed. A message from Romeo. It was almost three in the morning. *Are you okay?*

I replied quickly. *You should be asleep.*

You should be with me. Come over.

I can't, I wrote back. *Work. Got a new client I'm dealing with; she's a bit of a handful.* I didn't want to dump my problems on him.

Let me help.

I exhaled. I couldn't. This was my job.

Another message buzzed through. *I know what you're like, baby. You're trying to help everyone. You don't have to do it alone. Don't set yourself on fire to keep other people warm.*

Marie darted back into the room, holding my O-CPS training manual in her arms. "Why is there a big white goose asleep on your bed?"

"He's not a goose," I told her absently. My head swam. Suddenly, the thought of collapsing in Romeo's arms was just too overwhelming.

Another message from Romeo buzzed through. *I can make all your problems go away...*

Marie thumped my O-CPS manual down at the table

and frowned at the blood sausage. "I'm not eating that shit."

Myf gave a loud groan. "Tell her to fuck off!"

We got takeout from Il Fornaio for dinner. Lasagna. There are lots left over. I ordered two extra servings, just in case you decided to join us.

Lasagna. Damn him, he knew my greatest weakness. I was so tempted.

No, I couldn't. I had to get Myf settled, I had to make sure Marie was safe, and I had to get some sleep.

Marie started reading. "Are all your clients so selfish and pathetically helpless, Daphne?'

"Look who's talking, you dumb cow," Myf snapped back. "You're stuck here with her, too."

"I'm only here because I need to know more about this Otherworld I'm a part of now," Marie said, her eyes snapping back and forth as she inhaled the training manual. "Knowledge is power. As soon as I've got the basics down, I'm jumping on a bus and heading back to my dorm."

A miserable noise escaped my lips. How did I end up with two feisty teenagers in my apartment? I was usually so good with kids. I knew how to get children to listen to me. Somehow, little kids seemed to fill my well, whereas these teenagers were sucking the last dregs of energy out of me.

This is going to end badly. "You can't go back to Harvard, Marie," I huffed out, exhausted. "And you're not supposed to be reading that," I added feebly, pointing at my O-CPS manual. I was done. Tapped out. "Some of that information is highly classified, you know."

"It's more informative than the vampire war book." Marie flipped the page. "This sounds interesting. Faerie, as an actual place. Goblins, pixies, trolls... There's a whole list of characteristics and poisons. Why do they choose to live here when there's so many things they're allergic to? But then again, I suppose I *am* lactose intolerant." She frowned. "Am I still lactose intolerant?"

"No, you fucking moron. There's no lactose in blood, and you're a vampire. You drink blood." Myf thumped around in the pantry.

"Actually," Marie said, flicking the page. "There are traces of lactose found in blood, particularly in lactating women—"

"Please stop," I moaned.

"Hey," Marie glanced up and grinned. "If that selfish idiot in the pantry is an animal shifter, shouldn't you be referring her to the Alpha to deal with?"

I buried my face in my hands. "It's complicated."

"I would," Myf shouted. "If she let me. I'd go straight to the shifter compound and get myself a bunk bed there. But nooo, Princess Daphne has her own reasons for keeping me away from Lennox Arran." She sniffed wetly. "She wants to keep all the boys for herself."

"You really let her talk to you like that?" Marie's eyes twinkled menacingly.

Oh, no, she's going in for the kill.

Marie gave an evil grin. "Daphne, tell that English bitch to settle down."

Cold silence gripped the room. It was so loud, my ears hurt.

Dwayne's chainsaw-snore broke the silence. Myf let out a deafening screech. "English? *English?!*"

Oh, dear gods, Marie had found Myf's Achilles heel.

"Myf, don't." I scrambled to my feet, as smoke began to billow out of the pantry. The boards creaked. Myf was going to change into her dragon. She was in my apartment. The whole thing was going to be destroyed.

Marie chuckled evilly, "Hee hee *hee*."

Boards creaked. Smoke poured from the gaps of the

slats in the pantry door. "Marie, you don't know what you've done." I leapt to my feet and rushed over. "Myf, please don't. Deep breaths. Long slow deep breaths."

Myf let out a heartbreaking cry.

"Please," I begged her, rocking on my feet. I was so tired, my legs weren't holding me up anymore. I crouched on the ground and began to rock back and forth. "Long... slow...breaths. In...."

"Drama queen," Marie muttered. She didn't say anything else.

Myf sobbed.

"Breathe." I sat on my butt, and rocked back and forth, wishing I could hold onto her, to hug her, smooth her hair back, and tell her everything was going to be okay. But Myf didn't like to be touched, and nothing was okay.

I liked to be touched. It brought me comfort. There was nobody here to hold me. It was cold. I was alone.

We have to help her. We have to help them all. We have to save everyone...

"That's good, Myf. Breathe in..." My voice felt like it was coming from very far away. "And out..."

Darkness pressed in on me. The apartment vanished, plunging me into a desperate void. There was nothing here—a heavy void. I couldn't move.

It was hopeless. *I* was hopeless. Useless, pathetic, stupid, I couldn't even handle two sassy teenagers, I couldn't do anything right. Despair squirmed inside of me, reaching out with pitch-black tentacles, wrapping up my heart, suffocating and stifling its beat.

Boggs and Hartshorn were right—I did kill Wesley. I was a whore that spread her legs for Troy, and I did deserve to rot in jail, squashed into a hard box with evils pressed up against me—

Oi.

I blinked. The apartment suddenly appeared in front of me.

I gasped for air, panting. I hadn't even been breathing. Where had I been just then? Did I fall asleep? Oh, gods, I did. I'd fallen asleep and plunged head-first into a nightmare.

What in Hades' pierced nipples is going on here? Dwayne strutted into the room. His eyes were pitch-black, his beak slightly open, displaying the razor-sharp studs on his tongue.

Tears pricked my eyes. I was at the end of my rope. "Sir..." I gestured helplessly towards the pantry.

Myf was hyperventilating. The smoke wasn't pouring out the slats anymore, but she was right on the edge. I had no idea what to do.

I got this. Dwayne stomped over and Spartan-kicked the fridge on its side. It fell over; the door swung open. He rummaged around inside for a second and pulled out a bottle of electrolyte water and dumped it on my lap. **Open this for me.**

I popped the lid. Dwayne dumped a small purple pill in it, then marched over to the pantry, ripped the door open, and hustled inside. **You're dehydrated. Drink this, you stroppy cow.**

"No," Myf panted. "I don't... I don't need—" Her words cut off in a wild gurgle as Dwayne forced the bottle into her mouth.

Drink it.

I hoped that it was Tylenol.

Marie, deliberately oblivious to the chaos she'd caused, flipped a page in the book and scanned it quickly. "I'm missing some fundamentals. These course notes assume a comprehensive core understanding of supernatural biology. I don't suppose you have a monster version of Grey's

Anatomy, do you? Or even some blood samples so I can do my own analysis? Mmm." Her eyes flashed scarlet for a second. "Blood. God, I'm hungry."

The sounds of furious wrestling came from the pantry. **Get the little pointy toothed one out of here,** Dwayne dumped the words in my head. **I'll take care of the dragon.**

I shouldn't. I'd neglected Myf so much. She needed my help; I couldn't just abandon her. But Marie needed my help, too. I had to help them both.

Something screamed from deep within me—a deep, primal scream, multi-tonal, made up of a billion different bodies my soul had inhabited. I had to save them all. Everyone.

My phone buzzed in my lap, wrenching me out of the memory my exhausted subconscious had plunged me into. It took a second for my eyes to adjust enough to read the words.

Romeo. *Will you please come over?*

I gave in. *Yes,* I texted back. *I'll be there as soon as I can.*

My heart leapt and sank almost immediately. I'd have to take Marie with me. We would have to walk across the Hidden City to the entrance and try to get a cab from the far end of the parking lot, outside the city. I'd have to—

There was a knock at the door.

I got up without realizing I'd even moved, flew at the door, ripped it open, and fell into Romeo's arms.

CHAPTER
SIXTEEN

"It's not safe here, anyway," he growled, staring at the ice rose when we left my apartment. "That thing is after you. I feel it in my gut."

"It attacked the church again, didn't it?"

"Yeah." Romeo practically carried me down the corridor, one arm wrapped around me. He used his enormous strength to take as much of my weight as possible, so I practically floated along beside him.

Turns out, Romeo had been in the Hidden City anyway. One of the witch residents contacted Levi when they spotted the alien insect monster charging through the undergrowth between the East and South towers, around four hours ago. Romeo, Micah, and Cole, who was a night owl, came to try to find it.

The monster had come back. And it had come bearing gifts for me, leaving a frozen rose on my doorstep. The timing was too close to be a coincidence to not be connected.

Romeo, horrified at the new threat on my threshold, didn't want to smother me. So, he defaulted back to stalker-mode and waited until I agreed to come to his house, charged in, swept me off my feet, and promised to take me far, far away to keep me safe.

He didn't even flinch when I asked if Marie could tag along. He took one look at her, examined the deep red flash in her eye, and made a quick phone call.

Romeo was here to save me. I wasn't the damsel type, but by gods, it felt good to be rescued. Cole was sweeping the perimeter of the City to see if he could spot the monster, and Micah was just outside, waiting by the car in the parking lot and covering the entrance.

We left the building. It was so cold. Cold and still like the world had frozen around us. But now, with Romeo beside me, it was less of a hell-frozen-over and more of a winter wonderland. It was funny how perspective changed everything.

Marie bounced along beside us. "So, you're the High Priest, and based on the information Daphne gave me, this means you're the strongest witch around. Yes?'

Romeo looked a little alarmed. "Uh–"

I caught her eye and mouthed. "Yes."

"So, you have extra magical power? Or even supplemental powers?" Marie trotted alongside us, peppering Romeo with questions. "... and this High Priest title, it means you're the head of all the witches, right? Is it, like, a democracy? Or is it a theocracy? I mean, you call yourself a priest, so I'm guessing you think you're the most holy one." She squinted up at him. "Are you?"

"No."

"Is there a witch god? Who is it?"

Romeo's eyes widened a little. He glanced at me. "Where did you find her?"

"Johan Van Eiken's lair. Oh, and we don't have to worry about the new nestmaster anymore."

His eyes narrowed, a question in his expression. I jerked my chin towards Marie.

Romeo's gaze dropped back down to the little vampire. She saw him looking, locked eyes with him and took the opportunity to ask another question. "And if Daphne gets a little witch kid referred to her as an O-CPS client, would that be a conflict of interest for you?"

Someone was heading towards us, coming from the East—my nose confirmed it was Cole. He surged out of the darkness, jogging lightly up the path and called out, "Hey, Daphne." I watched as his gaze shifted towards Marie walking next to us. Cole's jog changed to a swagger as he approached us. He puffed out his chest a little, and swung his wide, stocky shoulders. "I've swept the perimeter to the east, boss. No sign of the monster. There's a lot of broken branches in the woods near the East tower, though, so something big crashed through there." He smoldered at Marie. "Hey."

I'd almost forgotten how pretty Marie was. "God, sometimes I feel like a broken record." I sighed. Turning, I gave Cole a hard stare. "She's seventeen, Cole."

He shrugged. "I'm only nineteen." He gave Marie a soulful look and did something weird with his lips, the boy version of a duck-face pout. "How you doing?" he purred.

Marie stared at him, her expression distinctly unimpressed. "Who are you?"

"This is Cole. Cole, meet Marie. She's a brand-new vampire."

She eyed him suspiciously. "Why is he looking at me like that? The squinty-eye thing? And why is he rubbing his hands together and licking his lips? Is that a supe thing, or is it some sort of tic?" Her eyes narrowed. "Is it a self-soothing technique? Is this the new Havening method, maybe? Or is it like that emotional freedom technique tapping thing?"

"No." I was too tired to laugh.

She edged closer to Cole and sniffed him. "Are you a witch too?"

"No, honey," Cole puffed out his chest. "I'm a lynx shifter."

It was supposed to be a secret. Cole's brain had clearly turned to mush. I shot Romeo a look, but he just rolled his eyes.

"Really?" Marie perked up. "You're not defective, like Daphne, are you? Can you shift?"

Cole smirked. "Sure can."

"Oh, good, you can answer some of these questions for me." She flipped some pages of the O-CPS coursebook. "Now, when you change into a lynx, do you retain all your human brain function? Or is it a more primitive train of thought? Like, hunt, kill, eat, procreate? Have you ever tried using tools in your animal form?"

We fell back a little, letting Marie and Cole walk ahead of us.

Now that Romeo was beside me, I could think a little clearer, but nothing made sense. "So, the alien attacked the church again but didn't get through this time?"

"Levi took a leaf out of Christopher Jupiter's book and layered a hard ward next to a ghost ward. We figured that if it could stump you, it might slow the insect down. And it did." Romeo frowned. "It blasted away a big chunk of the fence, though. We got it on the security cameras, but all you can see is sharp flares of light."

I shook my head, bewildered. "I don't know what it is. And that frozen rose on my doorstep... My instincts are telling me it's all linked somehow."

"My instincts are telling me it's coming for you."

"But it's not attacking me. It's attacking *you*. It's leaving off-worlder blades and frozen roses on my doorstep. And suddenly there are two human cops stalking me, threatening me with prison, because Wesley's body didn't get handed over to Otherworld, and it's stuck in the human police system." I hissed through my teeth. "Something tells me this is all linked. There's a monster out there trying to ruin my life, I just can't figure out what it is!"

Who was doing all this? Who had the ability to keep Wesley's murder in the human system? Who could plant evidence on his body so the coroner found my hair in his hands? Who could sneak into my building twice and leave what I assumed were clear threats on my doorstep? Who could break through the wards around the church and stab Romeo with a human-made iron blade?

I was good in a fight, but only if I knew who I was fighting. The picture in my head of my enemy grew bigger and bigger—a shapeshifting, smell-changing, multi-dimensional being.

By the time we got to the entrance of the Hidden City, Marie was still interrogating Cole, and he was on the verge of tears. "But that's nonsensical," Marie gasped. "Inbreeding leads to an accumulation of dangerous recessive genes, which means weaker mammals, not stronger ones."

"I know!"

"I'm appalled that anyone would be stupid enough to think it was a good idea. If you're going to run an experiment, the second step of the scientific method is to do background research. If your dad had just cracked open a book on genetics—"

"Why do you think I ran away?" Cole wailed.

"A wider gene pool leads to greater evolutionary potential. Adaptability, disease resistance, improved functionality... Look at what they did to French bulldogs. They can barely breathe. You inbreed a canine for long enough, you're going to get a dog that can barely function. Your father is clearly an idiot."

"I *know!*"

As we walked up to the brick wall, Marie turned and caught my eye. "So, Daphne," she said, her voice casual. "What was your gene pool like?"

"I'm not defective because of my gene pool, Marie." I sighed.

The Ironclaw pack was a horror show for many reasons, one of them being that the Alpha, Braxton Myles, would often invite out-of-state shifter VIPS to impregnate the females. Someone knocked my mother up, and I had no idea who it was. "And no," I added. "I'm not giving you a sample of my DNA."

Marie mumbled something under her breath. It sounded like "I'll get it one way or another."

We moved through the brick wall. Romeo's huge Escalade waited in the parking lot. "Oh, look," Cole said loudly. "There's Micah. Micah's a vampire; he can help you. Micah, come and meet Marie!" He ushered her towards the Escalade.

"He's a vampire?" Marie narrowed her eyes and trotted forward. "Hey! Hi, there! I've got some questions for you!"

Romeo opened the door for me. I climbed in, grateful for the heated leather seats. The cold seemed to have sunk into my bones. Marie got in the front next to Micah and began peppering him with questions. Thankfully, Micah had a bag of o-positive in a cooler in the car for Marie.

It was great that she got fed. It was even better that she kept her mouth shut for the three minutes it took her to drain the bag, keeping her quiet for most of the ride back to the church. "Mmm. If you think about it as a raspberry Capri Sun, it goes down a lot easier. So, Daphne, you're taking me to your boyfriend's house for the night. Is that approved procedure, or is this wildly unprofessional?"

Romeo leaned over and hit a button. A partition rose up, blocking the front from the back.

Unfortunately, we could still hear her clearly. "I'm going to take that to mean that it's wildly unprofessional. Okay... so, Micah. You live with a bunch of non-vampires, right? Did you kill your maker? Or was there some other horrific incident that caused you to be cast out of your nest and exiled?"

"Uh... no."

"Can vampires be exiled? You've obviously done something terrible to be shunned by your own kind. These course notes don't cover much vampire stuff, because of the whole "no vampire children" thing, but it does clearly state that vampires are exclusionary and have a heightened superiority complex." She paused. "Are you a self-hating vampire?"

"No, I... uh. I'm young, like you."

"And you never found a vampire nest to join? Did one of them try to kill you, and what methods did they use?" The sound of flicking pages filled the brief silence. "I can't find a list of limiting factors or threats to survival of the vampire species in here. I'm assuming it's common knowledge and not applicable to a CPS coursebook because, again, because of the whole 'no vampire children' thing. Typical." She sighed. "I had to go ahead and be an anomaly as a vampire as well as a human. Go, me." She paused for a second to take a breath. "Anyway, how does one go about climbing the ranks of the vampire hierarchy? It says here it's a monarchy with four kings or queens ruling over each corner of the globe. Is it a hereditary monarchy, or is it elective? Or is it conquest or divine mandate? Is there a vampire god?"

"Uh..."

Romeo wrapped his arms around me, drawing me closer. "I thought you must be joking when you said she killed the new nestmaster."

"Nope." I popped the P. "She decapitated him with a few rough calculations, some razor wire, and a dentist chair."

"Like a homicidal ginger MacGyver." Cole caught my eye. "Should we... y'know..." He made a throat cutting gesture. "Before she starts gunning for the vampire royal throne?"

"Cole. No."

"I'm just saying. That girl has got world domination on her mind, I can tell."

He's not wrong, Brain-Daphne chipped in. *The whole Iron Man thing is a bit of a green flag.*

You mean red flag.

I said what I said.

"She's scary-smart," Cole hissed, keeping his voice down so Marie couldn't hear. "She's so friggin pretty, but she dresses like a dorky middle-aged dad. She's terrifying."

I gave him a sharp look. "Smart women who dress like they don't care about what men think are terrifying, are they?"

He stared back at me. "Yes! Of course they are! Daphne, I don't think I've ever felt more intimidated in my life! I'm having some very weird feelings here!"

I wriggled into Romeo's arm and sighed wearily. I'd been wearing my bike leathers and heavy jacket all day. Now, with over twelve hours of wear, it felt like it had sunk into my skin, and I'd be uncomfortable forever.

"How can you not know?" From the front seat, I heard

Marie give a little hiss. "You mean you don't know anything about being a vampire? Well, do you have access to a manual? I'll even take an online course at this stage."

We reached the church and drove straight through the gates, pausing for a second so Romeo could retract the wards. I felt the tingle of magical residue as we passed through. There was a hell of a lot of power in these defenses.

A little of the tension drained out of my shoulders. We would be safe for now. I could rest. God, I needed rest. It was just before three in the morning, and if I cleaned up and wolfed down my lasagna, I'd manage at least a couple of hours of sleep before I had to get up and go to work.

We stopped right outside the church steps. For once, Marie was speechless, looking up at the big gothic building. The silence only lasted a few seconds, though. "Whoa. This is incredible. This has got 'evil lair' written all over it."

"Don't get any ideas," Romeo said to her.

We walked inside. Marie's eyes flicked over the newly installed temporary oak door, the battered refrigerator, and scanned the safety board and tape over the shattered library door. The guys had cleaned up, putting the room back in order after the alien bug tossed it, but it was quite obvious something had gone on in here recently. "What happened here?"

"Giant alien insect invasion," Micah said.

"Cool." She nodded, impressed. "Where did it come from?"

"We don't know."

"What did it want?"

"Micah," Romeo said loudly. "You're on watch."

The vampire heaved out a sigh of relief. "Thank you, boss."

"Cole..." Romeo looked at the lynx shifter, who was

staring at Marie with very wide eyes. "Check in with the other guys."

Cole jerked and shifted on his feet uncomfortably. "Got it."

"And you." Romeo turned to me, his expression softening. "Go take a shower and warm up. I'll heat up the lasagna."

"What about Marie?"

He gave me a crooked smile. "I think I can handle her."

I scuttled off to the bathroom. Romeo's ensuite felt like a masculine luxury spa. The soft lights overhead were heat lamps, throwing a delicious warmth on my skin. The stone floor under my feet was also heated.

Peeling off my leathers felt like a religious experience. They'd become tighter and more uncomfortable as the day went on, as all the problems that cropped up accumulated, squeezing me tighter, burrowing into me, and pinching me with sharp needle teeth—

My brain kicked me in the sinuses. *What the hell is wrong with you?*

"Too much," I muttered. "Too much has happened today, and I can't deal with all of it. This multi-dimensional alien creature is ruining my life."

Shower, my brain ordered. *Wash off the day. Good vibes only.*

I turned on his waterfall faucet and lost myself in a heavy deluge of warm water. After a while, the buzzing in my head quietened down. I didn't realize how long I'd been gone until I put on Romeo's huge cozy hoodie, wrapped my hair in a towel, and padded out into the living room.

Voices came from the kitchen. "I still don't understand why you would run away. You could have at least got a sample of the alien."

"I was wounded."

"It sounded like it just scratched you, though." Marie was sitting on the counter in the kitchen with my O-CPS manual in her lap. The antique ceremonial athame lay next to her. "If you're a big bad warlock with lots of magic, couldn't you—"

"I had two other souls to protect." Romeo moved into my line of sight. Next to Marie, who was perched on the counter like a pretty little goblin, he looked like a giant. Romeo had gotten changed at some point and now wore a plain white t-shirt and gray sweatpants. It seemed incomprehensible that he'd look more dangerous and more brutally handsome out of his combat gear, but this Romeo —relaxed, calm, in comfy clothes, and wrangling that little ginger devil with ease—took my breath away.

And... I swallowed. Gray sweatpants.

"There were a few options I could have employed, but ultimately, I had no idea what was attacking us. I still don't."

"I'll figure it out," Marie muttered, flipping through the pages again. "You just gotta find the Achilles heel, and you can kill anything."

He put a slice of lasagna on a plate, put it in the microwave, and picked up his phone from the counter, tapping on it. "I can't be sure I can destroy something if I don't know what will kill it."

"Well, you can." Marie said. "Just chop off their head. You have to admit that it's kind of a foolproof way to destroy literally everything."

"Says the girl who has never met a hydra."

Marie jerked her head up. "Really? A hydra?"

Romeo shrugged. "Sure. There are a lot of creatures who can live without their heads and come back stronger. You're just lucky that vampires aren't one of them."

She pursed her lips. "Hmm. Touché, I guess."

"So, you see that a strategic withdrawal was the only option."

"Yeah, about that." Marie flipped the pages of her manual. "It doesn't make any sense. You're the only witch who can move through shadows? From what I've read here, mortal realm-based creatures can't render themselves noncorporeal or sublimate, as in, change from solid matter to a gas state."

"I'm not changing to a gas state," Romeo said mildly. "I'm becoming shadow and sending my consciousness through the darkness to emerge wherever I want."

She tapped her chin, staring off into space. "Theoretically... I've heard of light being transformed into supersolids, I guess this is just the reverse, but instead of a beam, it's the absence of a beam. Or maybe there's an undiscovered dark wavelength, something invisible to our current technology, and you're travelling through that." She glanced up, staring at Romeo with her intense eye contact. "If you can do it, but nobody else in your family line can, that would indicate a genetic mutation of some sort."

"I don't have a genetic mutation," Romeo said, pulling a steaming plate out of the microwave.

"You could. Or it could just be your ancestry. Can I get a sample of your blood?"

"No."

"Marie," I said firmly.

She turned. "What?"

I marched over to the huge piece of plywood covering the shattered library door, and pulled it off, letting the nails rip right out of the wood. I pointed at it.

Marie saw the library and all the books inside. She gasped. Her beautiful green eyes sparkled with ruby light. She moved so fast my hair blew back off my face. Within a split second, she was inside the library, gazing up at the shelves. Reverently, she slid a huge tome off the shelf in front of her and opened it.

"I don't know why I didn't think of that," Romeo said. "I like a challenge, I guess." He poured a glass of milk and walked over.

"I can't leave her," I said apologetically, sinking into the huge squashy sofa behind me. "She won't go to sleep until dawn, and I'm responsible for her until..." I trailed off and waved my hand wearily.

He handed me the plate of lasagna and sat next to me. "Until what?"

"Until I get fired, probably."

"You won't get fired."

"I might." Quickly, I told him about my latest run-in with the human detectives, leaving out the awful things they'd said. "Monica said that if I can't make this go away, she'll have to fire me."

"I've made some calls." Romeo wrapped his arm around me, propping me up so I could eat without spilling lasagna on my chin. It was, as expected, heavenly—with tomato, garlic, and a herby meat filling, smooth creamy sauce, and perfectly cooked al dente noodles, slightly crispy on one end, just the way I liked it. "I gave the Otherworld authorities a little push. They'll have taken over the case by tomorrow, so you won't need to worry about them anymore. Your job is safe."

It still felt like a stone around my neck. "The fact that they found my hair in Wesley's hands is worrying, Romeo."

He was quiet for a second. "Yeah, it is."

"This feels like a conspiracy."

"It does."

I looked at him. "You don't sound worried."

He gave me the ghost of a smile. "Everyone, everywhere, all at once, remember? I've had so many conspiracies against me, and I've survived countless assassination attempts—for me, it's just another Tuesday."

"It's Wednesday now." I took another bite of lasagna.

Suddenly, a pulse, a magical thump that made my heart pound, thrummed through the room. I lurched out of the sofa, tossing the plate behind me. Two small explosions shook the ground under my feet.

Romeo was already charging across the room. "Stay here."

Fuck, no.

Glancing quickly at the library, I spotted Marie sitting on the floor with her nose buried in a book that was almost bigger than her. She was safe and clearly not moving anytime soon. I dashed after Romeo as he slipped out the vestry door into the garage.

An intercom gave a tick. "South gate, boss!" Micah's voice boomed over the loudspeaker. "The alien is attacking again!"

Romeo hit a button on the wall; an alarm gave a whoop.

Another explosion shook the garage. Whatever firepower that thing had, it was unleashing it on the wards. I paused for a split second and focused. My hearing sharpened, and I tried to identify the ballistics it was using. I caught a sharp *zip* noise before the bang.

The intercom clicked again. "Sending up a drone," Micah said. "We can follow the heat signal."

I joined Romeo at the door, moving into my combat-mode low crouch, trying to spot the enemy outside.

The huge tree near the south gate burned. The smell of burning metal and smoke choked me. Through the dark haze, I saw something moving, something shiny, like hard armor with too many parts. Was it just one thing? Maybe it was a whole bunch of armored attackers working in perfect unison.

Zip—bang!

The creature fired again. The ground shook, and another tree burst into flames. There was no way it was getting through this many wards. Whatever it was shooting with, the explosive bullets were ricocheting off and tearing apart the trees around the gates.

A terrifying clacking noise came from the direction of the creature, which was hidden almost completely within the burning foliage outside of the gates. Was the monster making that noise? It sounded like a giant demented demon tap dancer.

I could sense its anger and frustration. But I couldn't see what it was. And, even more bizarre, I couldn't smell it. What the hell was that thing?

The shiny armor darted back and forth, but even with my enhanced eyesight, I couldn't make sense of what I was seeing. An insect, yes, with an armored carapace, but it was an odd shape, far more upright than a crab or a spider.

We need to see what it is! If we know what it is, we can fight it!

Romeo didn't bother. He stood tall, arms out, palms up, his shoulders firm and corded with tense muscles—violet magic turning his fingers to flame—and strode out the door like a warrior charging across a battlefield. "Stay behind me."

I joined him at his side, pulling my Orion blades. He held out his arms, shielding me, as we both ran towards the smoking fence.

In the street beyond the trees, blue and red lights abruptly flared. A siren whooped. The cops had become aware of the disturbance. Humans were on their way.

The clacking grew more demented. The alien fired one more time. *Zip-Bang.*

Then it turned and crashed into the undergrowth.

CHAPTER
SEVENTEEN

"It disappeared," Micah said, shaking his head in disbelief. "It disappeared completely. I got the tag on a giant heat flare coming from the creature, followed it, then suddenly, it was gone."

We gathered in the living room. I'd taken my spot back in the fluffy faux-mink rug next to Romeo. Brandon and Levi were awake, yawning and rubbing their eyes. It was almost four in the morning, and I was slowly losing the will to live. I wanted to burrow into Romeo's skin and sleep for a million years.

Marie was still in the library, sitting cross-legged on the floor, surrounded by books. Four huge grimoires lay open in a circle around her, and she flicked her focus between them, obviously cross referencing. Every now and then I heard her grumble something like, "well, that's hardly scientific," or "hmm, sounds like someone is a little delusional."

"The drone caught absolutely nothing," Micah continued. "It was like the monster blinked out of existence."

"I don't understand it." Cole scowled at the coffee table. "An alien shot at our wards for thirty seconds, then vanished into thin air. Why?"

"The wards held," Levi said through a yawn.

"Did it disappear when the cops came, or did it leave when it saw you?"

I shrugged. "I don't know what it is." Strangely, I wasn't scared. Maybe I was just over-tired. Adrenaline fatigue. Yeah, that was it. I hadn't recovered from the battle with Christopher Jupiter yet. Hell, I hadn't recovered from the battle with Alexei Minoff, or the battle with the ishkikys demon, or the battle with Zofia, the first nestmaster. "Maybe we should have sent Marie out to interrogate it."

I got the feeling Marie would crack the mystery with a quick game of twenty questions. "Whatever it is, we know now it's not an actual *alien* alien. Like a space alien, I mean. It's a magical creature. The cops pulled up on the street outside, and it vanished. It's safe to say it's bound by the Great Agreement."

An anguished cry came from the library; I shot to my feet. "Marie? Are you okay?"

She walked out slowly, her peaches and cream complexion paler than ever. "I can't go outside."

Everyone looked at her. Silence gripped the room.

She opened her mouth. A word fell from her lips. "Contraindications."

Another long moment of silence passed, this one loaded with confusion. The coven shot each other puzzled glances. I watched as Cole mouthed to Micah. "What does that word mean?"

"The sun." Marie's lip quivered. "That's why you can't send me back to Harvard. The sun will burn me."

"Well... yeah," Micah said slowly. "Everyone knows that." He cut himself off abruptly when he saw Marie's face.

She looked devastated.

My chest ached. I felt so sorry for her, and I felt like a

complete idiot. I didn't realize Marie didn't know she would be allergic to sunlight.

And how could she? The current pop culture didn't do vampire lore any favors. Even Valerie thought she had to stay out of the sun because she'd shine like a diamond, and she needed to stay hidden or else the Volturi would get her. Valerie existed in a constant state of sleep deprivation because she thought she didn't have to sleep. She got a few hours' sleep every time we found her frozen solid in the snow, though.

I sighed. "Marie... yeah. It's true. New vampires are allergic to the sun."

"I can't go back to my classes. Most of my lectures are mid-morning, and there are windows all around the lab." Tears flooded her big green eyes. "The sun will burn me to a crisp."

To be fair, it was only one of the reasons that she couldn't go back to Harvard. Vampires, like the rest of us, had to stay in the shadows and keep magic a secret, and Marie still hadn't processed the idea that she was completely different now. I had no idea what she looked like as a human, but the vamp-metamorphosis would have changed every aspect of her physical appearance. She was stronger, faster, harder, more beautiful, more resilient, and more powerful.

The humans who knew her before she was turned would notice the change in her instantly. Even if she still walked like a trotting show pony and dressed like Adam Sandler.

Consequently, it was standard practice that new vampires had to sever ties with their old lives immediately and were effectively dead from the moment they opened their vampire eyes for the first time.

"It's not so bad," Micah said soothingly. "After a year or

so, you develop more of a resistance. If you wear a hat and some heavy sunscreen—"

"Have you *seen* this *skin?*" Marie's screech made the glass in the coffee table vibrate.

Micah swallowed. "Uh... what?"

She jabbed a finger at her own face. "Can you not *see* this red hair? This corpse-like pasty glow? These tiny red volcanos on my face?" She waved her hand around her face wildly and screeched, her voice breaking through three more octaves. "I can't wear sunscreen! You think all this acne is bad now, wait 'til you see what a brief touch of UV light will do to it! I haven't felt the warm glow of far-infrared rays since I was a baby! And that's only because my mom didn't *believe in sunscreen!*"

I frowned. Acne?

"I'm a *ginger*, for Pete's sake!" Marie howled. "A ginger with acne aestivalis! Do you not understand how friggin' sensitive to the sun I am *already?* I have to wear SPF50 to go out in the sun anyway, or I'll burn to a crisp! I was a friggin' poster child for the Wear Sunscreen campaign even before I got turned into a vampire!"

Cole gazed up at her soulfully. "You have beautiful skin, Marie."

She tossed her head, snorting in derision, like a very offended horse. "Don't try to gaslight me, Mister Hillbilly Sister-Fucker."

"Marie!" I gasped. "That's mean!"

"He started it!" She jabbed a finger towards me. "I have a motto, Daphne, I don't start shit, but I will always finish it. I don't fight fire with fire. If you try to roast me, I'll dump napalm on your house."

"He wasn't trying to roast you—"

"You think I haven't had a lifetime to get used to people

bullying me about my skin? You think I haven't heard every single insult before?"

"He was just complimenting you on your complexion, Marie," Micah said soothingly.

Marie jerked a finger at him. "You can shut it. You're a vampire, goddamnit, you're the only person in this place with lived experience with vampirism, and you couldn't tell me anything about it. You're about as useless as tits on a bull, and I don't need your sarcasm rubbing salt into my wounds."

"He wasn't being sarcastic," I tried.

"Oh, right, so I guess the metamorphosis cured my acne as well as my eyesight, did it?" She glared at me. "See? Sarcasm!"

"Marie!"

She was like a little spitting kitten. "You can't hurt me even if you tried," she hissed, whirling around. "I've done the work. Eight years of intensive psychotherapy to accept myself as who I am—short, ginger, zitty. You all should try it, and you wouldn't feel so much shame around who you are. You." She pointed at Cole. "*You* were a minor. You were a victim! Get some goddamn therapy and stop hiding behind the big guy's skirt. And you," she said, rounding on Micah. "You're in denial, which I find absolutely bizarre. You were a scummy human assassin—why the hell would you want to hold onto your humanity and pretend to be a witch?"

"Marie..." Romeo's voice held warning.

She turned to him, eyes blazing, blisteringly unafraid. "Don't start with me. I like you a lot, Mr. Zarayan, but you're obviously in denial about your heritage, too. Come on, dude. Poisoned by a pure-iron blade? Unique magical abilities? Shadow-jumping? I've been a part of this world for a few hours, and—"

Stop her!

I flung myself across the room and tackled her to the ground.

Marie gave a yelp and wriggled like an eel. "This is *so* unprofessional!"

I clamped my hand over her mouth. I could feel her trying to take a chunk out of my palm with her teeth, so I cupped my fingers so she couldn't pinch them. "You think you're the first vampire to try and bite me?"

"OoMmm remmoor oo oo MMMM!"

A slightly hysterical bark of laughter slipped out my lips. "You're going to report me? To whom? This is the Otherworld, honey, and you don't have anyone to complain to. In case you missed it, I'm already under investigation for murder." I got her in a headlock, a leg-lock, wrapping her up so she couldn't move, and hissed in her ear. "You might be smart, Marie, but you're skating on very thin ice right now."

A pulse of magic punched through the room. The surge rolled over both of us. It felt like someone had thrown a bucket of water over me.

Marie froze immediately. Her eyes widened. Goosebumps rose on my skin.

Marie started to shiver. It was the first time she'd been hit by a spell, and it finally shocked her into silence.

"Get up," Romeo growled. "Both of you."

The room had gone dead-quiet. I untangled myself from Marie and stood up.

Uh oh.

Romeo stood like a statue, not moving a muscle. But the storm raged within him, turning his gray eyes almost black. His massive shoulders were somehow bigger than before. Every line in his body was hard, tense, about to explode into violence. A hurricane stood in the middle of the room. We could all feel it.

Marie stood next to me, then edged closer, until she was touching me. She gulped.

Oh, shit. He knows.

He's going to kill us.

Worse, he's going to hate us.

After what felt like a million years, Romeo unclenched his jaw and pointed at Micah and Cole. "Stay here. Don't move. If she opens her mouth," he growled, pointing at Marie. "You have my permission to kill her."

Marie gasped. Then, she clasped her hand over her mouth.

Romeo turned to me. It was like staring into the depths of a cyclone. "Daphne," he said, his voice thunderous. "Bedroom. Now."

CHAPTER
EIGHTEEN

I scuttled into the bedroom and moved all the way back as far as I could, trying to outrun the storm.

But there was nowhere to run; the storm was right behind me. I hit the far wall and turned around.

Romeo stalked inside and slammed the door behind him. I jumped.

"Daphne..." He looked furious. He took a deep breath through his nose, calming himself down.

"I'm sorry." It was probably best to get that out of the way. "I really am sorry, Romeo."

"You should be." His dark eyes glittered. "I can't tell you how angry I am right now."

Oh gods, he was so angry. The muscles in his chest were so hard; his forearms bulged. He fixed me with a glare that almost scorched me.

"I know you are mad," I said in a little voice. "You have every right to be."

Is it wrong that I'm really turned on right now?

Shush, brain, this is serious. "I should have told you," I continued. "In my defense, I assumed you must have suspected...." My voice withered away.

Romeo walked towards me slowly, a predator stalking his prey, never taking his eyes off me. "Yes, I did," he growled. "Of course, I suspected that my father might not be human. That evil genius in my living room was right, it's logical to assume that I'm not entirely human." He paused. A muscle in his jaw ticked.

Brain-Daphne fanned herself.

He took a deep breath through his nose, obviously trying to keep a hold of his temper. "Yes, I have issues. I hate everything about the cowardly asshole who knocked up my mother and ran away, so I don't like thinking of who he might be, because every time I think of it..." He clenched his huge fists.

The floor rumbled underneath me. It took a second to stop.

"This is why I didn't want to tell you," I said. I sounded so pathetic.

Romeo continued, "My mother died, leaving me an orphan with nothing. He never came back to find me. I hated all aspects of him. But now I realize you knew all along." He took another step closer, stalking me again. "Do you know who he is?"

I flinched. "No! Of course not. I just guessed he was a high fae royal, because your magic is so similar to theirs."

"Because I will find him, and I will kill him." Romeo glowered down at me, moving closer. "A coward like that does not deserve to live."

I backed away until I hit the wall again. Trapped, nowhere else to run to. I held up my hands, palms out. "And that's another reason why I couldn't drop it on you without the proper support. You already hate the high fae. Killing one of their royals could trigger a diplomatic disaster that could lead to the extinction of the human race—"

"You think I'm a savage." He moved closer. Heat radiated off his skin.

He definitely looks like a savage. Brain Daphne shivered with longing and licked her lips.

"Of course not." I had to tilt my head up to meet his eye. "You've been through so much lately. Emotionally. I mean. I didn't want to overload you—"

"Instead, you lied about it." Romeo put his hands on the wall on either side of my head, boxing me in. "You cured my iron poisoning with a fae remedy, not once, but twice, and you lied to me about it."

I shivered. "I knew how much of a delicate topic it was, because of how much you hate your bio dad. I wanted you to come to the realization yourself—"

"So, you avoided telling me the truth for so long, leaving the door open for that redheaded she-devil to drop it on me like a bomb," he growled. "And you tried to silence her when she announced it to everyone."

"At least I *tried*." I sounded so pathetic. Tears pricked at my eyes; I blinked them back furiously. It would be so unfair to him to cry right now. "I just... I just didn't want you to be hurt, Romeo." I swallowed the lump in my throat. "I'm so sorry. I was trying to protect you, and the truth ended up hurting you even more."

He glared down at me for another long moment. In the silence, my legs buckled. I was so damn tired.

Romeo saw it and swore. The fire in his eyes vanished immediately. His arms wrapped around me. Scooping me up, he carried me to the bed. "We're not done here." He laid me down gently. "I'll be back in a second."

He turned and stormed out the door. I heard his footsteps heading towards the living room. I'd been so scared, I forgot that the others were still waiting there, not moving, not speaking.

I hid in his room like a coward and heard every word he said. "Marie." Romeo's voice made me shiver. "I understand you are going through an enormous adjustment period right now."

Okay, he sounds calm. He's going to give her a lecture. He'll come back and give us a lecture too, and we'll be okay.

Except Romeo's voice was still dark, vibrating with the promise of violence. "I'm not going to make any assumptions about your life, and why you act the way you do. To jump to conclusions based on a handful of facts is not particularly scientific. Worse, you decided these assumptions were correct."

"Ouch," she said very quietly.

He's hit her where it hurts.

"I invited you into my house, with my friends, at a very vulnerable time in your life, and you've insulted us. My capacity for mercy can only go so far. This isn't a warning, Marie, it's an order. You need to adjust your behavior quickly, because I mean it when I say you won't survive long in this world if you keep offending the people who are trying to help you. And we are trying to help you."

She was silent for a moment. "I know."

"Daphne has gone to extreme lengths to try and make sure you're safe and fed, and I've provided you with sanctuary. You might have survived in the human world with your brain alone, but right now, you are being unfathomably stupid."

There was another awkward pause. "That's fair," she muttered. "I'm sorry."

"Now, I'm guessing you've had a rough childhood. You've been raised to think that everyone is a threat to you, and you act accordingly. Everyone is an enemy, and you're just waiting for them to strike. Is that right?"

"Well..." Marie said grudgingly, "It has been my experience, yes."

"And you don't trust anyone."

"Of course not."

"You think of people as either enemies or pawns you can move around until you get what you want." Romeo's tone softened a little. "That must be a lonely existence." He paused for a moment, but Marie didn't respond. "You don't have any friends, do you." It wasn't a question. He already knew.

It took a while for Marie to reply, and when she did, her voice was so tiny, it almost broke my heart. "No."

"Thought so," a surly voice muttered.

"Cole." Romeo's voice was like a boom of thunder.

"Sorry, boss." Silence held the room for another long moment. "Uh, and... I apologize, Marie. That wasn't very mature of me."

Romeo sighed. "Marie. Apologize to Cole."

"I'm sorry I called you Mister Hillbilly Sister-Fucker." Marie's voice sounded grudging.

"Now apologize to Micah, too."

Marie groaned. "Fine. Sorry for calling you a shitty human and a self-hating vampire. Look, I'll admit, I can go a little overboard when someone is being mean to me. I lashed out. It's a defense mechanism. When you said I had nice skin, I got a little reactive. Sarcasm is the lowest form of wit, you know."

"I wasn't being sarcastic," Cole whined. "You *are* pretty. You've got the personality of a cheese grater on my nuts, and you're so insufferable that I'm—"

Romeo cleared his throat, cutting him off. Cole sighed. "I apologize for being shallow. And for that last comment, which was also mean. You do have nice skin."

"Yeah," Marie snarled. "If you like pizza, I suppose."

"Marie." Romeo's tone shifted a little. "If you had acne before, it's gone. The metamorphosis cures all human diseases and ailments."

"Wh— What?" Marie stammered for a second. "Mirror," she whispered. "I need a—wait. Can I see my own reflection?"

"You can."

"Here," Micah said.

I waited to hear her talk. Then, I waited some more. Marie must be examining her vamp-enhanced features in the mirror carefully. The silence dragged on for longer than it should have. Nobody said anything.

My brain sniggered. *She's going into shock again.*

I couldn't think why. Why would she be going into shock? Marie was a beautiful girl.

"I'm done here. Micah, look after her and make sure she has somewhere safe to sleep," Romeo ordered. "Cole, you can switch out with Levi. Make sure he checks the wards again."

Marie's scream echoed from all the way down the hall. "No! This... nooooo! I can't look like this! I put so much work into loving myself as I am! Thousands of dollars and hundreds of hours of therapy to be okay with myself, and you mean to tell me I'm pretty *now?*"

Micah tried to shout over her. "It's a good thing, Marie!"

"It's not! I can't look like this! Do you even know how hard it is to be a woman in STEM *already?* Nobody will ever take me seriously ever again!"

Romeo appeared in the doorway, grimacing. He shut the door firmly, leaned back on it, and pinched the bridge of his nose. "And I thought I wanted to have kids one day."

"You should," I said. "That was awesome. Very paternal. Strict but fair."

He looked up, glared at me, and stalked towards me again. "I'm still mad."

I shivered, this time, in longing. But we had to talk this out first. "I'm sorry," I said. "You're right. About everything. I'm a hypocrite and a coward. I should have brought up my suspicions about your biological father much sooner, and I definitely shouldn't have cured your iron poisoning without initiating a conversation about it."

"I understand why you didn't." He sighed roughly. "And you're right—deep down, I knew. I just didn't want to have to deal with it. I'm just so..." He clenched his fists and cursed under his breath. "I'm angry. I've been angry for my entire life. Some high fae asshole got my mother pregnant and ran away, and when she tried to find him, she lost one hundred years of her life and got thrown out on the streets by Wesley Jupiter. I've gotten even with everyone who has ever done me wrong, except for the man who ruined my mother." Romeo wiped his face with his hands, exhausted. "I'm just so tired of carrying around this hatred," he said quietly.

"You don't have to hate him—"

"It's not just hatred for him. It's for me."

"You?"

He clawed his hands, gesturing to his chest. "He made me, Daphne. I'm half him. The darkness inside of me—the part that screams for blood, the part that demands vengeance, the selfish, pigheaded, self-absorbed, power-hungry side of me. Even the part that seduced princesses and movie stars and dumped them like they didn't matter... That's my biological father. I'm his legacy." He swallowed roughly. "I became exactly what he is, and I hate it."

I shook my head frantically. "Romeo, no—"

"You can't say it's not true. Everyone is scared of me. The Warlock. The bad boy heir who overthrew the Jupiters.

The dark prince of Philadelphia. I was too scared to admit what my father might be, because if I knew who he was, I'd have to find him and kill him." He took a deep breath. "And then, when we meet in battle, he'll be proud of what I've become, and that makes me hate myself more than anything."

"Okay, wait." I held up my hand. "This might be a little abrupt, but Romeo... And I'm trying really hard not to be ableist when I say this, but are you *actually* delusional?"

He scowled at me.

"Can you even hear yourself? You're literally the most selfless, self-sacrificing person I think I've ever met in my life. You took the High Priest's job even though you didn't want it, because—even though you hated that Aunt Marche did it to you—you knew you were the only person strong enough to withstand the pressures of rebuilding our Otherworld after the Suffocation. You were the only one who would keep the balance. Even though all the other supe leaders despised you for killing Aunt Marche, you did the work and bore the weight of their hatred anyway."

His eyes narrowed.

"You're the only impartial supe in this whole city," I continued. "All the others—the Alpha, the nestmaster, the diplomat—they only serve themselves and their own race, but mostly themselves. You treat everyone equally. You believe everyone deserves respect."

"I kill without remorse, Daphne," he said quietly. "Without hesitation, and without mercy."

I shrugged. "So do I. Am I like your father?"

He glared at me. He didn't say anything.

"You're assuming way too much. You don't even know what your father was like. And"—I pointed at him—"I'm sorry if I'm getting harsh here, but I'm trying to make amends for not discussing this with you earlier—you don't even know that he abandoned your mother!"

"He did," Romeo growled. "He left, and he didn't come back."

"You told me he left to get things to ease the burden of her pregnancy and help with her labor. Fae reproduction is wildly volatile and incredibly dangerous. My friend Prue is half-fae—"

"The daughter of the Beast," Romeo interrupted. "I know."

"Then you should know that she's nothing like her biological father. She inherited his incredible magical power, but her personality is her own." I bit my lip before I said anything else. Prue was kinda nuts, but in the best way possible.

"It's not the same," Romeo said.

"It's exactly the same. You know her history. I happen to know that in order for her mom to give birth to her, there were certain magical rituals she had to complete. Maybe your dad had to go and do some sort of pilgrimage. He would have returned home, back to the mortal realm, and found your mom missing. She didn't come back for one hundred years, Romeo."

"And he *never* came back."

"You don't know that. You don't. Nobody knew that your mom had come back—how the hell could anyone know that you existed?"

He exhaled roughly and looked away. "Okay. Logically, I know you're right. I just... I know what the high fae are like. They're merciless and power-hungry and bloodthirsty, Daphne."

"They are." I smiled at him. "But so are we. Nobody can be more inhumane than a human. You've carried this burden of hating your biological father your whole life, and this vision you have of him... it's grown into a monster that just isn't real. Don't you see that?"

He wiped his face with his hands again.

"I don't know who your father is. But I know who *you* are. You just scolded a seventeen-year-old-vampire girl. You could have killed her or thrown her out, but instead you gently admonished her." I shuffled forward on the bed, hating the distance between us. I needed to be closer. "You literally activated my school headmaster kink," I murmured.

Romeo stared down at me. "I know you're just trying to snap me out of my mental breakdown."

"Is it working?"

"Yeah, it is."

I held out my arms. "Then let's leave behind all the self-doubt and self-loathing and pick it up again tomorrow. We both need to sleep."

He let out a short huff of breath. "You're unbelievable." He pointed at me and walked over to the bed. "Okay, fine. But we're not done with this conversation." He stopped at the edge of the bed and looked down at me. "You lied to me." His eyes glinted silver in the darkness. "There will be consequences."

"Consequences?" My voice was squeaky.

He crawled onto the bed, holding himself over my body, that enormous hard-muscled chest hovering only inches above mine. "Punishment." His cool breath washed over me.

Yes. In my head, Brain-Daphne flicked some handcuffs over her own wrist and popped a ball gag into her mouth. *Let's go.*

"Wh— What kind of punishment?"

"I'm going to give you a taste of your own medicine."

My mouth dropped open. "You know who my dad is?"

He hesitated for a second, then his eyes twinkled. "No, Daphne. That's not what I meant."

"Oh." I slumped back down. "Sorry. I'm really tired."

"I know." He wrapped his arms around me, forming a deliciously masculine scented, strong blanket made of manly muscles. Every single bit of resistance vanished. "We'll pick this up tomorrow," he said, his voice soft. "You can sleep now. Your punishment starts tomorrow." He leaned down and pressed his lips to mine gently, then smiled, his eyes devilish. "And I can't wait."

In my head, Brain-Daphne stomped her feet like a brat. *But I want to start nowwww.*

Romeo's arms were so warm, and I was so, so tired. My eyes kept rolling back in my head. And besides, I told my own brain quietly, I didn't think he was going to spank me.

"So..." I said sleepily. "What's my punishment?"

"You were trying to protect me, so you deliberately kept some very important information from me—information that I deserved to know. You disregarded my autonomy, so you're going to get a taste of your own medicine."

I think I know where this is going, Brain-Daphne sighed. *It's not as good as a spanking, but I'll take it.*

Romeo's arms tightened around me. "I've been working really fucking hard not to be too overprotective with you, Daphne." His voice was low and dangerously seductive. "I've been keeping my distance. I've respected your wishes to handle your own problems." His eyes glinted—the dark fae prince looked right into my soul. "No more. Your problems are now my problems. And I'll be solving your problems however I see fit."

"No murder," I said sleepily, trying to boop his nose with my finger.

"I'm not promising anything." He leaned down and kissed me. "Now sleep. That's an order."

I was already gone.

CHAPTER
NINETEEN

There was an eyeball in my face.

Beady black, fathomless, a vast, endless void waiting for a spark so that it could unleash ultimate anarchy on the world. Along with the void, a weight sat on my chest, heavy, almost crushing me.

The eyeball blinked and narrowed. **You awake, little one?**

"I am now," I croaked. My mouth was so dry. "Of course, it's a little hard to snooze when you've got the physical embodiment of chaos poking you in the face with his beak and crushing you to death. Can you get off me, please, sir? You're really heavy."

Dwayne did a little hop, jumping off my chest onto the bed beside me. **Thought you'd never wake up.**

I moaned and gave a little stretch. I felt stiffer than I should have. "It's weird. I feel like I've slept for days." Reaching up and out, I felt my joints pop. There was something heavy right beside me...

I patted the blankets, feeling cold metal underneath my fingertips. "Is that a shotgun?"

Yeah. Dwayne sounded gloomy. He wrinkled his beak,

grimacing. **I wanted to do the overprotective father gag on your boyfriend. It didn't work as well as I hoped.**

"I'm sorry." I stroked his beautiful white neck gently. "You still haven't figured out how to hold a shotgun, huh."

I could have used the Glock, I suppose. Dwayne gave a goosey shrug. **But it ruins the aesthetic of the gag. It's a shotgun or nothing. Besides, your hot piece of man-beefcake doesn't scare easily. He saw me on the church steps with a shotgun in his face and he just opened the door wider and invited me in for pancakes.**

I smirked. "Ah, pancakes, your Achilles heel." I sat up. A giant yawn shook me and unclicked my jaw. It felt good. "What time is it?"

Baby girl, time is an illusion created by creatures with limited perception.

I squinted at him. "I'm only asking because happy hour starts at five." Sometimes, you had to put questions to Dwayne in a language he understood.

Oh. He frowned. **In that case, it's just after two. We can have tacos before we hit the happy hour.**

"Two?" The panic hit me like a truck. "Two in the *afternoon?*" I scrambled up, looking for my phone. "I've slept for almost the entire workday? Oh, no. No, no, no. I'm on thin ice as it is. I'm going to get fired. I'm so dead. I'm so dead."

The door opened, and Romeo's smooth, confident voice interrupted my mental breakdown. "Relax, baby. You needed to sleep. Levi ran your vitals before dawn, and you were dangerously low on literally every single thing needed for basic functioning."

Even the sight of a freshly showered Romeo, wearing black sweatpants and a sleeveless t-shirt that showed off his insanely bulging muscled arms and shoulders, wasn't enough to calm me down. In fact, the sight of him spiked my heart rate, so now I was panicking for both good reasons and bad reasons.

"There were two meetings scheduled for this morning," I stammered, lurching out of bed. My legs felt stiff. "New clients. I've missed them. I didn't even show up at the office. Monica is going to kill me."

"You didn't miss anything." Romeo walked over to the bed, moving so confidently and so gracefully for such a big man. A jaguar on the prowl, complete with a hint of playful menace in his eyes. "I intercepted a phone call just before five this morning, from your colleague, Judy Sagwood."

I froze. "You... you did?"

"I spoke to her myself. Apparently, she was calling to make sure you were okay." His eyes darkened, turning slightly stormy. "Is there a reason your colleague might be calling you at five in the morning to make sure you were okay?"

My eyes widened. "No."

Yes! Brain-Daphne hissed. *That bitch was calling to fuck with us! Go ahead and rip her head off, Romeo, baby!*

Hell, no. I couldn't tattle to my boyfriend just because Judy was a bitch to me at work. He *would* rip her head off. I'm very much a fight-fire-with-fire kind of person, and unleashing the Warlock on my colleague just because she was mean to me was more like fighting fire with nuclear weaponry.

Romeo watched me carefully for a moment. "Well, you'll be happy to know that after our little talk, Judy graciously offered to take over your new client meetings today. She also agreed to speak to Monica, your boss, and let her know you will be working from home today."

A trickle of relief dulled a little of my panic. Judy wouldn't dare lie to her High Priest. She was probably still sweating from the conversation with him. "But... I was... I was on-call," I stammered. "There might have been emergency callouts."

"There was," Romeo said. "The Otherworld Enforcer called. He found four young new vampire girls in their death-sleep under a bridge downtown first thing this morning."

Dwayne settled down on the bed beside me, tucking himself under the covers. **I took care of it.** He let out a huge yawn, waggling his barbed tongue, before laying his head down on the pillow beside me. **You're welcome.**

I looked at him. "How did you take care of it?"

Got a UPS truck, piled the sleepy vamp girls in, and drove them over to Dennis in D.C.

"Oh, no." I put my face in my hands. There were so many details missing in that story. Dwayne couldn't drive, and the nestmaster of Washington D.C. was almost three hours away. "Sir, did you carjack a UPS driver with that shotgun, too?"

I don't think that's any of your business, baby girl. He waved his wing. **Look, I helped, nobody died. That's the main thing.**

"But..." I blew out an exasperated breath. "You took them out of state? To a different nestmaster's territory? To *Dennis?* Are we allowed to do that?"

No idea. But Dennis was delighted with the new employee intake. When I left, he was preparing to put them through his H.R. induction program. Got out of there before he fired up the PowerPoint presentation on what it means to be a good team player. Dwayne yawned again. **I like Dennis, but that man is batshit crazy.**

"Oh." I liked Dennis too. Dennis Pritchett—the only vampire in the entire continent who insisted on using a surname—had been a call center manager in the early nineties when he was turned, and he still behaved like he'd never left the call center or the nineties. The vampires in his nest in Washington D.C. had to endure performance reviews, Monday Morning Motivation meetings, and team building karaoke nights. Where other nestmasters might discipline their vampires by ripping out their fangs or encasing them in concrete while the sun crept slowly towards them, Dennis preferred to call in H.R. and make the naughty vampire sit through days of additional training presentations.

Dennis was, as Dwayne said, absolutely batshit crazy. Most of the vampires in D.C. adored him, but there were a handful who'd ran to nests in other cities when he took over. Some vamps would rather have their fangs ripped out than endure another karaoke pizza party.

But he was the best nestmaster in the whole country. I should have called him as soon as I found out about the new underage vampires. Although, since there was no procedure for dealing with under-age humans turned against their will, it would take him eight months to draft a process map.

"Thanks for taking care of it for me," I said to Dwayne. "Did you take Marie there, too?"

"No. She's asleep in the library," Romeo said. "There's no natural light, so it's the perfect place for her right now."

Speaking of sleep... Dwayne shut his eyes and snuggled down on the pillow next to me. **Nap time. Wake me before happy hour, would you?**

I barely heard the words he dropped in my head. As soon as Marie woke up, she would run back to Harvard. Her screams last night sounded desperate and delusional, and based on the few hours I'd spent with her, I knew she wasn't the type to give up on something she wanted. "She could escape—"

"We boarded her in," Romeo cut me off. "Nailed some big plywood planks over the door."

I stared at him. "You say that like it's supposed to reassure me."

The hint of a smile touched his lips. "Don't worry, we'll take down the boards at dusk. And we'll figure out what to do with her when she wakes up." Romeo's confident expression wavered for a second. "I shadow-jumped into the library to check on her just before dawn, and she was a little calmer. She asked me for some odd materials. Said she wanted to build a portable particle accelerator and a laser confinement grid. I assumed it was some kind of protection field from the insect monster."

"She's probably building a bomb." Sinking back on the pillows, I exhaled with a mixture of relief and fear. "You did the right thing leaving her in there, though."

He let out a low grunt of agreement. "I don't think Dennis is a good fit for Marie."

"That's a diplomatic way of putting it."

"I was trying to be charitable. Dennis is certifiably insane, but he's the only nestmaster in the entire continent that I actually like. There's no way in hell I'm sending that demon redheaded girl his way. In five minutes, she'd figure out his Achilles heel and use it to manipulate him until she was the head of his entire vampire company."

"Yeah." I grimaced. "I'll have to think of something else for her."

"*We'll* think of something else for her." Romeo climbed onto the bed next to me.

"She's my problem. One of many." I sighed.

"Your problems are my problems, remember? Hit me with one, and I'll solve it."

Guilt squirmed in my chest. "I've got to go and check on Myf."

Just then, the door opened, and Brandon walked into the room holding a tray. My mouth watered—the delicious smell of toasted sourdough with bacon and eggs wafted towards me. Mmm, hollandaise sauce, made from scratch.

"I actually checked on Myfanwy a couple of hours ago," Brandon said to me.

"You did?" I shot a look at Romeo, who threw me a wink. He really was taking this punishment seriously.

"Yeah," Brandon said.

"And she's okay?"

"Hell, no, she's not okay." Brandon put the tray down on the bed next to me. "She's self-absorbed, wracked with guilt, and severely depressed. She needs therapy in the worst way."

"I know," I muttered, slumping back against the pillows. "I'm trying to get my friend Cindy to help, but she had to run out of town."

"We'll figure out something for her," Romeo said. "In the meantime, inspired by Marie, I had Brandon drop off some books to her that might help. There was one in particular that I thought Myf should read. It's a history of the conflict between the People of the Claw and the Welsh Guardians. I know you told her about it, but she needs to learn the details of why they did what they did to her—In black-and-white."

"That was an excellent idea." It would help her a lot. At the very least, she'd know she wasn't alone. "Thank you," I said passionately.

Romeo's beautiful mouth twitched into a crooked smile. "I told you I'm not asking permission to take care of you anymore. On that note, I've got some bad news." He dismissed Brandon with a nod.

"What is it?"

He tapped the tray. "Eat some carbs first."

"Oh, God, it really is bad, isn't it?" I snagged a perfectly toasted slice of sourdough off the tray and layered a piece of bacon on it. Brandon had rubbed a slice of garlic into the bread and had melted a glistening slick of butter over it. It smelled divine. "Is being a good cook a dragon thing?" I bit into the slice and moaned in pleasure. "Okay, hit me with it."

"There was another little gift on your doorstep." Romeo's jaw tightened. "A wooden doll with the head snapped off."

"Huh." I took another bite of toast. My stomach gave a grateful rumble. "That's interesting. Did the doll look like me?"

"No, it was a baby doll. A little baby, missing the head."

I chewed for a moment, then picked a piece of bacon off my plate and held it next to Dwayne's beak. He snored once, smelled the bacon, nibbled it up, and went right back to sleep. "That's a weird threat."

"It might not be a threat." Romeo's voice darkened. "It might be a gift."

"Hmm." I smooshed the perfectly poached egg with my fork, then dipped a piece of sourdough in the yolk and hollandaise sauce. If there was a breakfast heaven, this is what they'd serve. "Did they leave a receipt with the decapitated doll? Because I think I want to return it if it's a gift."

"I don't know why I have to remind you that a demon was literally leaving you dead bodies, tied up in bows, as little gifts for you only a month ago," Romeo said, a touch reproving. "Monstrous creatures will leave monstrous gifts."

I took a deep breath. "I don't know. A baby with its head missing kinda feels like a threat."

"It's not a threat. It's not attacking you—it's attacking me." His eyes narrowed. "I think it *wants* you."

I didn't say anything. My intuition told me the same thing. The giant alien bug thing wanted me. But the odd items left on my doorstep felt like threats.

"Here's what I think," Romeo continued, leaning back on the bedhead, careful not to disturb Dwayne. "I think one of your captors—some powerful dark elf sorcerer or some fae warlord—has decided he can't live without you. He set out to try and find you, and he's found you, but you're under my protection. He's leaving you gifts to try and entice you back and sending one of his creations, a vicious giant bug monster, to attack me to take me out of the picture."

I chewed thoughtfully for a second. "It's a good theory. It would explain the strange rampaging monster. I've travelled through infinite realms, and I have no idea what kind of off-world creature that could be. The closest thing I can think of would be a Bonnacon."

My friend Imogen had fought a Bonnacon before, and she'd told me all about it. It was a fae cow that could shoot burning lava-like poo out of its anus when it was scared. "I didn't get a good look when it attacked last night, but I definitely saw an armored carapace, not a sad cow with turned-in horns and lava poop. You could be right; it might be a magical Frankenstein monster designed specifically to bring me in. There's just no such thing as a giant bug with embedded bio-weaponry. That belongs in a sci-fi novel, not a fantasy world."

"My gut tells me I'm right. Someone wants you back desperately, and they're willing to do anything to get to you."

But the gifts on our doorsteps say, "you're dead meat, bitch."

I agreed with Brain-Daphne. "It doesn't explain the Wesley Jupiter mystery, either," I said out loud. "Someone wants me to suffer in human jail. Or they just want me to suffer the indignity of being questioned by the human detectives over and over and not be able to do anything about it."

I didn't want to mention the horrible things Boggs and Hartshorn had said to me during the interview.

Romeo frowned. "It might not be related."

"I just feel like it is." I rubbed my stomach for a second. "I feel like *all* this stuff is related. In my head, there's a giant puppet master pulling all these strings to ruin my life. He's laughing maniacally, watching the chaos unfold. And yours, too," I added. "That bug is trying to kill you. Not me." I pointed at him with a piece of sourdough for emphasis. "You." Dipping a small piece in hollandaise, I fed it to Dwayne, who ate it mid-snore.

Romeo was quiet for a moment. He looked thoughtful. I watched his face carefully. There was something in his expression... "What is it?" I asked him.

He shook his head once. "Nothing."

"Tell me."

After a few seconds, he let out a weary sigh. "It's probably just a coincidence, but there *have* been some unexpected problems crop up with some of the Jupiter companies in the last week or so," he admitted grudgingly. "It's the reason why Cole has been losing his mind."

I peered at him. "What kind of unexpected problems?"

"Mundane, corporate human problems. The I.R.S. started digging into Scorptec last week, and I just got word that a corruption watchdog is investigating the whole Juplex board."

"Oh." I blinked. "Is that going to be a problem?"

"Not for me personally, but it is a nuisance. Unfortunately, the things being reported to the authorities are true. Eight years ago, before I took control, Jupiter Inc. was a cesspool of corruption."

I made a face. "I mean, it's the Jupiters, so I'm not surprised."

"I did my best to clean house when I took over. I fired the whole Juplex board years ago because Wesley's fatcat friends were lining their pockets and awarding contracts to their family members. Tax evasion, bribery... you name it. There was plenty of insider trading going on, too." Romeo heaved a weary sigh and held out a tiny piece of bacon for Dwayne, who gobbled it up without missing a snore. "Everything has been above board since I took over—I made sure of that. But someone has been feeding the authorities some very specific, very sensitive information about the inner workings of Jupiter Inc." He scowled for a second. "A former employee has decided to turn whistleblower, and it's a pain in the ass. I've had to take over from Cole because he's not coping with the heat."

I chewed on another piece of toast. "See?" I said, raising my eyebrows. "Someone *is* trying to ruin all our lives."

"It's probably unrelated," he muttered. "In other possibly unrelated news, I know why Wesley's murder hasn't been transferred to the Otherworld authorities."

"You do? How?" I dropped my toast and put my hands together in a prayer position. "Please don't tell me that you abducted the Liaison and beat the information out of him."

"I would have," Romeo admitted. "Except he's gone on vacation—as of yesterday."

"Hmm." My eyes narrowed. "That's convenient."

"It is. The Otherworld Liaison's name is Lieutenant Chet Stanley, and he's currently on an island in the Bahamas, out of cell phone service. He left his backup in charge. She's a nice lady, but she refused to reopen any of Chet's processed files."

"But the file was processed incorrectly!"

"Turns out, it wasn't."

"What?" I narrowed my eyes even further. "Of course it was."

"Wesley's murder was combined with Mina's missing person case, with Mina's case taking precedence because she might still be alive. Mina's magic had been bound, so she was considered a vulnerable human when the mansion collapsed. So, her file was stamped by the Liaison as belonging to the human department. And Wesley, because he died of stab wounds and not from magical means, was forwarded to the human department, too."

I ground my jaw. "And only hours later, Lieutenant Chet Stanley went on vacation."

"Yes, you're right, it's suspicious as hell. I've filed a motion with the Court to have the whole mess looked into," Romeo sighed. "The case will get transferred."

"I might get hauled into jail while this bureaucratic nightmare gets sorted out," I grumbled. My insides squirmed. Suddenly, I wasn't so hungry anymore. "Monica might fire me. She said I had to get this whole mess cleaned up quickly. She's getting pressure from the human managers in the D.H.S because it looks bad to have a suspected murderer on staff." I paused. "And then there's the other problem. What happens when the case *does* get transferred to the Otherworld Court?"

"Nothing." Romeo shrugged. "Wesley's a witch under my authority, and you killed him in self-defense. I'll make sure the case disappears. You won't even need a lawyer."

The dark, squirmy feeling inside me wasn't letting up. "What if the case doesn't disappear?"

"It will."

"I don't know, Romeo." The vision of the puppet master—an evil genius pulling the strings behind the scenes, hell-bent on ruining my life—popped into my head again. "I don't think any of these things are coincidences. And if they're not coincidences, then it's painting the picture of a very powerful entity with their tentacles in every single world. In the human world, the Otherworld, and off-world."

Romeo didn't say anything. He fed Dwayne another bit of bacon.

"The alien insect is off-world," I continued, pressing my point. "The gifts on my doorstep are off-world, possibly fae, judging by the bozan blade and the frozen fae rose. Wesley's murder is stuck in the human world; your company problems are in the human world. If someone can plant evidence on Wesley's body to get me implicated in murder and send a giant insect with laser guns to attack you, while at the same time sinking your companies, then it's only a logical deduction that if I stand trial for Wesley's murder in the Otherworld court, I might go down for it."

The penalty for murder in Otherworld court was death.

The temperature in the room suddenly plummeted. Romeo's eyes glittered with silver. "They can try. I'll burn the whole Court to the ground first."

I smiled at him. "Thank you, baby."

"I mean it. Whoever is behind all this, I'll find them. And they'll beg for death before I'm done with them." His phone buzzed again. Then again.

I raised my eyebrows. "Work?"

Romeo didn't even look at it. "Probably. It doesn't matter. If this whistleblower is another puppet out to destroy me or even distract me from you, I'm not going to let it." He stared at me. "From now on, you don't leave my side. I can get a team of human lawyers to deal with my human problems."

"A lawyer." A thought hit me, and I grabbed it. "Hmm, actually, that's not a bad idea. I should get a lawyer. Holly LeBeaux works for the Otherworld court." I grabbed my phone. "Last I saw her, she was dragging Troy out of the mansion. Maybe I'll check in with her to see if there's anything suspicious going on in Court. It's time we tried to get on top of this whole conspiracy." I fired off a quick text, asking Holly to meet me somewhere for a late lunch.

To my surprise, she answered immediately. "She wants to meet for coffee in an hour," I said.

Romeo met my eyes. "I'm coming with you."

"Oh. You really don't have to."

"My punishment still stands, Daphne," he said, his tone rumbling through me. A smile pulled at his lips. "Holly won't mind. She's one of the rare people who isn't scared of me."

I sighed. "One of the *only* people."

CHAPTER TWENTY

I had no clothes with me apart from my motorbike leathers. The idea of squeezing myself back into them after wearing them all day and most of the night yesterday made me want to roll into a ball and cry. But, since Romeo's clothes swamped me and made me look like a little girl playing dress up, there were no other options. Miserably, I hung my leather pants and jacket on the back of the bathroom door.

When I got out of the shower, my leathers were gone, and I found a brand-new outfit waiting for me—designer jeans in the perfect size, tan ankle boots, a beautiful, structured corset-type top that felt both silky and bulletproof, and a soft periwinkle-blue cashmere sweater that complimented my lavender hair. "I guess we're not riding today, huh?"

Romeo sat at his desk, tapping on his laptop. He didn't look up. "Not today. When I'm satisfied with your punishment, I can go back to chasing you around the streets while you ride like a demon. Today, we're going in an armored car, and we're taking Brandon and Levi for muscle."

I held up the corset and winked at him. "Is this Kevlar?"

He smiled back. "Yeah. Put it on."

"You're lucky that I find ballistics gear incredibly sexy." I dropped my towel and picked up some very lacy black panties with the tags still on.

Romeo froze.

I took my time. We hadn't gone any further than deep, intense kisses so far. It was another unspoken thing between us—we'd come together when the time was right. The moments we'd spent in each other's arms, recovering from battle, were far more emotional and intense than passionate, all-consuming sex...

But the anticipation between us was building to a fever pitch. Idly, I snapped the tags on the panties and slid them on.

Romeo watched me while I got dressed, not saying a word. The heat in his eyes almost scorched me. My core tingled as I wiggled the jeans over my hips. He let out a manly groan when I pushed my boobs into the Kevlar corset.

The anticipation was everything.

I pulled the sweater over my head, brushed out my hair with my fingers, and turned to check myself out in his slightly foggy antique mirror by the door.

Wow. We look expensive.

We certainly did. The clothes Romeo had picked out for me radiated wealth and luxury, and they were exceptionally cozy. No man had ever treated me this way before, probably because I was so good at taking care of myself. Now that I thought about it, no man had ever tried. I'd never felt so cherished in my life.

Brandon and Levi came with us downtown, driving in the Escalade to a pretty French bistro. Holly, willowy and gorgeous as always, waited outside. Brandon pulled over at the curb to let us out.

Something is wrong. She's not wearing a sexy pantsuit.

I ran my eyes over her. My brain was right; Holly wasn't wearing her usual uber-chic professional clothes. Instead, she wore a very expensive looking sports luxe outfit—yoga pants, a bomber jacket, and a cap pulled low on her face. She tapped the toe of her sneaker impatiently.

That's unusual. She's normally cool as a cucumber. And I'm sure she's packing more than a Glock today. Brain-Daphne focused. *She's wearing at least two holsters under that bomber jacket.*

Holly arched her eyebrow when she saw Romeo looming beside me, huge and graceful, wearing black jeans and a dark gray henley that matched his eyes. His huge black sheepskin jacket made his shoulders look bigger than ever. Holly met my eye and nodded towards him. "That's probably a good idea."

"What is?"

"Bringing some muscle with you."

Romeo gave a low grunt. "It's nice to see you too, Holly."

She rolled her eyes. "Come on, I've reserved a booth."

We walked inside, handing our jackets to the hostess. The place was filled with mostly older people—ladies in Chanel suits and men wearing flamboyant shirts and sportscoats. The air in the bistro smelled like French pastries—vanilla and custard and caramelized sugar. I inhaled the delicious air gratefully, trying to calm my nerves.

Holly slid into the curved seat. Romeo and I had a little stand-off when we fought over the seat that had the best view of the bistro, facing the door. I gave in and let him usher me into the booth first.

"Don't get used to this," I told him.

"I'm enjoying it while it lasts," he murmured, sliding in beside me.

I settled in and faced Holly. "What's going on? How come you wanted to see me in such a hurry? Is there something going on in the Otherworld Court?"

She hesitated for a second. "I don't know. All I know for sure is I've been fired."

My eyes popped. "You've been *fired?*"

Holly was a hotshot litigation lawyer employed by an Orbiter firm that took cases in both the human and the Otherworld courts. From everything I'd heard about her, she was the shining jewel in the legal industry.

"When?" I spluttered. "And for what?"

Holly shifted in her seat uncomfortably. "For 'unbecoming conduct,'" she said, making little air-quotes with her fingers. "That's all I got before the firm let me go. I managed to get a couple more details out of one of the partners, and one of them told me that there have been several complaints filed against me recently. My boss ignored the first couple, then in the last week, there's been a lot more. The directors decided to search my company laptop." She scowled down at the table. "Apparently, their search led them to the conclusion that I'm a revolutionary with links to terrorist groups."

My mouth dropped open. "What?"

"One of the complaints suggested I was planning to do something very illegal, and the firm decided to let me go before they got any blowback if I was arrested."

Romeo sat forward, fixing Holly with a hard stare. "Were you planning on doing something illegal?"

"Of course not," she said, arching her eyebrow at him.

"Why did they think that, then?"

She sighed. "One of the complaints filed against me included a transcript of something I said in a private phone conversation with a friend in Louisiana. She'd been passed over for a promotion for a very mediocre white man. I was joking around, talking about how I was flipping through my copy of the Anarchist's Cookbook, looking for a nice cocktail recipe."

Romeo's face was stony. "They fired you for jokes."

"Private jokes made in the privacy of my home on my own personal phone," Holly said pointedly. "And it wasn't just that. The original complaints filed against me included accusations of racism, suggesting I threw two of my cases last year because I didn't like the white clients I was representing." She made a face. "To be honest, I didn't—both were absolute assholes who were guilty as sin, but I did my best to defend them, because that's my job." Holly exhaled, a sad, tired sound. "Unfortunately, I didn't exactly hide my disdain for both these men, and the complaints included private emails where I was very forthcoming about it. When you put all this stuff together—the emails, the recordings, the cases I lost, the social media profile where I liked a few BLM posts—you get a picture of a very violent, angry Black woman who hates white people and who is ready to blow the whole world up." She dusted off her hands. "So, they fired me."

Romeo let out a rumble, deep in his chest. "I can get you reinstated. With a raise. And an apology from the partners."

"I don't need you to fight my battles for me, Warlock," she snapped. "And it won't make a difference. People talk. My reputation has been shredded."

"I can hire you myself," Romeo said. "I don't care about reputations, and I need a good lawyer. You're a good lawyer, Holly."

She stared at him for a minute. "Right now, I don't feel like a good *anything*. I feel..." She pinched her eyes closed for a second. "I feel like a fool. Like someone has gotten the better of me. Someone beat me in a game that I didn't even know I was playing. I've been blindsided, and I have no idea what happened."

"I'm so sorry, Holly," I whispered.

"That's not all," she sighed. "I got outed."

I frowned. "What?"

"They outed me. As a lesbian."

The gasp left my mouth before I could stop it. That was not what I'd expected. I shut my mouth again with a click.

In my head, Brain-Daphne threw up her hands, popped some champagne, and squealed. *Wheeeee!*

"I didn't realize," I said weakly.

"I know you didn't." Holly's mouth dropped back into a frown. "But that's the thing that's got me so worried. *Nobody* knew I was gay. I've had one relationship with a woman my whole life, and I had to break it off when my family coven forced me to move here and get engaged to Troy."

"I see." I squinted, trying to think of a way to put it delicately. "Do you think your ex-girlfriend might have...?"

"No." Holly shook her head abruptly. "I checked. Ava has been waiting for me. The second the ink dried on the dissolution of the marriage contract, I was going to move her up here to join me. But now, I got outed, and it's been used against me. It's bad enough that I'm a violent, racist Black woman and a terrorist, but now I'm also a secret lesbian, a liar, and a cheater. My only option is to get out of this city and start fresh. I didn't want to have to go back to Louisiana, but now I have no choice."

I exchanged a meaningful glance with Romeo. Holly's reputation had been ruined in the blink of an eye. The puppet master was pulling some serious strings here.

"I know what that look was about," Holly said, watching us. "Someone is hellbent on ruining my life. Not just mine, but yours, too. I heard about the mysterious giant insect attack on the church and the whole debacle about you getting arrested for Wesley's murder. I was going to offer my services, and bam, the whole mess came tumbling down around me." Her gaze sharpened. "I'm not blaming you, but I need to know if this is all because of you. Is someone trying to stop me from helping you?"

"I don't know," I admitted. "Maybe."

"It could all be because of me," Romeo said. "I'm getting attacked on all fronts, too. I've been thinking. The Jupiters are gone, but Mina was a Mannix. The Mannix covens in Europe still rule the magical community, and they've been putting a lot of pressure on me lately. I suspect it was their UK High Priest who sent Brandon to assassinate me." He glared at the table. "They want me out. Maybe they're making a move now that I killed Mina."

Holly shook her head. "Whoever did all this knows too much personal and sensitive information about me. If it is some foreign coven trying to muscle in on your territory and overthrow you, then it's got me really worried. With you getting attacked by alien bugs and whatnot"—she nodded at me—"and you getting arrested, and me getting fired, we're looking at an incredibly powerful magic user."

The puppet master in my head morphed until he was as big as a genie towering over the whole world.

"Who, though?" Romeo frowned. "There's nobody strong enough in the Mannix coven to challenge me, even if I were weakened financially by attacking my companies and emotionally by attacking Daphne," he said, brushing his hand over my shoulder.

I met his eyes. The alien insect had cut him with an iron athame. It would have poisoned him and made him very sick by now if I hadn't cured him. Did the puppet master know he was part-fae, too?

Romeo glanced away first. "The only people dumb enough to try to challenge me were the Jupiters, but there are no Jupiters left."

"Except for Troy, but even Troy is struggling right now," Holly said, grimacing. "Incidentally, he got fired from his internship yesterday, too. He was working at a commercial law firm downtown. But," she added, shrugging, "if it was a targeted attack, they didn't have to work too hard to get him fired. Mina got him that job, and he barely ever went into the office. He never actually did any work."

That sounded about right. I remember him convincing me to do some of his homework for him when he was with me in Castlemaine. He was so charming and so spoiled.

Holly huffed out a sigh. "He's been crying about his mom and dad nonstop. That poor guy hasn't left his apartment since he had to I.D. Wesley's body. He sits at his computer in the dark playing video games, surrounded by Mina and Wesley's precious things, with tears pouring down his face. He barely says a word. He's lost his mind."

Troy had lost more than that. My chest gave a half-hearted squeeze. Troy was a selfish, cheating asshole fuckboy who had played me, but he wasn't evil like the rest of the Jupiters.

Holly pursed her lips. "I actually feel really bad for him. Mina spoiled the crap out of him. He's an orphan now. He's got nothing."

I felt bad for him too. "Will you keep an eye on him?"

"Sure. I've moved out already, but I'll drop by and see him." She stood up and exhaled. "In the meantime, I'm going to lay low and think about my options for the future."

"My offer still stands," Romeo said. "If you want a job, I'll hire you."

Holly hesitated for a second and glanced at him.

"I just didn't think you were the type to roll over," he

added a little pointedly. "I thought you had more fight in you than that."

"Yeah." Holly heaved a sigh. "I've just been so tired lately. So defeated, you know? For the first time in my entire life, giving up and running away is *so* tempting."

I voiced my thoughts out loud. "Maybe you should get your iron levels checked."

She gave me an amused smile. "I might do that." Her smile vanished. "Before I go, a warning. Whoever is doing this, they're an evil genius with phenomenal magical powers, so be careful." She tossed cash on the table, gave me an air-kiss, and left.

CHAPTER
TWENTY-ONE

"That was interesting," I murmured, watching Holly walk out of the bistro. She was still incredibly graceful, but there was a weariness in her posture—her shoulders were a fraction curved in, and her head wasn't held as high as usual.

"No, it was worrisome," Romeo said quietly. "Holly is the only witch in this entire city who I would be reluctant to fight. She's magically powerful and smart as a whip. There's a reason why the Jupiters were desperate to integrate her into their family. And she looks absolutely defeated."

Something occurred to me. "Does Holly know she's related to you? Your grandmother was her great-great-great aunt. You're like her..." I counted on my fingers. "Second cousin, thrice removed?"

"Oh yeah, she knows. My magical profile indicated that I had LeBeaux blood." He took my hand and helped me out of the booth. "And she gives me cousin sass nobody else would get away with. It's another reason I like her—she hasn't pressed me on the details yet. I think she probably figured it all out ages ago. My mom was her great-great-aunt, and it's common knowledge that Gwendolyn LeBeaux disappeared."

As we left the bistro, an older woman wearing a lace veil reached out and touched Romeo's shoulder. "My lord," she whispered. "May I have a word?"

Brain-Daphne scanned her carefully, noting the veil, the smell of herbs and candlewax, and the fact that Romeo was wearing a glamor to hide his true nature which the woman could see right through. *A crone from Sweetgrass coven. She's safe enough.*

Romeo clearly thought so, too. He glanced down at me apologetically. "I'll just be a second."

I smiled. "No problem. I'll wait right outside."

"Right where I can see you," he ordered.

The hostess handed me my wool coat, and I walked out of the bistro.

The sunlight had dipped low behind the buildings of the city, turning the late winter streets chilly and dark at only four o'clock in the afternoon. I shivered and hugged my wool coat around me. An odd sensation, a deep longing for seasonal awakening, sunk deep into my bones. An intense yearning for the spring crept through me.

Winter was necessary, but I'd had enough of death and decay. My soul longed for the bright spring mornings, the first flowers, the new green shoots. It will happen very soon; I could feel the rebirth in the air. I took a deep breath in, trying to taste a hint of spring.

I froze. The two detectives were coming this way, I could smell them.

I whipped around. Boggs and Hartshorn were striding towards me from the other side of the street, deliberately choosing to approach me from behind—Boggs in a camel trench coat that strained across his belly and Hartshorn swamped in a grey wool overcoat. They swung their arms as they walked.

"Ms. Ironclaw," Boggs boomed, holding up his hand. "Stay where you are, please."

Damn, damn, damn. I had my Orion blades nestled in the sheathes at the small of my back as usual. If they decided to arrest me right now, they'd have the murder weapon, and I was doomed.

I froze like a deer in headlights.

Hartshorn reached me first. "Late lunch?" He smirked at me.

I don't answer questions, Brain-Daphne said sullenly, taking a cue from Marie.

Boggs moved in on my other side, boxing me in against the wall. "Who were you meeting here today, Ms. Ironclaw?"

They already know, Brain-Daphne snarled. *They'll use this against you.*

Gods, she was right. This wasn't a chance encounter. Maybe Holly's phone had been tapped or something, and the detectives had just caught me having a coffee with my ex-boyfriend's fiancé—a woman who had just been fired on suspicion of being a domestic terrorist.

I opened my mouth, unsure of what to say. "This feels like harassment," I managed.

"It's okay. We know all about Holly LeBeaux," Boggs said in a conversational tone. "Heard some crazy stuff about why she was fired. Funny crowd you hang out with, Ms. Ironclaw."

Hartshorn wiped his red nose with the back of his hand. "What were you two discussing today? Troy? I hear she broke off the engagement, and she's out of the closet. A new out-and-proud dyke." He smiled at me. "I suppose you were fucking her, too. Was she in on this with you? Or did you seduce her and turn her against the Jupiters?"

"Was she there when you killed Wesley?" Boggs asked.

My heart began to pound faster.

A shadow fell over them. Suddenly, it got very cold. Boggs fell silent. Hartshorn shivered.

Romeo's voice rolled over them like a tsunami. "Is there something I can help you with, gentlemen?"

Both detectives spun around.

Romeo had dropped his glamor. He stood there in all his overwhelmingly handsome, brutally masculine glory.

Boggs recovered first. "Mr. Zarayan. Good afternoon." He straightened his shoulders, looking determined not to be cowed by Romeo's presence. "We don't need your assistance at this time, thank you."

Romeo's eyes glinted dangerously. "No?"

"No, sir. You can move along." Boggs did an awkward half-turn, desperate to not have to look at Romeo anymore, but too savvy to turn his back on the dangerous thundercloud looming over him. "Thank you for your cooperation," he added.

There was a beat of silence; I could have sworn I felt the pavement under my feet shake ominously. Romeo's eyes flashed. When he spoke again, his tone vibrated with menace. "Is there a reason you're speaking to my girlfriend?"

Hartshorn's eyes widened just for a second. "Girlfriend?"

"Yes. Daphne is my girlfriend. Why are you talking to her?"

They didn't know. Maybe, like everyone else, they refused to believe Romeo would date a nobody like me.

Brain-Daphne let out a snarl. *At this stage, we're going to have to ride him like a rodeo bull in Washington Square before anyone will believe we're together. Yes, let's do that.*

Detective Boggs rocked back on his heels for a second. I could almost hear his brain tick. "We're conducting some inquiries into the death of Wesley Jupiter," he began. For the first time since I met Boggs, he didn't sound so confident.

"I see," Romeo rumbled. The atmosphere grew impossibly tense. "And is Daphne a suspect?"

Hartshorn tried, and failed, to look stern. "We're conducting inquiries, that's all, sir."

Romeo let the silence hang in the air for a moment. "I think you have conducted enough inquiries for now," he said coldly. He moved closer; both detectives edged away.

Romeo took my hand. "Come on, baby. Let's go home." He pulled me away.

CHAPTER
TWENTY-TWO

"You can't kill them." I feinted left, then right, and spun, attempting a roundhouse kick to the face.

Romeo let my kick brush his chest. He was so damned tall. "Yes, I can," he said, throwing a straight-right punch towards my face. "It would be easy. Like falling off a log. Nobody would ever know."

I ducked back and watched his fist as it whistled past my nose in an attempted jab. "They don't deserve it. They're just doing their job. I did check them out, Romeo, and if I thought they deserved to get the crap knocked out of them, I would have done it myself." I tried a side kick; he blocked it with his shin.

Ow. It felt like kicking a concrete post. "But the truth is," I continued, "neither Boggs nor Hartshorn has ever been investigated for corruption, and neither of them have had any complaints of brutality. They're tough men, but they do things by the book. That's why they haven't arrested me yet." I threw a random combination. Romeo held up his arms, taking every single punch, not flinching, as I panted through my next sentence. "There's not enough evidence to hold me now that the hair sample from the autopsy has been destroyed. They're just watching and waiting for me to slip up."

Romeo bounced up and down on his toes, hesitated for a second, dropped his guard, and frowned. "Okay, I wasn't expecting that. Judging from the expression on your face back at the bistro, I assumed they were monsters."

"What do you mean by that?"

He paused. "You were scared, Daphne," Romeo said softly. "They made you scared. You don't get scared." His fists clenched so hard, the bindings on his knuckles ripped. He'd refused to spar with me without gloves, but I hated wearing them, so he'd wrapped up his hands and was pulling his punches. "They frightened you, and I hated it," he growled. "I want to rip their spines out of their bodies."

"Oh. Well, it wasn't them who scared me." I sighed. "Not exactly."

"What was it, then?"

It was a second before I could speak. "It was the thought of being arrested and thrown in human jail. It sounds so cowardly when I say it out loud. I've been trapped in multiple dungeons and locked in numerous towers in my lifetime, but the idea of being locked in a concrete box kinda triggered me." I shrugged, backed away, and started to unwind my own bindings. Sparring with Romeo wasn't working—he pulled his punches, and he smelled so good it was hard to stop Brain-Daphne from biting him. "My body had a visceral response to the threat of human jail. I don't know why."

Something flashed in Romeo's expression—an understanding that I couldn't comprehend. "Oh." He started to unwrap his own ruined bindings, tearing them off his hands.

I looked at him. "Is there something you want to tell me?"

He turned back to me and grimaced. "Yes and no. Remember that memory we took from you before the hunt for The Tear of Zeus? The one we stored in the mnemosyne?"

I shuddered. "Oh, yeah. I forgot about that. Some terrible trauma that was causing me pain, and we had to remove the memory so I could function properly. I suppose the memory was about me being buried in concrete, unable to move." My gut suddenly lurched up, threatening to choke me. Oop, that felt about right.

"Do you want to talk about it?" Romeo asked me tentatively.

"Oh, *hell*, no." I swallowed the echo of darkness, pushing it down, and felt instantly better. "Let's ignore it until we're forced to deal with it. How much time do we have left on the mnemosyne?"

He shrugged. "A month or so."

"Okay, that's good news," I said cheerfully. "For now, it's enough that I know that all this discomfort is because of the deep-seated trauma of some terrible thing that happened to me a long time ago." I exhaled a deep breath, shaking my arms and legs. "*Wooh!* I feel much better now."

Romeo stood very still and stared at me for a moment. "I adore you, did you know that?"

I stared back at him. My cheeks warmed. "Thanks."

"But I still need to do something about those detectives. If they're as good as you say they are, they're not going to stop harassing you. They might not even stop after the case gets handed to Otherworld. Some of those human guys are intuitive, obsessive, and they might chase you forever."

"You can't kill them because they made me uncomfortable, Romeo. And besides, I keep thinking that once I get my act together and get over my trauma heebie-jeebies, I can find out the deal about why they're so sure it was me who did it. Get some clues on who is behind all this, y'know? I don't think they would plant evidence, but my hair was found on the body, and I know I didn't leave it there. If it wasn't them that planted it, then they might know who had access to the body. I could get a name."

Romeo scowled at me. "Okay, then I can maim them a little."

"No maiming!" I threw myself at him, trying for a flying kick. He caught me, spun me around, and slammed me on the mat, pinning me down.

I wiggled with pleasure, gasping for air, grappling with him half-heartedly, our skin slick with sweat, sliding together. The smell of him drove me crazy.

Bite him.

He was so big, so... hard. I felt like the blood rushed to my core all at once. A pulse pounded between my legs.

Bite him!

My breath came in shallow pants. He let his weight rest on me for a brief, delicious moment. I needed more. More...

A voice echoed through the church. "Ew."

I wriggled out from underneath Romeo reluctantly. "Good morning, Marie."

Marie trotted into the training gym like a show pony, coming towards us. Romeo had arranged for Levi to go shopping for clothes for her, and Marie had written a list of what she wanted. She was now wearing wide-legged, high-waisted jorts that came down to her knees, fluffy purple socks with Birkenstock sandals, and a baggy purple-and-fluro green striped shirt that hurt my eyes so badly, I wondered if it was a deliberate choice.

Oh, it's definitely a choice.

Maybe it was. I could barely stand to look at her. The bright stripe color combo reminded me of a highly poisonous beetle.

I kept my gaze fixed between her neck and the top of her head, and my eyes breathed a sigh of relief. Marie was astonishingly pretty. Her creamy skin glowed almost translucent like it was lit from beneath, with a gorgeous peach blush warming her cheeks and button nose. Her eyes shone bright like two emeralds. Thick copper-color hair fell in a smooth wave over her shoulders and down her back.

"Good morning?" Her shell-pink lips pursed up in disapproval. "It's seven-thirty at night, Daphne."

"It's morning for you," I said in my kindergarten teacher's voice. "How did you sleep?"

Marie appeared to be thinking about her answer. "Like a corpse, actually. I read that vampire sleep is like super-charged human sleep, as in, it's supposed to be healing, but the deathsleep only occurs when you have injuries. I didn't have any injuries, but I slept like a corpse."

"It heals mental and emotional injuries too, Marie," I said gently.

She hesitated for a second. "Oh." She nodded approvingly. "That's a good point. I suppose it's likely my brain was damaged by the events of the last few days. My amygdala would have shrunk, and my hippocampus would have enlarged. But now, after my deathsleep, the shock appears to be gone, and I feel a lot more accepting of my current predicament." She gave me a beautiful smile. "Mystery solved. Thanks, Daphne."

"You two are insane," Romeo muttered. "This is like listening to a conversation between a kindergarten teacher and a nutty professor."

I smiled at her. "Does that mean you're okay with not going back to Harvard?"

"Oh, no." Marie laughed like I'd said something silly and shook her head. "I'm still going back. I've already got plans for a full-face UV latex mask"—she held up a finger—

"complete with acne, and I'll get some non-prescription glasses so I look exactly like I used to." She let out an evil chuckle. "Nothing is going to get in my way."

"Except the deathsleep," I reminded her. "Every time you stub your toe or drink too much at a frat party, you'll be deathly unconscious during the daytime. You'll miss a lot of classes."

Marie huffed out a snarl, clenched her fists, threw up her hands, and roared, "God*damnit!*" towards the ceiling.

I exchanged a glance with Romeo, while Marie threw a little tantrum that involved her pacing back and forth on the mat for a minute, stomping her feet, and muttering a combination of imaginative swear words and science-babble under her breath.

What the hell were we going to do with her? I couldn't unleash her on Dennis. But any other nestmaster would either pull out her fangs or brick her into a wall for all eternity.

Romeo frowned and shrugged. I took it to mean, "she can stay here until we figure it out."

I exhaled with relief. Good, because there were no other options.

"This is bullshit," Marie moaned. "What am I supposed to do?" Her shoulders slumped jerkily, and she thumped onto her butt on the mat. "I can't go home."

For the first time, I wondered if Marie was a little delusional. I had already used the DHS records to check the Harvard students, and there was nobody called Marie enrolled in any of the science departments.

Marie was possibly the most least-popular name for a girl her age. But because she said it with so much conviction, it never occurred to me that she might be lying.

"We'll figure something else out," I said.

She wiped her face with her hands. "I suppose I can occupy myself with sorting out your defenses."

"What defenses?"

"The sorry excuse you have for security in this place," she sniffed, wiping her nose. "I get that there's magical wards. Levi explained it all to me, and they sound too basic. Sub-standard, even. You need something offensive, or else that dumb bug will keep smashing against the ward until it gets through."

Romeo stared at her, his expression patient. "Is that why you asked for the particle accelerator?"

"Oh, no," she chuckled, as if it was a silly thing to say. "That was for a little craft project." She tugged a tiny strap around her neck, pulling out a glass vial on a leather necklace. "Made a mini proton pack and caught myself a ghost. I hope you don't mind, Mr. Zarayan, but I triboelectricity-charged some resin and used your 3D printer to make an unbreakable, positively charged container."

I stared at her. Then, I looked at the glass vial, sniffed carefully, and caught the tiny hint of closely packed, negatively charged ions with a hint of burned wool and smoke. "Marie..." My eyes narrowed. "Did you ghostbuster Father Benedict?"

"Yeah." She eyeballed me back. "But he deserved it, Daphne. He was bugging me in the library. I swear I kept hearing him shouting about me being the whore of the devil." She shrugged. "I'm an atheist, so I don't believe in the devil. I'm just a whore, thank you very much."

I put my hands over my face. Vampires had heightened senses just like I did, so I wasn't surprised that Marie could sense Father Benedict berating her from beyond the veil. After a moment, I dropped my hand and fixed her with a stern stare. "Let the ghost out, Marie."

"No!" She clutched the vial. "He's mine. He can be my pet. I'll take good care of him, I promise!"

This girl is nuts, I love her.

I looked at Romeo, who shrugged. "Benedict *is* a bit of an asshole," he said under his breath. "Maybe this will force him to move on. It could be good for him."

"See?" Marie scuttled over to Romeo and leaned into his side like a cat—an odd display of what I assumed was affection. "Mr. Zarayan thinks this is a good idea!"

I heaved a sigh. "Just... okay, we'll revisit this topic at a later date. What were you saying about the defenses?"

"Right. Well, there's one thing that will stop a giant alien bug..."

"Beheading?" I said, a little moodily.

"No, Daphne," she said in a *duh* tone. "I mean, that might work with the bug, but I remembered what Mr. Zarayan said about the hydra. We can't take any chances." She gave us a brilliant smile. "So, I think forty thousand volts of electricity would do it."

"Of course," I muttered.

"I found a roll of electrical cable and a generator in your storeroom, and I think with a little maneuvering, I can set up a perimeter on the inside of the wards. A tripwire that will send a giant bug to hell if it gets through the wards."

"You terrify me," I said, shaking my head.

Marie blushed. "Thanks."

I glanced at Romeo. "Yes, or no?"

He frowned. "Maybe."

"Too bad, I already did it," Marie said cheerfully, rocking back on her heels and clicking her fingers. "I can't stay here if your defenses aren't up to scratch. I'm not getting murdered by an alien on my second night as a vampire." She hesitated and made a guilty face. "You, uh.

You might want to tell the other guys to not touch the wire."

"Marie..." Romeo glared at her and sighed. "Forget it. I think most of the guys are in the garage. I'll go tell them." He moved backwards, stepping into the dark corner of the room.

The shadows moved around him... then stopped. They didn't swallow him completely like they normally did.

Something was wrong. "Romeo?"

He gave a little growl of frustration.

I shot a look over to Marie. She was watching the corner carefully, her lips pressed together.

It only took him a second. "Marie." His voice sent a shiver down my spine. "What... what did you *do?*"

"Sorry," she said in a little voice. "I couldn't help myself."

"You stuck a glow star on my butt?"

"I just wanted to test—"

Romeo loomed out of the shadows, his expression one of very tightly controlled fury. On the tip of his finger, a tiny luminescent star threw a faint greenish-yellow glow. He glared down at her. "Are you *kidding* me?"

Marie had the grace to look ashamed. "Sorry. My curiosity got the better of me."

He exhaled through his nose. "I'm not your enemy, Marie." He had to bite the words out through clenched teeth. "You don't need to find my Achilles heel."

"Yes, sir. You're right." She nodded seriously. "I don't." Under her breath, she added, "I already know what it is anyway, I just have to stab you with an old fork, and you'll go down like a lead balloon."

A dangerous rumble rolled through the room.

"Okay! Okay, I'm sorry. I have problems with impulse control, I know." She put her hands together, steepling her fingers. "I apologize, sir. Please, I beg you. I can't bear another lecture."

Romeo took a deep breath through his nose and exhaled carefully. "Marie, we're going to have to have a serious talk about respect. You respect my privacy, and I'll respect yours. Got it?" He pointed at her. "Otherwise, I might be compelled to start calling you by your real name."

I gaped at him.

Does he know her real name?

Of course he did. I hadn't had time to dig into her background, and now that she was a vampire, it was mostly pointless, because she couldn't go back to her old life, anyway. But Romeo had a whole security team who could find out who Marie was almost instantly.

Marie's gaze turned suspicious. "No. You haven't found out—"

"Don't test me, Mu—"

She flew forward. "NO!!! Oh, please, sir, no. Don't say it. Please!" Putting her hands together in the prayer position again, she fell to her knees on the mat in front of us. "Please! I hate that frickin' name more than life itself. I've been counting down the days until I turn eighteen so I can legally change it to Marie!"

Just then, I got it. I pointed at her. "You chose to call yourself Marie, because of Marie Curie, right?"

"Of course. First woman to win a Nobel prize, and I'm going to be the first woman to win a whole bunch of them." She shrugged. "It was either that or Mary Shelly."

Figures. Of course Marie was a fan of the woman who created Frankenstein.

Romeo scowled down at her, crossing his arms over his chest. It made his biceps pop in a way that made me almost swoon. "You're on thin ice, Marie. I understand you're a curious young woman with a thirst for knowledge, but if you continue to test my boundaries, I promise you I will start to call you by your real name, *and* I will use all my magic to force you to sit through a thirty-hour lecture on scientific ethics."

"*Nooo*," she moaned sadly. "Anything but that. I'll behave, I promise."

"First of all, you're grounded. You're not to leave this church, and you're not allowed outside in the yard. Besides," Romeo added, "you might electrocute yourself."

"I know where I put the tripwire," Marie said sulkily. "Ooh, yeah," she added, her expression turning guiltily, "you might want to go and tell your buddies about that wire really, really soon. If you want them to live, that is. Sorry again."

Romeo pointed at her. "Go to the security room, right now," he said. "Levi is in there, monitoring the wards. For the next six hours, you're on security detail. Watch the cameras. No experiments, no messing with anything electrical, no blowing anything up. Do you hear me?"

Marie pouted. "Yes, sir." Hanging her head, she stomped off, out of the gym.

"That was...that was certainly something." I turned to Romeo. "You will make an excellent dad one day."

"God help me if I ever have a teenage daughter like her," he growled, tapping on his phone for a second, letting the others know about the livewire around the church.

"She's not really a teenager, is she? More like a mad professor in a young woman's body." I frowned in the direction she had walked off to. "I didn't even know you had a security room."

"*She* does. Marie has already checked out our entire monitoring system and run tests on all our security. She criticized it so much, Micah got his feelings hurt, so I've sent him and Cole off to run some errands in the city tonight."

A huge sigh escaped my lips. "I don't know what I'm going to do with her."

"If she didn't drive us all so crazy, I would suggest that we keep her here," Romeo said mildly. "She's absolutely brilliant. But she's offended Micah, Levi is wary of her, and Brandon is downright scared that she'll do something to set him off, so he's avoiding her like she has leprosy. And Cole..." Romeo made a face and exhaled roughly. "Cole is head-over-heels in love with her."

"Really? I didn't expect that. She was so mean to him!"

"It appears Cole enjoyed it very much. Apparently, he likes being dominated by a smart-mouthed woman. Marie thinks Cole is a sad and pathetic young boy. Cole enjoyed the humiliation."

I tapped my chin. "I could have gone my whole life not knowing that."

"That's why I sent him out with Micah tonight. Don't worry"—he took my hand—"I'll get him some therapy."

I took a deep breath. "What am I going to do with her?"

"We'll think of something. Come on," he said, pulling me closer.

Just then, an alarm gave an ear-piercing *whoop*. I jumped in fright.

The hell?

"Incoming," Marie's tinkling voice chimed over the intercom like a bell. "We have incoming bogies approaching the southwest fence." She paused. "Wait. Confirming single bogie approaching the southwest fence. Just the one bogie."

Romeo cursed.

"We're taking heavy fire at the southwest fence," Marie

continued, sounding distinctly excited. "The alien is coming in. I repeat, the alien is coming in. *Wheee!*"

"Stay here," Romeo growled, stalking off towards the hallway.

"Not a chance." I followed him. I'd only taken two steps before a wild explosion came from outside. The stone floor shook underneath my feet. The acrid smell of burned steel hit my nose, making my head spin.

"Ooh, this alien has some heavy-duty weaponry," Marie added over the intercom, sounding impressed. "Not artillery. We're looking at embedded high-tech lasers."

Another explosion shook the church. Loud rumbling tore through the room. Romeo hesitated and looked up. "This monster is going to tear this whole place down trying to get in." He strode forward. "I have to stop it."

Boom. Boom boom boom.

Multiple explosions shook the church. I shifted my gait, moving into sea-legs mode so I could keep up with Romeo without losing my balance. We teetered towards the hallway, arms out.

"Southwest fence is now a glowing tangle of iron," Marie said cheerfully over the loudspeaker. "It looks like orange spaghetti." A male voice said something. Marie hissed. "What? No, I have the comm. Get off. I'll tell them." She cleared her throat. "Levi believes the hard ward is cracking. The alien is coming in."

Zip-Boom, zip-boom.

The church shuddered again. A carved gargoyle shook loose and fell from the ceiling, smashing on the floor in front of me. I leapt back just in time.

"Oooh," Marie gasped. "I have a clear visual on the bogie."

Romeo bolted down the hallway. I followed him into the living room, where he hesitated for a brief second. "I need to stabilize the grounds," he shouted, clenching his fists and spreading his palms in front of him. "Once the church is stable, I'll drop the wards and let it come." Power poured into his hands, glowing violet. "If Marie's electric tripwire doesn't kill it, it should at least disable it enough so I can finish it off."

Magic surged, dripping from his fingers as he muttered words of power while he ran towards the exit. He threw the door open. The air outside was thick with smoke.

It sounded like a space battle. The alien was firing at the ward near the front gate, over and over, trying to bash its way in. My senses reeled, overwhelmed.

"It doesn't look like an alien." Marie's voice over the intercom was scornful. "And it's not an insect, it's a giant scorpion. Scorpions are arachnids, not insects. Y'all are stupid."

I froze in my tracks. *No. It couldn't be.*

Another explosion shook me. I stumbled.

Romeo dropped to one knee, planting a glowing hand on the ground.

"A giant scorpion. It's the size of a frickin' big horse." Marie's voice perked up. "Wait. Wait! I think the lasers are coming out of its eyes. Whoa. That's *so* cool."

My heart leapt into my throat. No.

A giant scorpion with laser beams for eyes.

The ground beneath my feet suddenly stilled. "It's done. Levi, drop the wards!" Romeo roared. "Let it come!" He stood up, massive shoulders tensed, and spread his arms out, drawing more magic towards him, muscles bulging with the strain of holding so much power in one glorious, god-like body.

My heart hammered out of control. Oh, no. She's going to hit the tripwire. It could kill her.

How could we have been so stupid? Run, you idiot!

I ran.

The night air whipped past me as I bolted, pushing every ounce of strength I had. Adrenaline pulsed through me, and time slowed.

My senses went into overdrive. Burned metal, ploughed earth, smoke, and Romeo's explosive magical scent hit me like an ethereal punch as I blew past him...

The giant scorpion reared up in front of me, only ten feet away, her stinger hovering high up in the air, glittering with poison. She saw me. She came closer.

"No!" Romeo shouted. "Daphne! Get back here!"

My vision sharpened on the ground—there. A spicy current surging through a metal wire. I jumped.

"Daphne!"

There was no time to explain. I held up my arms right in front of the giant scorpion and skidded to a halt. "Stop!"

Romeo was too close. She was too angry. She didn't stop. A claw flung out, snatching me up by the waist, and she yanked me to her chest, holding me there firmly. Her legs splayed, cutting my vision completely. I was caught in a tiny cage made of impenetrable chitin armor.

Romeo's roar shook the heavens. *"Daphne!"*

With a clatter of armored legs, the giant scorpion turned around and dashed away with me caught in the trap of her arms.

CHAPTER
TWENTY-THREE

The scorpion didn't let me go until we'd gotten to the Hidden City, and by then, I was so furious, I could barely speak.

The City was silent as she carried me through the park, heading to the East Tower. In a blink of an eye, she clattered into the building, stomped across the atrium, climbed effortlessly up two flights of steps, and stalked down the corridor. She kicked open a door on the second floor and carried me inside.

I unclenched my jaw. "I see you got one of the four-bedroom places. How the hell did you manage that? The waitlist for anything bigger than a two-bedder is over five years."

She didn't say anything, but then again, she wasn't capable of human speech right now. Dumping me into a chair by the table, the scorpion clattered backwards, watching me with her terrifying pitch-black eyes.

I lifted my chin. "I suppose you need the extra space. Considering you're running around Philadelphia in your most monstrous form."

The scorpion twitched.

Magic punched me. Her body morphed, instantly melting into the shape of a woman—tall, skinny, with long pitch-black hair, pearl-colored skin, and flashing dark almond-shaped eyes. It had been years since I'd seen her, but she looked the same as she always had, ferocious and gorgeous. She even manifested a typical tiny outfit, a cherry-red crop top and skintight jeans.

She glared at me, wrestled a phone out of her jeans, dialed, and put it to her ear. "I've got her, Cindy."

My brain gave a whine. *We're so stupid. We're so, so stupid. Cindy even told us the whole story, and we didn't put it together.*

She spoke into the phone again. "Yeah, she's safe. And unharmed, from what I can see. Now, we just need to figure out how to break the spell she's under."

I heaved a sigh. "I'm not under a spell, Prue."

Prue Nakai, the daughter of the Beast, watched me suspiciously. "Well, she looks fine," she said into the phone. "But she did throw herself at me as soon as she was able to, so I think you're right, she is still in there somewhere. He was holding her hostage, but whatever spell she's under can be broken."

"Prue..." I pinched the bridge of my nose. "Romeo was *not* holding me hostage."

Prue turned away from me and hissed through her teeth. "What do you mean, you don't know how? Just ask Damon, he'll be able to come up with something to break it." She turned back, and her eyes ran over me. "How about I dip her in salt water? That should wash it off."

"Prue," I moaned. "Romeo *didn't* put me under a spell. I was with him voluntarily. There was literally no reason to bash your way into the church to rescue me."

Prue put the phone back to her ear. "Of course she's denying it, Cindy."

I cupped my hands over my mouth. "Cindy, Romeo is not a monster! I'm sorry I didn't get a chance to explain that to you before you flew out of the window of the office!"

I could hear Cindy's squeaky voice over the line. "Bullshit," she peeped. "He's the devil. He killed Aunt Marche!"

I groaned. This was all so stupid.

"And he put you under a spell to make you his sex-slave!"

My head whipped up. "He *what?*"

Prue hit a button on the phone, putting Cindy on the loudspeaker. "Yes, he did! I have evidence!"

"You don't have any evidence!" I shouted. "Because it *didn't happen!*"

Cindy snapped. "I didn't scrape up every single scrap of courage I had in my body to go to D.C. and make amends with my best friend because I was so scared for your safety just on a hunch, Daphne. The whole office has been talking about it!"

I shook my head, bewildered. "What the actual hell are you talking about, Cindy?"

Prue knelt in front of me and put her hands on either side of my face, squashing my cheeks. "Daphne," she said loudly. "I know you're in there. You. Have. To. Break. Free. Of. The. Spell!"

I smacked at her hands until she backed away. "Enough. That's enough!"

"Oh, she's *definitely* under a spell." Prue made a face. "She just got all snappy with me. That's not like her."

"I'm pissed you would think I was stupid enough to get myself put under a spell! I'm used to my enemies underestimating me. But Prue..." I shook my head. "You *know* me."

"He's the *Warlock!*" Prue roared back. "He murdered the most powerful and intelligent woman I've ever known!"

"Okay, stop." I stood up and held out my hands. "This is just one big misunderstanding, Prue. And I—"

A boom of thunder sounded in the distance. Oh, no.

My hand went to my chest, where the little crystal hung between my boobs. *He's coming.*

I took a deep breath. "Listen, Prue. And listen hard, because Romeo's coming, and he doesn't know it was you attacking the church."

"Well, he's about to find out. I won't shift this time." She squared her shoulders and glared into the distance. "I could fight that pissant as a little crested chicken."

"No! Please, just listen. Prue. Please?"

She huffed out a breath. "Fine. Go head, get it out of your system," she muttered, walking away from me. "Talk loudly so I can still hear you while I run the bath."

"Run the...?" I blew out an exasperated breath.

"Bring me the salt, would you? We have to get this spellbreaking bath going."

Bang. I ducked and covered my head with my hands as an explosion shook the apartment. A second later, I peeked, and saw the apartment door shattered into tiny fragments, floating like heavy mist in the air. Slowly, the fragments settled on the ground.

Romeo stood in the doorway.

Magic rolled over me, and behind me, Prue exploded too, morphing into a bigger, more terrifying scorpion. Her eyes glowed red. The air vibrated.

I took a step in front of Prue and held out my hands. "No."

Romeo let out an inhuman growl. "Daphne. Come here."

I swiveled on my feet to face him. Prue made little squeaky noises behind me and poked me with her pinchers.

"Daphne..." He slammed a hand against the doorframe and swore. "Why the hell did I make these wards so strong?" His jaw clenched. A steely determination shone in his eyes. "I can break it."

"NO!" I waved my arms frantically. "Romeo, no! For goodness sake, won't you two please listen to me?" I pointed at the scorpion behind me and fixed Romeo with a hard stare. "It's *Prue*. For some reason, she thought you had taken me hostage and put me under a spell. She's been trying to rescue me, not attack you!"

There was a pause. Prue made a chittering noise. If I understood scorpion language, I bet she was saying something like, "yes, but I was *also* trying to kill you."

I turned for a split second, so I could glare at her. "You could have called me. You could have picked up the phone and called me and asked me." I raised my voice. "You too, Cindy. You should have talked to me. I know neither of us realized who either of us were. I didn't know you were Prue's gothflower friend, and you didn't know I was Prue's little wolf girl friend who went missing."

"I figured it out the second I saw him waiting for you in the office," Cindy's voice squeaked out of the speaker. "I remembered the gossip posts that Judy was laughing about, and suddenly it all made sense."

"What gossip posts? And... you should have *talked to me!*"

The unbearable tension in the atmosphere died down a little, but I was still furious. This whole thing was such a stupid misunderstanding.

"It would have been pointless!" Cindy's voice floated out of the phone. "You were under a spell. The ultimate betrayal! We all saw the post, and we all heard the gossip! I know what you were doing!"

"What? Cindy, what are you *talking* about?"

"Judy has been laughing over those social media posts for days," Cindy explained, "The ones in the private coven chat groups. I like spying on her, and I saw her laughing about something from an anonymous member talking about how the High Priest was enacting his final act of ultimate humiliation on the former High Priestess by magically enslaving one of her beloved young friends. His plan was to use her as a sex slave until she was all worn out, then throw her into the street. It was his final act of dominance. He was pissing on Aunt Marche's grave by defiling one of her grandchildren!"

"What the...?" For a moment, I was speechless. "That's... that's horrible."

The air around me pulsed with magic. Romeo's face was terrible. He was disgusted, too.

The scorpion behind me chittered, skittering her feet on the linoleum floor menacingly. Her anger felt so potent. I took a deep breath and exhaled, feeling sick to my stomach.

But at least now, it all made sense. Cindy heard some awful gossip about Romeo's intentions, then realized all at once that I was Prue's little wolf friend who'd gone missing, and I was now in awful danger from the powerful evil warlock who killed Aunt Marche. So, she bolted back to D.C. to find Prue and sent her to rescue me.

And Prue, of course, attacked in her most favored battle form, the giant scorpion with laser beams for eyes. I'd never seen it before, but I'd heard Chloe talk about it. I should have realized who it was ages ago.

But— "Who would write something like that?" I exhaled, shaking my head. "Who would spread such awful rumors?"

The puppet master, obviously. Whoever it is, they knew too much. They must have realized that by posting such awful things about Romeo, it would stir up the supe royals to come and kick his ass.

My brain kicked me. *Judy. It's fucking Judy, I bet you.*

"Daphne." Romeo's tone was hard. "Can you please step away from the Beast's daughter?"

The scorpion clattered dangerously. Her eyes flashed red.

"Shush." I held up my finger. "Keep your lasers to yourself, Prue, I'm thinking. And no, I don't want to move, because I know that if I do, you two will attack each other."

It could be Judy, Brain-Daphne hissed. *She's a witch. She's got contacts in the human DHS, so it makes sense that she's got contacts in other places. The coroner's office, maybe. Someone could have planted our hair for her.*

It couldn't be. While it was possible she might have picked up a strand of my hair at some point, Judy wasn't influential enough to pull this off.

And she wasn't close enough to any of the players in this game. Whoever was doing all this had intimate knowledge of things that were secret. Someone had rummaged through Holly's personal life like a housewife at a yard sale looking for treasure.

And besides, Judy thought I was a dumb little nobody. Whoever posted that gossip on the coven group chat did it for this very reason. They would have known how important I was to both Romeo and to the supe royals. They would have known it would lead to a fight.

Who could have known that spreading that kind of gossip about Romeo and me would mean that Prue—or Chloe, or Imogen, or even Sandy, dragging the twins with her—would charge in here to try and kill him?

Romeo stood at the doorway. "Daphne... don't make me

do this. I can blow the ward, but the magical backlash might hurt you."

That was an understatement. The wards on the apartments were sewn into the fabric of the Hidden City pocket dimension. He could collapse the entire City.

He'd do it, too. He reached out his hand. "Come here," he said, his voice lowering. "She's dangerous."

"Romeo. So are you. Both of you are superpowered halfbreeds with balls of steel." I pointed at him. "You need to communicate. None of this would have happened if you had been honest about what'd happened between you and Aunt Marche."

Romeo's jaw clenched. He didn't say anything.

Behind me, Scorpion-Prue's legs skittered on the floor restlessly. I felt a throb of deep sadness fill the room. It was coming from both of them.

"You don't have to carry your grief alone anymore," I said to Romeo gently. "You can let it go."

He stared at me. The sudden silence felt enormous and loud. I could hear his heart thumping in his chest.

"Please," I whispered. "I'm begging you."

There was a pop of magic, and suddenly Prue was standing behind me again, back in her skinny jeans and red crop top. Her face was wet with tears.

"Go on, then, you fucking monster," she said, her voice thick. "Tell me why you killed her."

Romeo exhaled. His huge shoulders slumped, defeated, as if the weight of the world was crushing him. "Marcheline was dying of cancer. We were working together, trying to figure out what was causing the Great Suffocation when I found out. And as soon as I stumbled on the letter from the doctor, I realized what was causing the Suffocation. Christopher and Trion Jupiter had tied the Great Agreement back to her, hoping it would weaken her again like it had when she first nursed it back to life after the whole Conclave debacle."

"Oh," Prue gasped softly, raising her eyebrows. "Oh!"

"The death magic inside her fed the magic of the Agreement, creating a continuous power loop, so the Agreement ballooned out of control, suffocating magical creatures in the street. I knocked her out and severed the magical tie. The Suffocation stopped immediately."

Prue said nothing. She just glared off into the distance, refusing to look at Romeo. I watched her face as it all sunk in for her.

The cause of the Great Suffocation had been a mystery for years now. Aunt Marche tried to tell the world about it after her death, but Romeo stopped her letters from going out to the leaders of the Otherworld because he was so angry at her. He *wanted* to be the villain.

And Prue had always thought that Romeo killed Aunt Marche because he blamed her for it. Romeo closed his eyes. The pain in his face made me want to cry. "After it was all over, Marcheline asked me to perform a spell in public, in front of the local coven, to cure her cancer. Instead, she reversed the spell so it killed her." He paused and swallowed. "She was tired. She didn't want to live, and she wanted to have a clear and indisputable line of succession so I could take over as High Priest. By killing her in a public challenge, I could step straight into the role. She engineered everything."

Prue wiped her face with her hands. "What a bitch," she said, choking back her tears. "But... that does sound exactly like something she would do."

"Exactly."

She took a deep breath. "But why didn't you tell anyone this?"

"Because I hated her for it."

"That's fair. But dude... I was *actually* going to kill you once I got back from Delaware. It's even on my to-do list. Look." Prue pulled out a piece of paper out of her pocket, unfolded it, and held it up. Underneath "toys for the twins" and just above "new hat for mom" were the words "torture and kill new high priest in horrible ways."

She folded the paper back up and shoved it into her pocket. "Why didn't you—" Prue glanced up, met Romeo's eye, paused and frowned. "Have we met before?"

"No. I don't think so."

"There's something very familiar about you, that's all." She squinted at him for a moment. "You remind me of someone. I can't quite figure out who it is, though."

Romeo's expression turned grim. "If you're about to tell me that you murdered a fae man who looked like me at some point, I wouldn't be mad about it."

Prue chuckled. "Daddy issues, huh? Me too." She took one more deep breath, shaking off the ghosts of the past, and waved her hand. "Come on in, brother."

"No offence," Romeo muttered, walking inside. "But I *really* hope I'm not your brother."

Prue held out her hand for him to shake and grinned at him widely. "If you hurt Daphne, Warlock, I will pull your heart out through your chest."

He eyeballed her back, squeezing her hand. "And if you hurt Daphne, I will tear off your head with my bare hands."

Oh hey, it's a party. Dwayne strutted inside the apartment, gave a little hop, and jumped up to land on Romeo and Prue's hands. **How've you been, Bones?**

Prue's eyes bulged. "Dwayne? Where have you been, you bastard? Chloe has been worried sick about you!"

Ha ha. Whoops. Dwayne hopped back onto the ground and sauntered away, heading over to Prue's fridge. **Probably should have told her where I was going. My bad.**

I put my head in my hands. "This is ridiculous. Have none of you ever heard of a cell phone?"

Dwayne waved a wing at me. **I'm working on holding a shotgun before I tackle social media, baby girl. Priorities.**

Cindy squeaked out of the phone. "I would have called you, but I figured there was no point. You were under a spell!"

Romeo wrapped his arm around me. I leaned into him and said, "The puppet master pulled your strings too, Cindy."

"What?"

"The puppet master. Whoever posted that gossip on the coven chat was doing it on purpose to provoke a response from the people who care about me. If it wasn't Cindy, someone else would have gotten word to my friends and family that the Warlock had put me under a spell and was planning on ruining me just to stick it to Aunt Marche. This was a very well-planned, meticulous assault from some scheming mastermind who knows us all very well." I hissed through my teeth. "And I can't figure out who it is!"

Cindy piped up. "It's obviously Judy. Let's kill her!"

My brain thought so, too, but my gut—always the voice of reason between head and heart—told me Judy wasn't capable of all of this.

"What?" Prue squinted at me. "What puppet master?"

"Whoever is trying to ruin our lives. This is a coordinated, targeted attack." I pointed at Prue. "Why did you leave the fae stuff outside my door?"

She frowned. "I didn't."

"The bozan blade? The rose encased in enchanted ice? The doll with its head missing?"

She shook her head. "Nope, not me. They sound like very specific threats."

Romeo cleared his throat. "We thought it was you. We tied the attacks on the church and the items left on Daphne's door together because they happened at roughly the same time."

"And I couldn't pick up your scent or the person who left the stuff outside my door, so I figured it was the same person." But now that I thought about it, I did pick up Prue's scent outside the church—it was that fiery spice-berry I'd noted and assigned to a pizza delivery guy. I knew it was someone I loved. "We figured the stuff were either gifts or threats."

"Nope." Prue shook her head. "They're not either of those. I read about this in one of mom's books on fae culture. It's a challenge. The blade says, 'come and fight me,' the rose in ice says, 'you can't put this dispute on hold for any longer,' and the doll with its head missing"—she shrugged—"that's self-explanatory."

"Can you elaborate?"

"It means you are a stupid baby, and I will take your head off," Prue said. "It sounds just like a fae challenge. What fae have you pissed off lately?"

Romeo grimaced. "I've just accepted the fact my biological father was most likely a high fae. I've sworn an oath to destroy him for what he did to my mother, but I haven't even started the hunt for him yet."

"Huh." Prue gave him an odd look and held up her finger. "I'm going to get back to you on that one. Anyone else?"

"No." *Only the daughter of the Winter Queen.* "It still could be Asherah, I suppose. She can mask her scent."

I told you, Asherah is cool. I sent a letter explaining everything, and she sent back a message to tell me she understood and forgave me. Dwayne beamed up at me. **She also sent a little goblin to sing me a song about all**

the things she wanted to stick in my butt. It was very sweet.

I blew out a breath. "I can't think of any other fae who would want to challenge me, though. If you say you've smoothed everything over with your girlfriend, sir, then I believe you. But if she's changed her mind for some reason..."

I didn't want to think about that. The idea of someone being able to manipulate Asherah was terrifying.

"My gut is telling me this is all related," I mumbled. "It's the same person behind all of this."

"Everything okay, boss?" Levi appeared in the doorway, panting, with Brandon close behind. A quick inhale told me that Micah was lingering by the elevator.

"Who is staying with Marie?" I asked.

Brandon looked guilty. "Cole volunteered. By the way, there's two human detectives staking out the church. They're watching us closely, so we can't get out there to repair the wards."

The detectives were still stalking me. A soft snarl left my lips. Fury tore through me, hot and overwhelming. Suddenly, I could barely contain the surge of emotion.

I needed to stab something in the worst way. "We need to figure out who this puppet master is," I ground out. "But I can't even identify the puppets. I don't know who posted that horrible gossip on the coven group chat. I don't know who planted my hair in Wesley's hands. I don't know who set up Holly LeBeaux and outed her. The *one* concrete lead I have is Lieutenant Chet Stanley, the Otherworld Liaison."

"Ugh," Prue said, grimacing. "Liaisons are the worst. They're usually Orbiters with the biggest chips on their shoulders." She raised her eyebrows and turned to her phone lying on the table. "Cindy? Do you think you can do your thing?"

I frowned. "What thing?"

Prue smiled. "Cindy is an excellent hacker."

"I am," she chirped. "I developed my computer skills when I got enslaved to a methmage in Michigan. He abducted me to make aphrodisiac pills, but seriously overestimated my output, so he put me to use setting up webcam sites for his girlfriends. Give me a second, I'll see what I can find out. Let me see..." Faint tapping came from the phone. "Chet Stanley. Hmm. Nothing on the watch lists. Lieutenant at the Philadelphia P.D. and single, originally from Baltimore, both sets of grandparents from Ireland. No red flags so far. His socials are pretty boring. There's an aunt here on his Facebook who has a nice triquetra tattooed on her wrist. Yep, she's a witch. His own mom is an anti-vaxxer; she's posted some seriously unhinged stuff. Let me see... oh, yeah, his mom and his aunt are estranged. So, he's an Orbiter because of some immediate witch family, but nothing to suggest he's biased. He has a Jack Russell called Max. He's a boxing fan—"

I jumped.

He's a boxing fan.

My eyes met Romeo's. "How much of a boxing fan?" I asked.

"Huge," Cindy said. "He belongs to a ton of fan pages. I'm scrolling through his posts now. He's a fanboy, that's for sure."

There was a beat of silence. "Lennox fucking Arran," Romeo growled. "I should have known."

I couldn't believe it. Lennox Arran did all this? Nowhere in my imagination did I think he'd be the puppet master. Lennox was a blunt instrument—vainglorious, bombastic, and unapologetic. And besides, this kind of manipulation would require the cooperation of witches, and Lennox had always been righteously xenophobic.

He did use people, though. During the Suffocation, he travelled with a team of wizards who kept him safe, and he hired witches to secure the compound, layering wards to keep out anyone that didn't have a dual animal nature.

It didn't quite feel right. But finally, I had both a target and an outlet for my rage.

Romeo took my hand.

I looked up at him. "Let's go break things."

CHAPTER
TWENTY-FOUR

The shifter compound loomed before me, a squat building with hard raw concrete edges and minimal windows set back in deep porches—a modern castle and a perfect example of brutalist architecture. Behind me, a giant bronze statue of Lennox Arran loomed at the edge of the Woodlands, right on the edge of the public space so the humans could worship him. It was hard to walk past it without both cringing in secondhand embarrassment and snarling in fury.

I stood at the gate and pressed the buzzer. The intercom clicked. A male voice spoke. "Yes?"

"Daphne Ironclaw to see the Alpha."

There was a buzz, then the line opened again. "You may enter." A split-second later, I heard Lennox hoot in the background. "About time! Come on in, baby!"

I ground my teeth.

The gate clicked and rolled open. I walked inside the grounds.

A long gravel path stretched before me, leading to the thick iron double-doors. On either side lay a whole football field worth of dry, bare earth. It was a killing field, designed to hold off invaders. I knew Alexei Minoff, the former Alpha, stationed snipers on the roof of the compound, and Lennox wasn't a fool, so he would have kept them. At least two of them would be training their sights right between my eyes.

Romeo grunted in my earpiece. "I don't like this."

Tell your boyfriend to relax. Dwayne waddled next to me happily, his little webbed feet making adorable *crunch crunch* noises on the gravel. **I've got this.**

"Dwayne says to relax," I whispered.

"Is he... Is he planning on making himself any bigger?"

I glanced down at Dwayne waddling happily beside me. He *was* a little smaller than usual. "Probably not. To be fair, he *is* a god of chaos. They don't tend to be big planners."

Romeo let out a little grumble in my earpiece. He could see what was going on thanks to a tiny camera in my pocket. I'd gone for battle-casual gear—black cargo pants, fitted at the ankle, black combat boots, and a long-sleeved ballistics t-shirt with an armored puffer vest overtop to keep me warm.

Dwayne wasn't even packing his Glock. He just waddled next to me, letting out little cheeps and cackles. I couldn't even sense the fathomless depths of chaos within him.

"Don't worry, Romeo." I looked down at Dwayne fondly. "He's doing his little happy-feet dance and singing a little song, which is always a good sign."

Gonna rip out some were-spines, Dwayne sang. **Gonna bitch-slap some hairy hoes.**

Romeo didn't say anything.

It went against every instinct Romeo had to let me go into Lennox Arran's lair by myself, but there was no way around it. Only those with animal natures were allowed inside the compound. The wards were designed to keep witches, fae, and vampires out. Orbiters were allowed, but that was it.

Prue wanted to come too. She could turn into any animal she wanted, so the wards might let her inside, but I talked her out of it. I needed to question Lennox, not eviscerate him on-sight. We still didn't know for sure if he was our puppet master. So, Prue stayed behind at her apartment in the East Tower with Cindy still on the line, busy trying to crack whoever was behind those anonymous social media posts. Cindy had already compiled a list of suspects at the coroner's office that might have been bribed into leaving my hair on Wesley's body.

Romeo and the rest of the coven—minus Cole, who was with Marie at the church—were waiting in the SUV on the edge of the Woodlands, within quick sprinting distance. All of them were ready for battle, sheathed in ballistics gear, and packing more weapons than a gun show in Texas.

Romeo still wasn't happy about me going in by myself. But he understood that if he were to breach the wards and come with me anyway, it would be considered an act of war on the shifter population. He reluctantly conceded that the innocent shifters who lived in the compound's barracks would be sent to fight to protect their Alpha.

They didn't deserve to die for Lennox's pride.

I looked up towards the compound. Two grizzled-looking men in black suits and earpieces stood at the entrance. Werewolves, by the smell of them, both hairy men, one dark, the other with a mop of gray curls. They both leered at me as I approached.

"Look, it's Snow White and one of her woodland creatures," one of them snickered.

"Are you looking for your seven dwarves, missy?"

"I'm here to see Lennox," I said shortly. "Open the door."

Neither moved. They just eyed me lecherously. The one on the left leaned casually against the wall.

I groaned out loud. It had been so long since I'd spent any time in a pack, I'd forgotten all about Alpha shifter culture.

It was exhausting. The posturing, the standoffs, the unrelenting misogyny, the violence, the constant need to prove yourself. In these places, there was no room for softness. No room for the heart. Only the strong survived.

The strong and the cruel.

"You want me to open the door?" The dark-haired wolf on the left grinned and licked his lips lazily. "Make me."

They knew who I was. They knew that Lennox wanted me to be his princess. But they also knew that Lennox wouldn't be mad if they treated me like shit, because cruelty in a pack like this was a way of life. I was expected to take it or give as good as I got.

I hated it. I hated it so much. The cruelty, the suffering. The *evils*. My hands curled into fists and began to shake. Darkness pressed in on me.

The gray-haired shifter on the right chuckled and dropped into a crouch, looking at Dwayne, who seemed even smaller than before. "Who is this little guy? You're cute. A cute little duck."

A duck? Dwayne let out a series of cute little peeps and bustled closer to the wolf. **Fuck off, you dumb cunt.**

"Aww. You're a friendly guy. A nice plump little duck." The gray shifter smiled, flashing yellow teeth. "You've been fattening yourself up for us, little duckie?"

Dwayne preened. **I hope you like eating dick, motherfucker.**

The dark shifter laughed. "I love duck." He ran a fat tongue over his lips. "Peking duck, a l'orange, confit... But they're best fresh. Still wriggling. Ha."

The gray-haired werewolf snorted and got closer, grinning right in Dwayne's face. "You want to join us for lunch, little duckie?"

Sure. Dwayne shot forward, snapping with his beak. The wolf reared back, but it was too late—Dwayne had plucked out his eyeball. Dwayne whirled it around, threw it in the air, then caught it, swallowing it whole. **Nom nom nom.**

The man slumped down and clapped a hand over his eye socket, too shocked to even scream, while Dwayne bounced happily towards him. **You wanted to have lunch? I've got something you can eat, fuckface.**

Finally, I was shocked out of my doom-paralysis. The hiss-pop sound of a soda can opening suddenly echoed through my head, chasing the darkness away. *Hear that?* Brain-Daphne gave a cackle. *That's the sound of a can of whoop ass opening. I've been saving it just for this occasion.* She metaphorically pushed me away from the controls of my mind and cracked her knuckles. *No hesitation, no mercy. Let's go.*

The dark wolf shot forward, arms outstretched. My blades were already in my hands. I twisted sideways, out of his grip, and slammed the butt of the knife into his temple with a sickening thud. Still moving, I ducked low, spun, and kicked his feet out from underneath him, and he fell to the ground flat on his back.

Another quick kick to his head knocked him out. Beside me, Dwayne was using his claws to rake deep rivets in the gray wolf's stomach, honking happily.

I stood up, stretched, and cracked my neck. "I think we've made ourselves at home." My pulse instantly returned to normal. *Battle mode activated. They want a bad bitch? They got one.* "Let's go, sir." I opened the door, waited for Dwayne to hop off the body and waddle inside before me, and I walked in behind him.

We strode down the long corridor of the shifter compound. Dwayne's webbed feet left little tulip-shaped bloodstained prints all the way down—it was both gruesome and quite pretty at the same time.

Following my nose, I marched past the dormitories, ignored the mess hall filled with a couple dozen rowdy shifters, and climbed the steps. If I knew Lennox—and I did—he'd be upstairs. He would have turned a good chunk of the shifter compound into his own version of a penthouse lounge.

At the top of the stairs, we walked down another short corridor with ornate double-doors at the end. We passed another small kitchen on the right—Lennox's private butler's pantry—and a luxurious bathroom filled with manly scents on the left.

I kicked open the double door and walked into a heavy curtain of fragrant apple-flavored shisha smoke and testosterone.

At least the man was predictable. Lennox had indeed created his own little harem-style penthouse lounge, fit for a lion king. Low sofas, ottomans, and rich Persian rugs lay scattered around the open-plan room. Glassy-eyed, scantily clad shifter women surrounded jewel-colored hookahs sitting on antique tables.

The conversation in the room died instantly. Someone stopped the music.

"Little sis!" Lennox boomed. He stood up from where he was reclining on a lounge surrounded by his entourage. He was shirtless, displaying his muscular hairy chest and hard stomach, and only wore ripped jeans and heavy boots, his long blond hair freshly shaved at the sides and Viking braided into a messy topknot.

Brain-Daphne mentally mapped out where best to cut him so we could gut him like a fish. *Or maybe we should take a leaf out of Marie's book and de-bone him like a chicken,* she mused.

I didn't want to spend too much time on it, though. Even the sight of him revolted me.

On the floor opposite, a small Orbiter film crew had their equipment trained on him. A cameraman stood behind a massive camera on a tripod, another man wore headphones and held a boom mike, and a busty woman with a bouncy blowout and low blouse clutched a clipboard.

Lennox was filming content for his YouTube channel. Or his podcast. That weird feeling, a mixture of embarrassment and fury, tore at me again. The man was *such* an obnoxious asshole.

"Why are you up here, babe?" He scowled for a moment and held out his arms. One of his minions scuttled forward and wrapped him in a giant bear skin fur coat, leaving his chest bare, like he was an emperor of some sort. "The guards were supposed to bring you to meet me downstairs," Lennox continued. "I was going to come down to see you soon."

I was so angry, I thought I might burn a hole in him with the fury streaming from my eyeballs. Dwayne padded next to me happily, weaving through the furniture, leaving faint tulip blood prints behind.

Lennox jerked his head at his two security guards, twins —scarred, wiry middle eastern men—both Persian lion shifters. "Dave, Andy, take Daphne downstairs and wait for me, please."

Dave and Andy moved towards me. I didn't hesitate in my stride forward. "Oh, no, Lennox," I said sweetly. "I'm not waiting for you."

Dave and Andy's eyes narrowed. They blocked my path to Lennox. Dave held up his hand. I inhaled. Both of them were heavy smokers—I could almost taste the buildup of tar in their lungs.

"Sweetie," Dave said in heavily accented English. "Back up. You are not allowed in here."

The fucking arrogance.

"Turn around, now," he ordered, spinning his finger. "I will take you downstairs—"

I took his hand, broke three of his fingers, and unleashed a jab at his solar plexus that almost went straight through his diaphragm.

He collapsed into a coffee table. Andy, his twin, rushed me from the other side, his eyes bulging and hands outstretched.

Guys like this only had one mode when they saw a girl like me. Overpower her. Pin her down. Hold her.

Except he was just a man, and I was a lycanphage. Wolf-strong, wolf-fast, in human form.

I twisted effortlessly out of his grasp, punched him in the face, then spun and delivered a vicious backhand as I rotated. Turning to face him, I reared back and kicked him into a smoked-glass table. A shisha pipe shattered. Water poured everywhere.

"Daphne!" Lennox bellowed. "What the hell are you doing?"

The cameraman turned the camera in my direction.

I pulled out my blades and stalked towards him. "If you want to shift, Lennox, now's the time."

His mouth dropped open—he was truly shocked. "Daphne..." He gaped at me. "Are you *challenging* me?"

"No, you idiot, I'm not challenging you. I don't want to be the Alpha shifter. I don't want this," I snarled, waving my hand around the plush furniture and zoned-out groupies. "Only an idiot king would want any of *this*. Only a puffed-up, arrogant moron with an overblown sense of his own self-importance would want *this!*"

"But—"

I walked up to him and punched him in the nose. It squashed under my fist. He took it like a champ, though, his head snapped back only once. He stared down at me, shocked.

I'd never fought Lennox before. I'd offered to spar with him in Castlemaine a handful of times, and he'd just laughed at me. He refused because he didn't want to hurt me, and I let it go, because I didn't want to hurt his feelings when I beat him. And, in human form, I would beat him.

I love you, Heart-Daphne, but you're a fucking moron.

I should have insisted. I should have nipped this all in the bud back then. I would have beaten the shit out of him, smashed his ego to pieces, humiliated him as much as possible, and we might have avoided all this. "You got the wrong idea about me, Lennox," I snarled.

He grunted, wiping his bleeding nose with the back of his hand, swiped out with an open palm, lightning fast, and grabbed my upper arm. He gave me a little shake. "Woman, what the hell do you—"

He was fast, but I was faster. Two more punches later, I'd cracked his jaw and two ribs. He staggered back, grunting. His eyes blazed with fury.

A woman screamed. Groupies staggered to their feet. Lennox's entourage—a gaggle of out-of-shape hype-men and a couple of his grizzled, barrel-chested trainers—surged forward.

Dwayne gave a little hop, landing on a coffee table in front of me. **I've got this, baby girl. You take care of the lion.** He let out the most adorable angry honk and bounced towards them.

Lennox growled and swung.

I ducked, dodging his fist by miles, and unleashed a combination into his lower torso in the same time it took him to retract his punch. It was like trying to beat a golem to death. Lennox was all hard, scarred muscle and thick skin, but I kept up, slamming my fists into his solar plexus, aiming for the softest spots, ducking his outstretched hands with seconds to spare.

Three strikes later, and the blood from the cuts above his eyes had blinded him. I darted in like a matador, working the cuts open wider until the blood flowed right down his face, and he looked like a gender-bent Carrie on prom night.

Behind me, all I could hear were screams and curses and breaking glass. Dwayne, still in his little-goose form, flew back and forth, tearing off toupees, biting off fingers, and raking bare flesh with his razor-sharp claws.

Lennox let out a deep rumble. His eyes turned golden. He was going to shift.

We can still take him if he shifts.

No, we can't. Not without help and a whole barrel of luck. He's the delusional one, not me. And he can't answer any questions if he turns into his lion.

Let's finish this, then.

I unleashed a kick to his groin. Then as he curled over, I snapped my fist right on the point of his chin, rocking him up and sweeping him off his feet. He landed on his back, breaking the hardwood table behind him with a loud crack.

Snarling, I pulled my blades and jumped on top of him. I slammed one dagger into the table right near his head and pointed the other one at his carotid. "You know what these can do, right, Lennox? You're not still stupid enough to dismiss my blades as pointy little toothpicks, are you?"

Dwayne let out a little honk-chuckle. Someone

screamed long and loud, the sound turning into a tortured gargle at the end.

"Daphne... be smart about this," Lennox glared at me, his blue eyes bright in his blood-smeared face. "You know I don't want to hurt you."

His ego just wouldn't let him face reality. "Really, Lennox?" I held his gaze and nicked his skin with the blade. The metal burned. It would leave a scar. "Why don't you try?"

The film crew were right behind us. I could hear the cameraman's heart beating in his chest fast, like a hummingbird.

I leaned closer. "Tell me the truth. Did you bribe the Otherworld Liaison to keep Wesley's murder out of the Otherworld authorities?"

"I don't know what you're talking about," he grunted.

"Liar." I knelt on his stomach, digging my knee into him. "I can hear your pulse skip, Lennox. I can smell the cortisol. Don't bother lying to me."

He glared at me for another long moment. "Fine," he spat out. "I did it for us."

"For us?"

"Yes, you dumb bitch." He reared up, shoving his bloody, swollen face closer to mine. "For *us*. You haven't learned your lesson." His eyes were so hard, like rocks. "You're meant to be by my side, Daphne. You're supposed to be right here, as my princess."

I glared at him. "But not here, in your private suite, where you keep your whores and your hype-men, though, right? You mean downstairs, waiting in the kitchen." I was so angry my fists started to shake again. My blade nicked his skin, this time, accidentally.

He let out a hiss. "You're meant to be mine. You and me, it's written in the stars. Even the pack shaman agrees we are cut from the same cloth." His mouth twisted. "You should have fallen in line right after I won the challenge. You should have taken your place right next to me after I saved you from Alexei Minoff. So, because you're too dumb to see what's good for you, I came up with a way to show you."

"By ruining my life?"

He huffed out a grunt. "Letting you cool your heels in a human jail is hardly ruining your life, you fucking drama queen." He scowled. "Now get off me."

I nicked him with my blade again. He stiffened. "Is that it?"

"What?"

"Is that all you did?"

"What else was I supposed to do?" He sneered. "I suppose you want flowers and fancy lingerie, too."

Disappointment crushed me. *I knew it. He's not the puppet master. He's just another puppet.*

Lennox bucked underneath me, just a twitch. If he wanted to, he could throw me off, but I would bury my Orion blade deep in his face before he'd manage it, and now, he knew it.

I could almost hear his ego warring with his survival instincts. I moved the blade slowly, until it hovered over his Adams apple. "Move again, and this is going straight through your throat, and I promise you won't be able to roar ever again. Look at me, Lennox. Am I bluffing?"

He stilled.

"How did you arrange it?"

Lennox's face hardened. "The Otherworld Liaison is a big fan of mine. I heard Wesley got iced, and the cops were fingering you for his murder, so I reached out to him. He's not out of contact—I've got his private cell. He's going to transfer the file to Otherworld as soon as I call him."

"Did you arrange for someone to plant my hair on Wesley's body?"

"No!"

That sounded like the truth. I arched an eyebrow. "Was it your idea?"

"Of course."

"Liar." I ground my jaw. "You're not conniving enough for that. Who told you to do it?"

Blood dripped into his eyes from the cut on his forehead. He tried to whip his head. "Nobody told me!"

"You didn't come up with this plan by yourself. Where did you get the idea from?" I needed the puppet master.

"Some guy at O'Malley's," Lennox finally spat out.

O'Malley's was a supe bar in Point Breeze, heavily favored by the rougher men in our Otherworld. "Who?"

"He was a first responder, E.M.T or something, he was first on the scene of the Jupiter mansion collapse."

I leaned forward eagerly. "Who was he?"

"I don't know, just some guy drinking at the bar. A wizard but not a bad dude. He said they'd just found Wesley's body, and judging by the purple hair in his hands, it looked like Troy's ex-girlfriend finally got her revenge for being dumped."

I ground my jaw. "What else did he say?"

"I don't know. We had a good laugh about it. You getting all hormonal and going apeshit on everyone in the mansion. It's hilarious."

We saved the world from an evil genius summoning a Greek god, and Lennox just reduced it to us getting all hormonal and going apeshit. I unclenched my jaw. "What else did he say?"

"He just said it would be funny if you were forced to cool your heels in human jail. How hilarious it would be if the case didn't get transferred to Otherworld. It gave me the idea, so I made a few calls."

Holy shit. This man is a buffoon.

"It was just a prank, Daphne. But I was really trying to show you what you were missing out on by keeping this whole game of yours going. You don't need to do it anymore. I'm right here. I'm your knight in shining armor."

Whoever he was talking to was the puppet master. He has been manipulated, just like everyone else.

I glared down at Lennox. "What did this guy look like?"

"I don't know," Lennox blustered. "He was just some guy. White. Generic."

"Old? Young?"

"No idea. Early thirties, maybe. I barely looked at him. He wore a Phillies hat, that's all I've got. I don't understand why you're riding me like this, Daphne. I did it for us. And there's no harm done. I will save you again, just like last time." His eyes narrowed. "And maybe this time, you'll have the good manners to be more grateful about it."

A bark of laughter escaped me. "You're unbelievable. Lennox, I was winning that fight with Alexei Minoff. You muscled in on my challenge and stole my kill after I'd already beaten Alexei half to death."

A whiff of smoke hit my nostrils. Dwayne, still in his tiny-goose form, was standing at the hookah, taking a toke from the pipe, while a terrified little shifter man held the mouthpiece for him. Another skinny man was lighting the bowl. Both were shaking and bleeding profusely.

Romeo's voice rumbled in my earpiece. "Baby, you need to get out of there. Something has come up."

I think we're done here, anyway. "This is over, Lennox. We're done. I don't want to see you ever again."

"No. You're mine," he snarled into my face. "One way or another, I'll make you understand it. You can wave your silver blades in my face all you want, lil sis, but one day soon, I'll make you give in. The only reason I'm not beating your ass right now is because I want to ride it later."

He's not giving up. He never gives up.

Neither do we.

For a second, I watched him. Lennox's chest heaved, panting. Naked, burning rage flared in his eyes. I stared into his face...

And I noticed something.

Our eyes were the same shape. Our jawline, too. And there was a definite similarity in the way both our top lips dipped in the middle.

Holy shit. Was Marie right about this, too?

This was ridiculous. And disgusting.

And... ridiculous. But the evidence was staring me right in the face. "Your dad spent a bit of time at Ironclaw around twelve years ago, didn't he?"

Lennox frowned, confused. "Yeah. He was good friends with Braxton Myers. The Alpha invited him to stay a lot."

My gut lurched. *I think I'm going to puke.* "Well, we might want to call in Maury Povich, because I'm pretty sure he might be my father, too."

"What? Daphne, what the hell are you talking about?"

"I'm your sis, Lennox. Your actual little sis." I choked down a dry heave. Thank the gods, I'd never let him anywhere near me. "That's why you feel like you should be close to me," I continued, fighting a gag. "We're cut from the same cloth, just like your shaman said."

Lennox froze. He stared at me, horrified. I climbed off him, suddenly so grossed out, I didn't want him anywhere near me.

"Daphne," Romeo muttered. "Wind it up. Let's go. Now."

I was done here. Returning my Orion blades to the

hidden sheathes on my back, I dusted off my hands. "Let's never talk about this ever again," I said. "I mean *ever*."

∿

DWAYNE DIDN'T FOLLOW me out. I had no idea where he'd disappeared to, but I could hear screams coming from the roof of the shifter compound.

"What's going on, Romeo?" I asked as I bolted down the hallway, heading for the exit.

"The church has been attacked again," he said gruffly.

Oh, fuck me sideways on a racing bike, what now?

"Cole sent an S.O.S. The guys have gone back to help fight. I don't know what's going on," he said, his voice grim.

A chill ran up my spine. Marie was there.

"I'm coming." I bolted out of the building and up the path. A sniper's bullet whistled over my head. A second later, a dull spat told me the sniper had taken a dive head-first off the roof.

I glanced over my shoulder and caught Dwayne waving at me cheerfully with a blood-splattered wing. Behind him, the watchtower on top of the compound was engulfed in flames. **Godspeed, little one.**

CHAPTER
TWENTY-FIVE

The Woodlands was dark, so I sprinted as fast as I could until I reached the cemetery and threw myself into the SUV. Romeo hit the gas, and we sped away.

I held on as he drove like a bat out of hell towards Fitler Square. "Did you catch all that?"

Romeo nodded. "I got it. Some random wizard pulled Lennox's strings. We still don't know who it is."

"We don't know *anything*," I snarled.

"Well..." Romeo hesitated for a second, accelerated, spun the wheel and turned the car into a drift, taking the corner like an expert. "We know you're Lennox's sister. I didn't see that coming, but I should have. You do look alike."

I shuddered. "Romeo please. Like I said to Lennox, we're never going to speak of this ever again."

"Happy to oblige. It's not exactly bad news, Daphne. At least now he'll leave you alone. His obsession with you was getting out of control."

Romeo's phone buzzed. I picked it up and read the

message out loud. "It's from Micah. They're at the church. Cole's down."

Romeo swore viciously and sped up, weaving through the traffic like a stock car driver. I held on as we screamed around corners and weaved through traffic. In less than three minutes, he swung the car into the driveway leading to the church.

I caught a glimpse of a brown sedan parked on the other side of the street. The two men inside were both fast asleep, heads lolled back on the headrest, mouths wide open.

At least, I hoped they were asleep. Boggs and Hartshorn were a pain in my ass, but they didn't deserve to die.

Romeo didn't hesitate at the mangled gate—he smashed right through, skidding to a halt in the driveway in front of the church.

The scent of fae magic hit me the second I opened the door. Summer wine, soft leather, luscious fruit with a hint of decay... the shock of it felt like a punch to the head.

I knew this scent. "It's Asherah," I shouted to Romeo as we dashed inside. "It was Asherah all along."

She wasn't here anymore, though. That wild, dangerous fae scent had dissipated just a little. Romeo and I bolted up the steps and ran into the church. The rest of the coven were in the living room, crowded around the sofa.

Cole lay there, face white, eyes wide open, staring at the ceiling.

Oh, no.

Levi muttered a spell, his hands cupped over Cole's forehead, palms glowing with yellow light. He glanced up. His face was pale, too. "I don't know how to undo this."

Micah's voice broke. "His heart isn't even beating."

I inhaled carefully. "He's frozen. It's a fae stasis spell. A Winter Court curse." I shot Romeo a look. "It's death magic from the court of decay. You can counter it. I've seen fae mages break them using the essence of life."

Romeo had studied the theory of fae magic and understood what I was saying immediately. The essence of life was blood. He knelt down, made a shallow cut on the inside of his arm, and let a dribble of blood fall into his other palm. He muttered words of power under his breath. The scent of fireworks and smooth whiskey bloomed, making my head spin.

Power surged, thickening the air. I held my breath. Seconds ticked by. One, two, three...

Cole sat up and gasped.

I sagged with relief. Levi leaned back, clutching his chest.

We waited a moment for Cole to catch his breath. Romeo put his hand on Cole's shoulder, laying him back down gently. "What happened?"

"Asherah happened, that's what," Cole said, still panting softly. "Most of the wards are down for repair now that we neutralized the attacker. Asherah walked inside like she owned the place and demanded to know where Daphne was. She was..." He gulped. "She was so damned terrifying. I could barely say a word."

"Where is Marie?"

"Gone," Cole whispered. "Asherah took her. I was trying to hold her back—"

I gaped at him. "You were trying to hold Asherah back?" Cole was a lot braver than I thought.

"No, I was trying to hold Marie back. She kept trying to get me out of the way so she could ask Asherah a bunch of questions."

That girl is going to get herself killed.

Cole continued, "Asherah shoved me aside, looked into Marie's eyes, licked the back of her hand and laughed that goddamn terrifying laugh of hers." Cole shuddered. "She said Marie was a wayward ward, just like you were, Daphne. So, she said she would take Marie and teach you a lesson."

My blood ran cold. "No," I whispered. My lips felt numb. *Godamnnit, Dwayne, I'm going to kill you.*

"We'll find her." Romeo glanced up, meeting my eyes. The steely determination in his gaze gave me strength. For the first time since I was a child, I realized something.

I didn't have to do this alone.

Loneliness had haunted me almost my entire life. It was the specter that loomed over me since I was seven years old, threatening to break me into pieces. I'd split myself in two just to fight the loneliness and make it easier to do the hard things I needed to do to survive.

I wasn't alone anymore. Brain-Daphne, the hard, survival part of me, didn't have to be separate anymore.

I could love and stab things at the same time.

I didn't have to save the world all by myself. I didn't even need to ask for help. There was a man standing right in front of me, threatening to set the whole world on fire just to make me happy.

We'd find Marie together. We'd fight Asherah together, and we would find and kill this puppet master. The thought ignited the fire of fury within me, chasing the ice out of my veins.

I took a deep breath and clenched my fists, settling the simmering rage so I could think clearer. "We need to figure out where Asherah took her."

Cole took a sip of water, his hand shaking. "She would have taken Marie back to Faerie."

"No. Asherah has come back to challenge me. I'm guessing she got some of her Hidden City underlings to plant the threats outside my door, and that's why I didn't pick up a trace of her scent or her magic. She's back now, and she won't go where I can't find her. She wants a fight, and Marie is the bait. She will still be here in the mortal realm."

For the billionth time, I wished Dwayne would prioritize learning how to use a cellphone instead of a shotgun. I needed to get hold of him desperately, but he was probably still kicking the shifter compound into dust.

"Dwayne promised me he'd fixed things with Asherah," I ground out. "He believes he did too. If he thought she was still gunning for me, there's no way he would have left me alone. He's many things, but he's my Alpha, and he protects me."

Dwayne had felt so guilty when he realized he'd put me in danger by telling Asherah he wouldn't come to Faerie with her because of me. He swore he smoothed everything over, and that she wasn't jealous anymore. He never lied to me.

A new chill ran through me. "Clearly, something has changed, and she wants to kill me again."

"Someone might have pulled her strings, too, in the same way they did Lennox." Romeo cursed under his breath. "It seems impossible that one person could do all this. A cowardly Iago, stirring up trouble from the shadows, using those with far greater power to fight his battles for him. Just to bring us down."

"She's not going to hear me out." I glared at the floor for a second, thinking. "I doubt she's going to stop and explain to me why she thinks Dwayne is cheating on her with me. If she thinks I'm after her man, she won't stop until I'm dead. It will be a fight to the death."

"It's not like I ever needed a reason," Romeo growled.

"It might mean a diplomatic disaster."

His face hardened. "I don't care."

Fuck it, my brain hissed. *Let's just get Marie back.*

"Asherah wants a fight, so I'll give her one." I took a deep breath. "She'll be waiting on a battlefield somewhere." I thought about the two detectives asleep in the car outside. "Somewhere away from human eyes, so she won't be subject to the laws of the Agreement." I thought about it some more. "Somewhere that suits her aesthetic."

Suddenly it was obvious. "She's in the Hidden City by the lake. Let's go."

CHAPTER
TWENTY-SIX

The second we moved through the entrance to the Hidden City, I knew I was right. The atoms in the air tingled with nervous energy. The atmosphere was charged—overwhelming, overexcited, and terrified. Asherah's scent dominated the surroundings, like a perfume bomb had exploded by the brick wall. Marie's faint sweet, coppery-sandy scent was everywhere, too, tinged with cortisol.

Marie was very scared. I was, too.

Romeo strode next to me, his massive arms held lightly by his side, ready for anything, huge shoulders tensed. The rest of the coven fanned out around us, listening as he gave his orders. "As soon as we spot her, Levi, you and Brandon set up a perimeter," he said quietly. "We'll need to reduce collateral damage as much as possible."

Brandon stared around at the deathly-silent woods as we strode down the path. "I don't know if that will be necessary, boss. There's nobody around."

I reached out with my senses. "Asherah has scared everyone away," I muttered. "It's not surprising. The people of this City can smell danger a mile away." The residents would be doing what they did best, hiding in their apartments behind the strongest wards in the whole world. "Come on," I said, moving off the path. "This way."

We stalked through the woods of the Hidden City, keeping our footsteps light, our mouths shut and our breathing even. Despite trying to remain calm, goosebumps rose on my skin as we walked further into the trees.

Asherah was shedding her magic like a nuclear power station in meltdown. She'd come back from Faerie recharged, reinvigorated, and ready to rip the flesh from my bones. I could feel her everywhere.

The air thickened as we neared the lake, the atmosphere tingling with Asherah's strange fae magic. Signs of her were everywhere. The rough bark of the tree trunks around us shimmered with a dusting of pure gold. The stars above us twinkled, too-bright, almost frantic. I stepped over the bright-white bones of an odd, long-dead creature, newly disturbed from the earth. Evergreen leaves hovered in the air, unmoving, trapped in the frozen air.

A voice hit my ears. High-pitched and relentless. "I'm just saying, from what I've read, you seem to possess greater magical abilities than the usual fae creature that reside here on earth. So, I figure you must be a goddess. You can't blame me for being curious."

Asherah's voice sent a shiver down my spine. "Do you bite everything you are curious about, little mosquito?"

I froze, holding up my hand. The coven stopped.

"Look," Marie said. "I said I was sorry about that. I couldn't help myself. You smell great. Like... sexy and apocalyptic at the same time. You smell like Snow White's poisoned apple. Like a deadly Red Delicious."

Asherah gave a little laugh. "Well, little mosquito. You

are lucky we enjoy biting. And we must say, your flattery *is* exceptional. We have half a mind to leave at least some of you alive. Our mother would enjoy you immensely." She sighed. "But no, we are not a goddess, merely a female guarding our own bedchamber from one who would seek to invade it. Now hush, for we must continue your torture. We must draw in the viper who seeks to steal our beloved from us."

There was a beat of silence.

"But you are a royal, though, right?" Marie piped up again. "I can tell by the way you're referring to yourself using the majestic plural. You're either a royal, or you're absolutely bonkers. Or both," Marie added, her tone overcheerful with a tinge of hysteria. "I think it's both."

Asherah let out another long sigh. It sounded like the sweep of dead leaves over a gravestone. "We confess you are making this whole torture thing very difficult. You are quite bizarre and enjoyable. We understand why you are the Wolf Girl's most precious baby. But alas, little mosquito, we must dunk you again."

"Oh, please don't," Marie whined. "My sinuses aren't great to start with. I—" A gurgling sound cut her off. Frantic splashing sounds filled the air.

Asherah was drowning her. I jolted. Romeo waved us forward, and we ran through the woods, bursting into the clearing.

Cold moonlight bathed the lake, turning the emerald lawn around it silver. Asherah stood at the edge of the sparkling water, glorious and terrifying in a plunging, deep-scarlet robe, her skin glowing pearlescent in the moonlight. A spiked crown sat on her head. Her hair hung like a black silk curtain down her back.

She did look like a goddess. Adrenaline flooded me. My

pulse hammered under my skin so hard, I was sure she could hear it.

In a fraction of a second, my eyes flickered, taking in the whole scene.

Marie dangled out over the water, tethered by her feet with a vine, hanging upside-down, suspended from the branches of a willow tree. She'd tucked her baggy t-shirt up into her sports bra so it didn't cover her face, displaying the skin of her tummy.

Her head was underwater. She thrashed wildly, the water boiling around her.

Romeo whispered. "Levi, circle around, put down a ward, contain any explosions. The rest of you, get out of the line of fire. While we distract her, see if you can get Marie down without Asherah seeing you."

The coven darted away, melting into the darkness of the willows. Romeo and I walked out into the clearing, moving closer.

Asherah lifted her hand, and the willow tree pulled its branch up, yanking Marie out of the water. She coughed and spluttered.

Romeo stepped in front of me. A silver glow ran over his dark skin, an excess of magic pouring out all over his body.

"Asherah," he growled.

The fae princess whipped around, facing us. "Warlock! I am glad you are here. We were worried the Wolf Girl might do something silly like come on her own." Her beautiful scarlet lips stretched up into a snake-like smile. Behind her, hanging over the water, Marie coughed, vomiting up water.

My chest grew tight. "Let her go, Asherah," I called out. "It's me you want."

"We don't *want* you, Wolf Girl. We want to punish you," she giggled, a high-pitched tinkle of bells. "We wish to make an example of anyone who might stand between us and our most beloved." Her dark eyes glowed as she held up her hands and flexed her fingers. "You will watch as your own wayward ward fills her lungs with water until she grows soggy. Then, we will split your bones inside of you and suck out the marrow with a straw."

"You might find that difficult," Romeo let out a rumble, and flexed his fingers. A sheen of translucent violet appeared in front of us. He'd thrown out a shield.

Asherah smiled and lifted her lily-white hand. A silver knife blinked into existence, floating in the air in front of her. She flicked her fingers, and the knife shot towards us like a bullet. It hit the sheen of air six feet ahead of us and shattered, bursting into sparks like silver fireworks.

Whoa. I took a deep breath.

"Oh, you've taken your gloves off, Warlock?" Asherah tilted her head, letting out a pretty laugh. "This just makes the game more fun." Lifting her arms in the air, she whirled in a circle like a madwoman. "I feel the edges of the barrier your covenmate has put down. You came to fight. I like it. The Wolf Girl might be standing behind your shield, but you remain on the battlefield. You will shatter, just like her."

"You know me, Asherah," Romeo said. "You know I don't even bend."

"Indeed." She tilted her head, smiling. "You don't usually play games, Warlock. You have always been so boring. But if you insist on being involved, at least we shall have fun watching you try to save her."

Romeo clenched his jaw. "Try it."

The tension spiked.

A tinny sound broke the silence. A melodic beep noise. It took me a second to place it. Someone's phone was ringing, and the ringtone was the Donkey Kong theme song.

"Oh, that's me. Sorry." Marie wiggled on the end of the

vine, struggling to reach the pockets of her jorts. She swung, finally engaging her core, and grappled with the Velcro fastening.

Asherah turned to watch her.

We should hit her now.

I pulled out my blades, my heart in my throat. I'd need to take her by surprise, or else her magic could tear me to shreds before I could even blink. Asherah was standing right between us and Marie, and she was watching Marie with a fascinated expression on her face. She could turn at any moment...

Marie finally wrestled the Velcro pocket of her jorts open. A phone came loose and fell into her hand. She clicked a button and answered it. "Hey, Deborah," she said cheerfully. "No, not much, not much, just, er, finished meditating. Oh, no, that's bad news. I'm sorry Paisley and Tamara have gone home. No, I'm sure it wasn't anything you said; if it was, they're probably just being sensitive. Of course you're bored. I know, I'm sorry. Oh, yes, I'll be coming home as soon as I can." Marie's eyes flicked towards us. "Uh, you know, Deborah, you might want to check the kitchen to see if they stole anything. From what I remember, Paisley *did* have sticky fingers. Yeah. I'm just saying, it sounds suspicious to me, that's all, if they left in a huff, there might be a reason. Oh, yeah, I bet they *did* leave very abruptly! Okay. Alright. Love you too. Bye."

I ran.

Asherah whirled around. The air around me rippled. She suddenly thrust her hands down and clawed up. The lawn rippled like it was water.

I wobbled on my feet and stopped my advance. Little furrows appeared in the smooth grass and tiny molehills sprouted. The smell of ripped earth and fallow ground rose like perfume into the air.

Bones emerged from the earth. Little skeletons, the remains of things long dead, called forth by Asherah's winter magic. A fully formed possum skeleton crawled out first, snapped its teeth, and launched itself at me.

I swiped my blade through it, shattering the creature into shards.

Asherah laughed and thrust her arms out sideways. A current of air whipped around her, stirring her gown and rippling her hair back like a silk curtain. A gleaming scythe with a pitch-black handle and a wide, curved blade appeared in the air next to her, spinning as if suspended on a string. Asherah tossed her head back, and another scythe popped up next to it. Another and another until the field in front of us was filled with rotating, macabre death blades.

She twirled her hand in the air. The scythes began to spin faster. She flicked her fingers, and they shot towards us.

Romeo stepped forward, stretching out his arms and gathering power. A brilliant blue fire burst out of his palms, and he scooped up the enchanted fire and shot down the scythes as they spun at us, shattering them into starbursts before they even got close.

"Get her down," I hissed at the boys creeping through the willows, pointing at Marie. "Go around, through the water." Another half-formed dead thing I didn't recognize rattled its bones wildly and tossed itself into the air. I slashed it down. Another took its place. They fell apart and came together in bigger form—a Frankenstein skeleton made up of tiny dead woodland creatures.

"Ooh." Marie sounded both impressed and terrified. "That's *so* cool."

The skeleton—a monstrous upright creature with the skull of a dog and millions of tiny rib bones causing it to weave upright like a striking cobra—lurched towards me on the bones of a deer's back legs. The creature towered over my head, its chittering, clattering noise making my teeth hurt.

I swung low with my knife, dodging a snap from a million little rib bones as they opened and shut. I slashed at the leg bones of the deer. The Frankenstein skeleton collapsed onto the lawn, the bones scattering across the grass.

Right in front of me, Romeo clashed with Asherah, holding nothing back, and poured astonishing amounts of magic into parrying her strikes, shattering her spinning scythes into firework sparks and blasting her blades into explosive bright tiny flashes of light.

If I lived through this, I would never forget how magnificent Romeo looked at this moment. Like a god of war. Like the shadow fae prince he was.

Out on the lake, I spotted a lynx wading through the shallows—Cole, in his shifter form, coming to rescue Marie.

The lawn rippled. Five misshapen skeleton rats burst from the earth and bounded towards me, clicking broken jaws and gnashing tiny teeth. I moved into a crouch, narrowed my eyes, and whipped my blade through them, shattering the magic that held them together. They scattered like confetti on the grass, then twitched, rolling together again. I stomped forward, and kicked the bones before they could reform.

Romeo locked in on Asherah, stealing her focus, but her long-dead minions tore out of the soil, coming for me. We needed to get closer to her. I just needed one tiny moment of distraction.

I began my advance. The bone-creatures rattled across the lawn, tumbling towards me. I whirled and slashed with my blade, and the creatures collapsed around me. They kept coming, though, reforming, rattling, clattering loudly. One slashed a sharp broken jaw across my cheekbone, opening up a stinging cut before I punched it away. Another tore a deep gash in my thigh.

Romeo had gotten closer, incinerating Asherah's weapons as she flung them towards him. Power radiated off his skin like heat from a furnace. The shadows of the willows behind her suddenly surged forward, swallowing Romeo, and in the next second, he appeared right in front of her.

Both his hands wrapped around her neck and squeezed. She whipped her arms up, breaking his hold and slapped a hand on his chest. Magic exploded.

The shockwave pushed them apart. Romeo flew back, landing on one knee. No, no, no.

He was injured. I heard his heart stutter.

Asherah snarled—an inhuman sound. "You *dare* lay hands on me?"

"You hurt my lover." Romeo's face was terrible. "You spilled her blood, Asherah. I will take your head for it." He took a deep breath; his muscles tensed and bulged. Pushing up from the ground, he bolted towards her, his long legs devouring the space between them.

Three more bone creatures leapt towards me, I let out a scream of rage as a deep cut scored my arm. I swirled like a dervish, shattering them as they flew at my face, trying to rip me to shreds. All I could do was slash at them, breaking their enchantments. But more came. And more.

Through the veil of bone-monsters leaping towards me, I spotted Cole climbing the willow. He clawed on the vine that held Marie above the water. If we died today, maybe Marie and the guys would get away. Gods, I hoped they would get away.

Suddenly, Asherah screamed, clapping her hands

together. A burst of power erupted from her, bathing the battlefield in a punch of pure ice. The skeletons fell apart, bones littering the grass, inert.

The cold hit me half a second later. I couldn't move.

Nobody could. The world stopped. Time skipped a beat. Then, another.

The spell cost her, though. Asherah was drained. She slumped to one knee. I panted, desperate for breath, but my lungs wouldn't move.

We have to get to Asherah! We have to finish this!

Right beside me, Romeo lurched forward, moving as if in slow motion, fighting Asherah's stasis curse—the same one she'd thrown at Cole only an hour earlier. A spell of winter and decay.

Romeo's eyes glowed silver, the power and magic within him boiling like lava in a volcano without an escape route.

We need to do something...

With enormous effort, I cupped my palm, letting my own blood pool in my hand. It cost me every ounce of effort I had left, but I managed to flick my fingers in Romeo's direction.

The essence of life. Blood, willingly given.

A splatter of my blood hit him. Instantly, Asherah's curse dissolved, and he surged forward, muttering words of power and snapping off the shackles of the last of her curse as the magic rolled over him. He lifted his chin.

"Come!" Asherah rose, ground her jaw, and raised her arms, the motion ragged, exhausted. "Let us finish this! We fight to the end, Warlock. If it is ours, then we will go to our next life knowing that you won't be far behind us." Her crimson lips trembled. She looked at me. "You know who we are."

My brain whimpered. *Queen Maeve will kill us all. The whole world, probably.*

There was no winning this fight.

Romeo took a breath. The curse was broken. He could move, but he was spent. His heart stuttered again, begging for respite.

Neither of them could take much more. The next hit would kill. Him, her. All of us.

Suddenly, the air shivered.

A wolf whistle cut through the silence. *What was that?*

Asherah's attention wavered. Her eyes flicked to the woods behind us. Something was coming. Something big crashed through the undergrowth, snapping the small trees and pushing through the forest. I couldn't move. I couldn't turn my head to see.

Asherah's eyes widened. Her mouth dropped open, and she let out an astonished gasp. "Oh," she sighed. "*Ohhh...*"

The giant scorpion sauntered into the clearing, waving her stinger high above her head, swinging it side to side provocatively.

You've gotta be kidding me.

"Who... who are you?" Asherah whispered. She looked enchanted. Behind her, Marie splashed into the lake and surfaced, spluttering and swearing like a sailor.

Asherah didn't even turn around.

Romeo took advantage of her distraction and reached out to me, breaking the stasis curse that still held me in an icy grip. His eyes blazed, and I read the thoughts in his expression. He wanted us both to attack her, together, and end it now.

I grabbed his hand before he could move away, shook my head once, and stared at him, trying to get him to understand. *Please don't attack her. Just wait.*

Scorpion-Prue let out a little chitter and clacked her claws like maracas. For some bizarre reason, she was wearing a little pink bow stuck just above one of her round, black eyeballs. Prue walked forward, weaving left, then right, deliberately stretching out her terrifying legs in a little kick with each step, showing off, like some sort of nightmare monster chorus girl.

Asherah took a shaky breath, then giggled girlishly, fluttering her hand to her chest. "Why, you *are* a gorgeous beast. What is your name, beautiful?"

Prue waved her stinger. A glistening drop of poison dangled from the end. She clicked her pinchers again, making a chattering noise.

Asherah clapped her hands in delight, cooing. Ignoring us all, she gathered her skirts and tiptoed closer, not taking her eyes off Scorpion-Prue. "Such beautiful black eyes. Such shiny armor." She exhaled with longing. "Such... thick... claws..."

Prue skittered forwards and tickled Asherah with her claw, nibbling her like an affectionate dog. Asherah broke into giggles.

I didn't know if I should laugh or vomit. Scorpion-Prue preened, shaking her tail. At least she was enjoying herself.

I'm here! Dwayne burst out of the woods; a rocket made of beautiful white feathers. He flew and landed at Asherah's feet, honking. **I'm here, hot stuff. Welcome back. Sorry I'm late.**

"Oh." Asherah looked at Dwayne, then looked back at Scorpion-Prue.

Good to see you, baby.

"Yes, indeed." Asherah tapped her chin with a white finger. "You know what, beloved? We have been thinking. Perhaps we were hasty. And selfish." Her eyes lingered on the scorpion's stinger for a moment. She waved her head from side-to-side, enchanted. "Who are we to confine ourselves to monogamy?" Asherah said. "We think we should revisit your idea of an open relationship after all."

My legs gave out, but Romeo caught me. He ran his hands over me, smoothing off the blood, checking for broken bones. He met my eyes and whispered, "What the fuck is going on?"

"Chaos and mayhem," I mumbled back, blinking sweat out of my eyes. Behind us, Cole dragged Marie out of the water, pulling her away from the willows towards Brandon and Micah. Marie looked pissed, but she was safe, at least.

Scorpion-Prue turned in a slow circle, provocatively waving her stinger high above her. Was she... twerking?

Asherah let out a giggle and clapped her hands in delight.

I met Romeo's eyes again and whispered, "I think this is the part where we shut the hell up and see how this plays out. Mister Chaos No-Plan over there might actually have a plan."

Asherah trailed her hands over Prue's preabdomen, her touch loving, like a man admiring a sexy sports car that he secretly wanted to bang. "It is as you said, amore," Asherah said to Dwayne. "We should not limit the boundaries of our love. We conceded we might have been hasty in denying your request to share."

Gotcha. Dwayne made a show of looking around the battlefield. He kicked a little pile of bones with his foot. **What happened here? Are you fighting the undead without me, babe? Gotta admit, I'm a little hurt.**

Asherah waved her hand, still staring at Prue. "It's nothing. A little spirited match of wills, that is all."

Romeo stood up, his face hard. "You attacked my home, Diplomat," he said softly. "You hurt my love. You declared war between us."

Prue made a sad clicky noise and scuttled backwards, out of Asherah's reach. Asherah let out a pained gasp and moved forward to stroke her again. "No, precious, no, we would never go to war without you. Oh, you sweet thing."

Prue was playing the part perfectly. We needed answers, and we needed them now. I stood up, took Romeo's hand, and cleared my throat. "You abducted my client, ma'am. You were torturing her." Marie sat on the banks of the lake with the guys surrounding her.

Asherah glanced up at me once, her hands now gently caressing Prue's huge claw. "Wolf Girl, no." She paused and frowned. "That sounds like a wild exaggeration."

"I distinctly remember you saying you were going to crack open my bones and drink the marrow through a straw."

Asherah huffed out a sigh. "We will admit that we were enraged when we received the pictures of you with my white-winged warrior. He promised to stay true to us while we were away, and we were sent evidence of your lies. Of course we were unhappy."

Unhappy? She summoned the bones of the dead to attack us! But, wait...

I was already way ahead of Brain-Daphne. "What images are you speaking of?" I asked Asherah.

She clicked her fingers—two little squares appeared in her hand. She waved them at us. "You, the Warlock, and my feathered fuckbuddy in a wild embrace. We were consumed with jealousy." She scowled deeply.

Scorpion-Prue skittered closer to Asherah, giving her tail a sexy little wiggle and blocking Asherah's direct path to us just in case she decided to attack again. Prue twerked her stinger again. I got the feeling she was enjoying herself.

Suddenly, I realized—Dwayne had told Prue to do this. If Dwayne had crashed our battle alone, Asherah wouldn't have listened to him. He told Prue to come in first and flirt with Asherah, knowing Asherah would absolutely adore the nightmare giant scorpion with laser beams for eyes. Mister Chaos No-Plan *did* have a plan. I suppose stranger things had happened.

Babe, I told you, Dwayne waddled closer and nibbled at Asherah's bottom with his beak. **I'm not messing with anyone else. I promise.**

"These images I was sent suggest otherwise." Asherah fluttered her fingers, and the pictures drifted over to us in a light breeze. Romeo reached out and pinched one out of the air.

I caught the other one. It showed a grainy image of me, Romeo, and Dwayne tangled up on the steps of the Jupiter mansion four days ago—me, clothes tattered and ripped, trying to yank Romeo out of the hole in the door. Romeo's eyes were rolling back in his head as he struggled on all fours. Dwayne's giant head pushed Romeo's butt from behind. Out of context, the picture looked insane, and to Asherah, who was into that sort of thing, it probably *did* look like some sort of wild, kinky public sex on a doorstep.

The picture Romeo held was of us with our arms wrapped around each other, with Dwayne helping us into the car. He flipped his over. On the back, someone had scrawled the words—*Your lover is deceiving you.*

"This is us escaping the Jupiter mansion collapse," I told Asherah, who was distracted again, back to stroking Prue lovingly. "We were trying to get out before the pocket dimension exploded. You can see in the pictures I've got cuts and burns all over me, and Romeo is nearly unconscious. It might look to you like... like something else, but none of us are really, um, into *that* level of sex stuff."

Speak for yourself.

I swallowed. "Someone is lying to you, ma'am." My

relief was tempered by chagrin. Asherah wasn't the puppet master either. She was just another puppet. Although I'd have to explain it a bit more diplomatically than that, or she might unleash her fury on the whole city. "Someone has a grudge against me," I continued quickly. "And they're trying to do everything they can to ruin me. They sent these pictures hoping you'd kill me."

Asherah's hand froze, mid-stroke. Her eyebrow arched.

"Where did you get these?"

"Our diplomatic porter-sorter," she said, her voice tight. "T'was delivered to us two nights ago. Hence why we returned from Faerie so soon."

A porter-sorter was a magical mailbox. They were astonishingly expensive to make. Private ones were usually used by people who worked for the Otherworld authority so we could keep the lines of communication between us open. They allowed us to send and receive mail instantly, anywhere in the world, or even in the closest off-world realms. Asherah would have taken hers to Faerie so she could receive diplomatic mail from the Otherworld Authorities.

Not that she would read it or respond to it, or do anything, really.

She looked at me, her mouth thinned to a hard line. "Are you suggesting that someone was... was... using us?"

The temperature dropped.

Prue clicked her claws, and Asherah relaxed a bit. "You're right, precious, pretty beast. This is a happy occasion. It's hard to stay angry when you look at us with those beautiful big black eyes..." She chucked Prue under the chin, laughed, then gave a little squeak as Dwayne disappeared underneath her skirt. **Can't believe you got jealous, babe. That's so sweet.**

I turned my back on them. The sounds coming from

beneath Asherah's gown were making me feel very weird. "What the hell do we do now?" I whispered to Romeo.

"I don't know." He grimaced and lowered his voice. "I need to get away from her so I can think."

I did, too. Asherah's wild magic was dizzying and overwhelming. I turned back. "Uh, we're going to take our friends and head on out, if that's okay, Madam Diplomat."

"Yes, yes." Asherah waved her hand dismissively, then jumped, letting out a delighted squeal.

Dwayne had obviously bitten her on the ass. **You should say sorry first, babe. Beating up my friends without checking facts first is kinda mean.**

Asherah let out a dramatic sigh. "We are a passionate being. We cannot help ourselves."

And I love that about you. But come on. This lawn looks like Stalingrad.

"Ugh. Fine." She called out. "Warlock, Wolf Girl? We hope we can move past this like mature adults."

Romeo let out a little growl. He, too, was nearing his limit.

"Sure, no worries," I mumbled.

"Oh, and... Warlock?" Asherah sounded uncharacteristically hesitant. "We *may* have been so cross to hear of your dalliance with my lover here... that we shared the news of your existence with your kin."

"Kin?" I whipped my head around. "His father? You know who his father is?"

"Oh, no." Asherah laughed like it was an absurd thought. "We do not mingle much with those who dwell in our shadow. Our mother does not care for the Court of Inbetween; they are small and insignificant to us. It's obvious, however, your blood is of the Shadow Fae. We merely mentioned your existence to a courtier. They were... perturbed to hear of you, to say the least."

Scorpion-Prue suddenly jerked. She turned around and stared at Romeo.

"We imagine that they may seek to make contact at some stage," Asherah added, trying to get Prue to turn back towards her. "Their blood is precious to them. No, no. Face us, precious beastie. Let us kiss your sweet head."

CHAPTER
TWENTY-SEVEN

I licked my lips and met Romeo's eyes. He stared down at me and shook his head. "One thing at a time, baby. We'll worry about the Shadow Fae another day." He took my hand, and we walked over to join the coven, waiting on the edge of the battlefield.

Marie stomped towards me. "Are you okay?" I asked her.

"No," she said, wringing out her hair. "That woman scared the shit out of me, Daphne. Gotta admit, I've always thought I could withstand torture. Especially waterboarding. I mean, all you have to do is hold your breath and not panic." Her lip trembled for a second, and her eyes shimmered with tears. "I don't like being wrong."

"Oh, honey..."

She blinked back the tears abruptly and grinned. "It's a good thing I practice strict compartmentalization. I'm just going to shove all this trauma into a box, and bury it deep down inside me, and try not to think about how terrified I was at the idea of going to my final death."

I opened my mouth. Brain-Daphne closed it for me. *People in glass houses shouldn't throw stones, girlfriend.*

Instead of lecturing Marie, I put my arm around her instead and gave her a hug. She leaned into me awkwardly, like a cat that wants affection but isn't sure how to go about it.

And, just like a cat, Marie probably didn't trust herself not to give into the temptation to bite me.

I let her go. "Let's get out of here." The guys spread out in a circle around us, covering all angles as he headed through the woods back to the path. Romeo stayed close to me. Marie trotted at my side. Rummaging around in her jorts pocket, Marie pulled out her phone and groaned. "Ugh, it's destroyed. If Deborah can't get hold of me, she's going to flip out. I might as well see if that mad faerie woman wants to adopt me, because she's not near as bad as my mom when the spotlight is off her. Does anyone have a container of dry rice on them?"

"Marie," I said. "I'm glad you're okay, but we're a little preoccupied with some other stuff." The fight with Asherah had given me no relief. I had no idea where the next attack was going to come from. I was wound so tight, I felt like I could snap at any second, and Romeo's heartbeat was still unsteady.

"Oh yeah, the puppet master. Cole filled me in." Marie suddenly had more spring in her step. "Some evil mastermind is trying to destroy you." She grinned at me. "I'm guessing it wasn't the Alpha shifter, then."

"No."

"And it's not the Diplomat back there. Face it, Daph, you guys put up a good fight, but she would have squashed you like a bug if she wanted to," Marie chuckled, a note of hysteria in her voice. "She was *terrifying*."

We reached the path. The bubble of Asherah's wild magic receded, and we all exhaled with relief. All the thoughts in my head stopped bouncing around. "Well, we know that the puppet master has access to a porter-sorter," I said, grasping at the only clue we'd gotten. "I'm going to take a wild leap and say it was a private one, because you can't send anonymous mail through the public porter-sorters. So, who would have one?"

Romeo glanced down at me. "Lots of people do. The richest families all have private porter-sorters. The nest-masters, the Alpha... we all use them. But if you don't have the recipient's box key, it won't go anywhere."

"The puppet master is a supe leader that knows Asherah's box key," I gnawed on my lip. "It could be any one of them."

"It's not anyone. It's someone who knows you *intimately*," Marie bounced alongside me. "They know exactly what buttons to push. They knew you were at the mansion, they knew you most probably killed Wesley, and they knew you're in a relationship with the big guy here," she said, jerking a thumb at Romeo. "And they knew enough to make a social media post, twisting it, so it pulled your guardian's strings so they'd come running to save you."

Marie was right. When she put it like that, the puppet master seemed omnipotent. Marie wasn't done. "Not only that, but they had some of your hair. The puppet master knew you'd go running to your lawyer friend if you got in legal trouble, and they knew enough about her to ruin her life, too. They knew dirty secrets about Jupiter Inc, so they could ruin Mr. Zarayan's companies. They knew the Alpha would do anything to soften you up, including have you arrested and put in human prison so he could ride in and save you. It has to be someone in your inner circle." Marie turned her head, preternaturally fast, and her eyes suddenly narrowed on Cole, shadowing her. "If he wasn't such a moron, I'd say it was him."

"It's not any of them." Romeo was gruff. "But she's right; it's someone close."

"They knew enough to send the fairy princess compromising pictures of you guys with her boyfriend, knowing it would drive her nuts and she would attack you. They knew her box-key address. Who has her box-key address?"

"I have it," Romeo said. "The Alpha, the nestmaster, the Otherworld court. All the supe leaders need it so we can send her diplomatic messages."

"The nestmaster is dead," I hissed softly. "I'm sure Lennox didn't do it... someone from the court? I don't know anyone from the Otherworld court! We've got all these puppets, but I've got no idea who was pulling the strings," I bit out through clenched teeth.

He was laughing at me. The puppet master was hovering in the shadows, sending his puppets after me to ruin my life.

"Then *you* pull the strings," Marie said perkily, bouncing along beside me. "You just have to grab a puppet and tug the strings, and he'll be forced to poke his head out. I have a thing for evil geniuses, Daphne—"

"I bet you do."

"—and this one is someone close to you, someone you've dismissed as unworthy of your attention. I bet you anything, somewhere out there, there's a man limping down the street, and suddenly, his gait is straightening up, he's smoothing his hair back, he's pausing at the corner, lighting a cigarette..."

I stopped and stared at her.

"It's a movie," she explained. "The Usual Suspects. You've got yourself a Keyser Soze."

"A what?"

"He's a character from a movie. Nobody suspected him,

but he was the crime lord all along." She whipped her head sideways to glare at Cole again.

"Well..." I started walking again. The brick-wall entrance to the City was just up ahead. "How did they find this Keyser Soze in the movie?"

She shrugged. "A police sketch."

"That's not helpful."

"Well, go back to the start. Who are the usual suspects? Someone planted your hair on the body. Who I.D.ed the body?"

"Troy did."

"Right. Who is Troy?"

"My ex."

Marie looked at me with a *duh* face.

I laughed. "No, it's not him. Troy is—"

It hit me. All at once, like a shovel to the face, so hard, I stumbled back. "Oh my God. Oh my *God!*"

Troy.

He was there that night when the mansion collapsed. Holly carried him out. He saw everything. Those pictures I'd seen just moments ago were taken from across the street from the mansion.

He could have come back after Holly got him out. He could have sent the pictures to Asherah using his father's old porter-sorter. They'd been kicked out of the mansion, so Wesley would have taken his most precious things to the family apartment downtown. Wesley used to be High Priest; he'd have Asherah's box-key address.

No. It was impossible. Not Troy.

But it was. It wasn't just possible, it was...

My God.

My head spun. I was only vaguely aware of Romeo's arm wrapping tighter around me, as if he were trying to hold me together as the twisted fragments of my reality asserted themselves in my mind.

Troy knew *everything*. Nobody kept their voice down around Troy, because Troy was a simple guy with golden retriever energy—a happy, good-natured boy just content to coast through life.

But Troy knew everything about me and my Castlemaine family. He knew about how much they hated Romeo for killing Aunt Marche. He knew exactly what buttons to push to get them to come and fight the High Priest—all he had to do was spread a rumor that Romeo had me under his spell.

"He lived with Holly," I whispered. "She dismissed him as a selfish moron, too, but he would have seen everything she did. He had access to her personal phone and laptop. He listened to her calls. He would have known about her girlfriend." My voice shook. "He knew exactly what to do to get her fired. He knew all about Lennox's obsession with me. He loved drinking at O'Malley's, too. Oh. *Ohhhh*."

It was so obvious, but still, I couldn't believe it.

Something else hit me—Lennox, on the street outside the police station, insisting that he knew I was just pretending not to like him, and it was all part of my grand plan to manipulate him into marriage. I thought Lennox was just being delusional, but Lennox said he'd gotten it straight from the horse's mouth. He meant my ex-boyfriend. Troy had told him that.

Holy shit. It all fits. All of it makes sense.

"Troy wasn't a moron, but we all thought so little of him. He passed the bar exam easily, though. I can't believe it," I mumbled, my lips numb. "It was him all along." My eyes flicked back up to meet Romeo's. "He'd interned at his father's companies before you took over. He knew all the board members. They would have been family friends. He would have heard all their corrupt dirty little secrets. He identified his father's body. He used to love playing with my hair. It was him. He'd done all this."

How the hell did I not see this? How did I not see him for what he really was?

Troy was a lying, selfish idiot, but he wasn't evil. That's what I always told myself. Even Holly thought so. All of us did. We dismissed him, just like Marie said. He was a laid back, cheerful, ramshackle boy...

Until someone said no to him. I'd said no to him before, and I remembered the switch in his personality. He turned cold, icing me out, until I capitulated to whatever he wanted. It was such a horrible contrast; I would have done anything to get back into the sunshine of his life.

And now, for the very first time, I realized the truth. Troy wasn't stupid. When he couldn't get anyone to do his assignments for him and he was forced to do them himself, he got top marks. The simple, good-natured, laidback boy was just a mask he wore. It wasn't the real Troy.

The real Troy was the cold, manipulative bastard.

He'd played me like a fiddle once. And I let him do it again because I was too blind to see who he really was. I thought he was different from his brothers.

Romeo squeezed my hand. He was watching this play out on my face, reading me like a book. "It makes sense. Troy is a coward, too. Just like Trion. Just like Christopher."

A horrible sense of shame sunk into me. I didn't want this to be true. I didn't want to be *that* stupid.

If it was true, then Troy was probably as intelligent as his brother—maybe even more so, since Christopher wore his cunning publicly like a badge of honor. Troy deliberately kept it hidden so that everyone would underestimate him.

Doubt gripped me again. "I just... I don't know. What if I'm wrong?" I was wrong about Lennox.

Marie was giving me an odd look. "Why? All the things you were muttering sound like nails in the coffin of his guilt. You can tie him to every single puppet. He's got means and motive. It makes sense that he's the puppet master."

I didn't know how to explain it. "Because... because it's *Troy*."

Romeo held me closer and rested his lips on my forehead. "I know what you're feeling," he murmured. "It's not your fault you didn't know."

Oh. Of course. Bella. Romeo didn't realize his foster sister was playing him like a fiddle, either.

It made me feel a little better. "I still really hope it's not him," I muttered into Romeo's chest.

"I know. I feel like an idiot for not suspecting him, too. Troy is Troy," Romeo said, pulling me back and stroking my cheek with his thumb. "But he's still a Jupiter."

"I need to know for sure." I took a deep breath. "There's only one way to find out."

It was time to pay a visit to my ex-boyfriend.

CHAPTER
TWENTY-EIGHT

The Jupiter family penthouse apartment downtown was more heavily warded than any place I'd ever been before. Another thing I'd blown off as insignificant—Troy, the coward, used to run and hide behind his wards whenever he was threatened. His wards were always insanely strong, so much so that I could never break them. I used to beg for him to let me in.

At first, I mistook his cowardice for self-preservation. Then, like everyone else, I mistook it for stupidity.

It never occurred to me that his unusually strong wards were a sign of his magical abilities. He was more powerful than I'd ever given him credit for.

I still don't want us to be right about this. Brain-Daphne was almost sobbing, still in full self-disgust, self-flagellation mode. *Because if it is him, then I'm the most useless survival entity in the history of the universe. I'm an idiot. A stupid moron.*

We'll work through this in therapy, I told her. Besides, if Troy was the puppet master, then it wasn't just me he'd fooled. Nobody that knew him could have predicted this, not even Holly, who was far smarter than I was. It took an outsider, someone that didn't know him—Marie, an evil genius herself—to point it out.

It was midnight. Romeo and I stood on the sidewalk across the street from the Jupiter family apartment building, deep in the shadows of a big oak tree, far away from the streetlights. I inhaled carefully, taking everything in. The air was cold in my lungs. I held it for a moment, tasting the flavors of magic around the building.

Troy had laid an alarm spell—an early-warning alert spell that would let him know if I was coming—over the entrance of his apartment building, right in front of the revolving doors.

Me, specifically. He'd used another strand of my hair to guide the spell's intention. I didn't need any other evidence to convince me of Troy's guilt, but if I did, it was there, right in front of me.

Romeo had already disabled the alarm spell. There was only so much magic Troy could do out in public, so it wasn't as strong as he could have made it. But right at the top of the building, ten stories up, in the last remaining property that solely belonged to the Jupiter family, the entire penthouse suite was ringed in a series of unbreakable wards. One was coded for me, another for the High Priest. He had an ill-intent ward, a hard ward, a ghost ward, and a door locked with several deadbolts.

There was also a mirror ward surrounding the whole penthouse. Witches usually used mirror wards on top of protective wards to reflect any offensive spells so they'd bounce right off, but Troy had clearly messed up this one. He'd put the mirrors facing inward, not outward. It was a silly mistake.

Maybe it wasn't him after all. Maybe he was just a coward, trying to hide.

I took another deep breath in. For the first time in

months, I could smell a hint of churned earth. The zing of fresh leaves unfurling. The stirring of hibernating furry creatures.

I could taste the coming spring in the air.

It gave me courage. New life, new beginnings.

Romeo squeezed my hand. "Are you sure you want to do this alone?"

"She's not alone." Marie adjusted her bright orange shirt.

Guilt churned within me. "I'm deeply uncomfortable with this." Marie was my client. She was a vulnerable supe kid under my care. "I'm supposed to be protecting you," I said to her. "Not letting you come on dangerous missions with me."

"So far, while under your protection, I've been attacked by an alien bug at your boyfriend's house and abducted by a mad faerie princess. You're doing a stunning job, Daphne." She smiled up at me. "The least you could do to make amends is to let me come on this field trip with you."

"It's not a field trip," I ground out. Marie had even bullied me into letting her drive here, so she could "get into character." I tried to put my foot down, but Romeo told me to pick my battles. Turns out, Marie was an excellent driver.

I tried one more time. "You shouldn't be here."

"Too bad." She grinned. "You have no choice. Besides, this was my idea." She heaved a bag over her shoulder. "Let's go. I'm excited to see if this works."

Romeo pulled me back, turned me around, dipped his head, and kissed me deeply. I lost myself in him for a too-brief moment. Soon, when this was all over, we'd have time. Time to sink into each other, time to adore and cherish every inch—

"Ew." Marie muttered. "Come on, Daphne. I'm not going to get a tip if we don't hurry."

Romeo slipped a little golden ball on a leather thong over my head, held the charm, and whispered an incantation. I felt a tingle of warmth blossom out from the ball. The don't-see-me charm ran over my skin, covering me completely. He bent his head to kiss me again, and missed my mouth, nipping my nose instead of my lips.

I gave a nervous chuckle. "I guess the spell works."

"Good luck," he whispered.

"Daph-*nee*." Marie tugged my arm impatiently. "Let's go."

I followed her as we crossed the street, staying only inches behind her. "You are far too excited about this," I said quietly.

"Why wouldn't I be? I get to see if I'm right. I *love* being right."

"Remember, you have to hold the intention that you're not going to harm him."

"I got it. I'm not going to harm him. *You* are."

"I'm not, either." I ground my teeth. "Not until I'm sure."

"I got you covered," Marie sang happily, trotting next to me in her platform sneakers. "You're lucky, Daph. Evil geniuses are my specialty."

"Takes one to know one, I suppose. Now shush," I whispered. "No more talking."

"Copy that," she whispered back, grinning like a madwoman. "This is Red Rocket, we got the go-code, confirming radio silence and zero talk."

We walked straight up to the revolving doors. During the day, there was a concierge service and a chic cafe in the lobby. Now, after midnight, the revolving doors were locked, and the only way in was the call button next to the door.

Without even hesitating, Marie punched the penthouse apartment number in and pressed the call key.

The intercom rang, then clicked. "Yes?"

"Hey, honey," Marie drawled in a terrible Philly accent. "I got your food down here."

"Step to the left," Troy ordered, his voice cold. "Look into the camera."

"Whad? Whaddaya wand me to do?" *Holy guacamole, we've found something Marie isn't good at.*

"Move to the left!"

"Huh?" Apparently, she wasn't great at playing dumb, either. But, thanks to Marie, I'd homed in on Troy's Achilles heel.

He was lazy. He'd always been lazy. There was no way he would be making his own food. With Cindy's help, we managed to hack into his favorite delivery service website and waited until he placed his dinner order.

"Look into the camera," Troy snapped.

"Oh. Right, I got you." Marie shuffled to the left a bit and smiled into the security camera.

There was a beat of silence. "Okay." His tone changed instantly. "You can come on up, beautiful."

To Marie's credit, she kept the dazzling smile on her face while we walked under the cameras in the revolving door, and all the way across the gleaming atrium floor, heading to the elevator bank. "Beautiful? *Eww*. What a fuck-head."

There was no point giving her my speech again. "I thought we were radio-silence no-talk," I whispered.

"We are." She pressed the button for the penthouse, and we rode up in silence. The floors blinked by quickly.

The elevator stopped, dinged, and opened up into a very short corridor with one door at the end. I took a deep breath, inhaling the flavor of Troy's anti-glamor charm that filled the corridor, a spell that would have dissolved any disguise someone might have used to get in. That was another reason Marie had to do this. She was the only person that Troy didn't know.

I followed her at a distance, praying my don't-see-me charm held up. It was a simple spell, more of an optical illusion rather than magic. We'd used it because there was no counteracting defense spell for it—it was considered too weak to bother with. A don't-see-me spell dissolved the second someone got suspicious. We only needed a second, though.

Marie trotted straight up and knocked. A series of snaps, clicks, and clunks came from behind the door, and it swung open.

I took a small breath, steadying my pulse.

Troy stood in the doorway in his usual relaxed slouch, wearing designer sweatpants and a loose gray t-shirt. He ran his hand through his shoulder-length, messy blond hair and smiled at Marie, looking as handsome and laidback as ever.

Was I wrong about him?

Marie held up the bag. "Here you go, sir."

Troy took the bag, still smiling his happy, wide smile. "Thanks, gorgeous." He let out a whistle. "Man, you got some nice skin."

Damn it.

Marie valiantly kept the smile on her face, but it grew tighter. I could sense her whole body bristling in rage. With effort, she extended her arm, palm out. "It puts the tip in the hand, or it gets the hose again."

Troy laughed, his wide blue eyes warm and so friendly. "You're funny. Hey, you know what? I think I might have over-ordered," he said, waving the bag. "Do you want to come in and—"

It was the invitation we needed. Quick as lightning, Marie shoved him backwards, stepped into the apartment, and rolled the ward-breaker charm back over the threshold.

I bolted inside. Before Troy could roll to his feet, I dashed over and slapped a cuff on his wrist.

"What the... what the hell?" He turned to Marie. "Bitch, what are you doing?" He held out his hands, reaching for his magic.

Nothing happened. The anti-mage prison cuff I'd slapped on him was clearly working. Troy let out a snarl and wrenched at it. "You fucking bitch, I'm going to—"

"You're not going to do anything."

The charm dissolved. Troy saw me. His eyes bulged. "Daphne."

I glanced around the room quickly, and any doubts I had vanished in an instant. There, on a workbench, was all the evidence I needed to know he was guilty. There was a lock of lavender hair scattered amongst sheaths of foxglove and oleander. In the corner of the room, a porter-sorter, a glowing golden metal box, sat on a plinth. A Phillies cap was tossed carelessly on the dining room table.

Most shocking of all was the rancid punch of blood in the air. Blood magic. Troy had been doing blood magic.

Just then, I realized something, and it was like another punch to the gut. The mirror ward he'd placed on the apartment wasn't a mistake. It wasn't there to protect the apartment's wards from offensive spells. It was there to bounce the vibrations of the blood magic back inside the wards, so they didn't ripple out through the ley lines. Troy was doing blood magic and making sure no one could detect it.

It'd happened *again.* I assumed Troy had done something stupid with the mirror ward. I thought he'd made a mistake.

But it was the work of a genius. "How long?" I asked him.

"What?"

"How long have you been doing blood magic?"

He didn't say anything. There was no denying it, anyway. Troy stood there, looking at me. I'd never seen that expression on his face before. I couldn't decipher it.

"It was you," I said. "It was you all along."

He stared at me, his expression blank. There was an odd resignation in his eyes. An acceptance. But also... defiance. "You can't blame me," he said tonelessly. "You deserved it all. You took everything from me. My parents, my brothers. My fiancé. You destroyed my whole life. You deserve all this and much more."

A hint of guilt wiggled in my chest. Brain-Daphne stamped on it like a bug.

"Blood magic," I exhaled. "You've been doing blood magic, Troy."

"You still have no idea." He let out a bark of laughter. "This is priceless."

I shook my head, confused. "I can understand you wanting revenge on me because you've lost your family. I'm not even going to bother trying to convince you that your family did it to themselves. But... *Troy*." I exhaled heavily. "I could have forgiven you for everything you did to me. All the manipulation, all the lies. You'd have to face Asherah and Lennox, and you might have to answer to your crimes in the Otherworld court, but blood magic?"

He shrugged like he didn't care.

I stared at him. He really *didn't* care.

There was no saving him. "This means death, Troy." Romeo wouldn't hesitate. And I couldn't stop him.

I wouldn't stop him.

"You're unbelievable." Troy huffed out another laugh. "I

loved it when you used to cry about people underestimating you. You really are the dumbest girl I've ever messed with. And I've messed with a lot of dumb girls. Even Holly is a moron. I thought she'd catch on ages ago, but she's an idiot, too."

He took an idle step forward and wagged his finger. "You know, this was so much fun while it lasted. The best part was listening to you cry over that old bitch's death. I wish I could have told you sooner what we did to her." His eyes twinkled. He stared down at me. "And that it was me who did it."

The breath left my lungs. "Aunt Marche. You... you didn't."

He laughed out loud. "Are you kidding me? The ritual to weave a magical tie between a sentient magic and a human being would require a times-three. Three wizards of the same blood. Are you telling me that even your Warlock didn't figure that out?" He chuckled, shaking his head. "He's a moron, too. Brawn over brains, huh?"

I couldn't believe it. I needed him to say it. "*You* cursed Aunt Marche? You tied the tie to the Great Agreement?"

"It wasn't even hard." He paused. "I mean, none of us could have predicted what happened right afterwards. The Great Suffocation was an interesting side-effect. We wondered how long we should let it go on for, but in the end, I convinced the guys to leave it. I needed a vacation, anyway." He leered down at me. "And Castlemaine made a great vacation spot."

My whole world tipped sideways. "You... knew?"

"Sure." He shrugged. "None of us died. It took out mostly vamps, anyway, and they needed culling. They were getting out of control, Daphne. As far as the rest of us... Well, only the poor supes were affected. The whole thing worked out really well in the end." His eyes were so cold, so empty. So... soulless.

The man was a monster. "It cleared out all the dregs," he added carelessly.

I let this man put his hands on me. I'd never felt dirtier in all my life. My hands began to shake.

Troy had caused the deaths of thousands of innocent people. And he was gloating about it.

He put his hands in his pockets and sauntered towards me, like he didn't have a care in the world. "It's a shame it has to end like this, Daphne," he murmured, looking down on me.

This isn't right. He doesn't look upset. He looks... smug.

"I know it's probably the last thing you want," he continued. "Going to your death with me by your side. But the fact that you know almost everything now makes me very happy."

I stammered. "Almost everything? What else is there?"

Bitch, listen to him, he says you're going to die. He's up to something!

He couldn't do anything. Not with that cuff stuck on his hand. Only the Otherworld court could unlock it. He couldn't hurt anyone anymore. I gave him a hard stare. "This is it, Troy. You're done."

"I might be." His eyes glinted like chips of ice. "But so are you." He leaned closer and smirked. "Goodbye, Daphne." Suddenly, his pulse spiked.

Adrenaline flooded me. I jerked. *He's going to do something!*

I reared back, pulled my blades, and braced myself. My heart hammered wildly in my chest.

Nothing happened.

After a moment, Troy's eyes narrowed slightly.

"Whatever you're waiting for, champ, you might not

want to hold your breath," Marie said brightly, trotting out of the bedroom. She held a strange electrical device in her hand.

Brain-Daphne exhaled in relief. *God, I love that girl.*

"You can stop clicking the remote too, bitch-boy. I've already disabled it." Marie waved the device above her head. "A little clippy-clip of the red wire, a twisty-twist of the blue, and your bomb might as well be used as a doorstop."

A bomb. Troy had rigged a bomb to blow up the whole apartment if he was ever caught.

I turned my head to look at him. His face twisted in fury. I'd never seen him this angry before. He looked just like his brother, Christopher.

"You messed up right at the end, bitch-boy." Marie kept talking, her voice bright and happy. "There's only one reason an evil villain would ever start monologuing like that. It didn't take me long to sniff this sucker out." She rolled the bomb over in her hand, examining it. "Normally, the explosive would go here. I'd use C4 or RDX if I could get hold of it, but I'm assuming this is a magical equivalent based on some of the components in here—"

"Marie," I cut her off.

"Yeah?"

I spun my blades in my palms. "You might want to turn away for this part."

EPILOGUE

I hugged Marie one more time. "Are you sure this is what you want?"

"Are you kidding me?" She wriggled out of my embrace and tossed her thick hair out of her eyes.

It was a little warmer tonight, but I made Marie wear her puffy jacket anyway, just to keep up appearances. Her luggage was piled up beside her, her carry-on packed with sunscreen, hats, gloves and balaclavas. She was ready to go.

"Yes, it's what I want," Marie said. "I can't believe you didn't tell me earlier that it was an option."

The bus depot was almost empty. Only a small handful of people were taking the last bus out of Philly, heading south.

A strange nostalgia gripped me. Last time I'd been here at the bus depot, I was a starry-eyed idiot, excited to join my loving boyfriend in his family home.

That family was all dead now. So was the loving boyfriend. I didn't make Troy suffer; not really. But, before I ran my blade over his throat, I made sure to thank him for leading me here, to Philadelphia, so I could meet the love of my life. I'd live the rest of my life with Romeo, in pure, happy bliss.

The look in Troy's eyes when I told him was vengeance enough for me.

My brain poked me. *Pay attention!*

Oh, right. I was farewelling my very own wayward ward.

"I can't believe how well everything worked out. I'm kinda mad I didn't think of it myself," Marie added a little bitterly. "But I'm gonna miss you, Daph."

The coven had already said goodbye. Cole, Brandon, Levi, and Micah had come with us to see her off and were standing a short distance away, watching me bid Marie farewell before she got on the bus. Romeo had business with the Otherworld Court tonight, so he'd dropped us off on the way to pick up Holly LeBeaux, who he'd retained as counsel. He was going to put the whole Jupiter mess on record, so everyone knew what had happened.

Finally, the Otherworld would know what caused the Great Suffocation. They'd know who was responsible, and they'd know that Romeo was the one who stopped it. No more secrets, no more misunderstandings.

My heart felt so full it was almost bursting. I smiled at Marie fondly. "I'm going to miss you, too."

Marie was transferring schools. She'd been adamant that she was going back to college no matter what, so I looked for alternatives that might suit a seventeen-year-old, terrifyingly intelligent newborn vampire like herself.

Turns out, there was a small college in a town called Eternity, just south of Lafayette, Louisiana, that ran night classes. When I called Holly to ask about it, she told me Eternity was a Veil town—a town where the human population had been spelled to ignore the supernatural, fixing the veil over their eyes so they would never See.

The same spell had been placed on my guardian, Chloe, when she was in high school. I couldn't imagine how much blood magic it would take to spell a whole town. The thought frightened me, but Holly reassured me that Eternity had been a Veil town for almost a hundred years, so whoever did the spell was probably long gone.

Subsequently, Eternity had been a sanctuary during the Great Suffocation—albeit a very unpopular one due to the heavy-handedness of the Enforcer who lived there. Enforcers were supposed to keep the peace between supes, but sometimes, they were a little more like modern-day Gestapo.

I would have been reluctant to send Marie there, but the heavy-handed Enforcer had died a year ago, so I felt like it was a good option. Even better—there was a physics professor there who Marie had not only heard of, but she admired him a lot. Professor Mannheim headed up the science department, and, according to Marie, he'd conducted some groundbreaking research at MIT around twenty years ago before he disappeared into obscurity.

Marie gave a happy, dorky little jiggle. "Don't get me wrong, Daph, I'm mortified that I have to go to a tier five school, but..." She sighed and clutched her chest. "I can't believe I'm going to get to study under Professor Mannheim." A dreamy look came over her face. "He's so brilliant. And *so* handsome."

"Marie..." I peered at her. "He's in his late fifties."

"Yeah?" She stared back at me. "And?"

I opened my mouth and shut it again. My brain gave a whistle. *Let's back away from that one. Marie can get some therapy. She'll be fine. Hopefully.* "Are you sure about this?"

"Yes, I'm sure." She grinned up at me.

"Because you can stay with Romeo as long as you like, he said so himself."

Behind her, the boys all shook their heads frantically and made cut-throat motions. Except Cole, who blew his nose miserably.

The bus driver announced the bus's departure. I gave Marie one last hug. "You better get going."

"Thanks for everything, Daph." She hugged me back, then turned, tossed her bags unceremoniously into the bus's luggage compartment, and trotted up the steps. "Bye!"

Godspeed, my baby. Brain-Daphne gave a wet sniff. I backed away, and the bus drove off.

My phone buzzed. I pulled it out. It was Holly LeBeaux calling. I hit the answer button. "Hey, Holly!"

"Hi." She sounded irritated. "Is Romeo with you?"

"No." A pulse of fear ran through me. "He went to pick you up an hour ago."

"He did pick me up," she said, sounding pissed. "We were walking into the atrium, headed to the Otherworld doorway just now, but he disappeared."

"What do you mean, 'disappeared'?"

"He was right beside me. One minute he was there, and the next, the lights blinked out for a second, then he was gone. Our session is about to start, Daphne," she said testily. "We have to go in. I've called him a bunch of times, but his phone is switched off. I figured he was running off to see you."

"He's not with me." My chest felt so tight, I could hardly take a breath. "Did you say the lights blinked out?" My voice sounded so faint in my ears. "He didn't move into the shadows?"

"Yeah. He's never abandoned anyone mid-sentence like that..." Holly trailed off. "Oh. Oh, shit."

"He didn't let the shadows swallow him?"

"No." She swore. "It was like... they stole him."

They stole him.

To Be Continued...

ALSO BY LAURETTA HIGNETT

Go back to the start with Imogen Gray series:

Immortal Ghost (freebie prequel novella)

Immortal

Immortal Games

Immortal World

Immortal Life

Immortal Death

Then follow Sandy in the Foils and Fury series:

Oops I Ate A Vengeance Demon

Dancing With The Vengeance Demon

Dating With The Vengeance Demon

Dying For My Vengeance Demon

Then go on to Prue's story with Blood & Magic:

Bad Bones

Bare Bones

Broke Bones

Blood & Bones

Burned Bones

Bitter Bones

Head on into Chloe's series, The Waif in the Wilds:

The Waif in the Wilds (freebie prequel novella)

Vicious Creatures

Fractured Gods

Ravenous Beasts

Savage Daemons

Duck Duck Motherf*cker (freebie epilogue novella in Dwayne's POV)

And then Daphne's story in the Hidden City Supernatural Sleuth:

The Wolf Vs The Vampire

The Wolf Vs The Warlock

The Wolf Vs Santa (Holiday Novella)

The Wolf Vs The Shifter

The Wolf Vs The Witch

The Wolf Vs The Monster

And detour into a new universe with Susan in Welcome to Midlife Magic:

Susan, You're The Chosen One

It's Called Magic, Susan

Susan, Break The Curse!

You Can't Fight A Prophecy, Susan

www.ingramcontent.com/pod-product-compliance
Ingram Content Group UK Ltd.
Pitfield, Milton Keynes, MK11 3LW, UK
UKHW040625110625
6336UKWH00015B/215